# SHADY CREEK

# SHADY CREEK

RUSSELL GILWEE

Createspace, Charleston SC

Author Disclaimer

This is a work of fiction. Names, characters, businesses, places, events, and incidents are either the product of the author's imagination or used in a fictitious manner. Any resemblance to actual persons, living or dead, or actual events is purely coincidental.



ISBN: **1976483115**
ISBN-13: **978-1-9764-8311-0**

# DEDICATION

This book is dedicated to my wife, Lauraleen, and our golden doodle, Sophie; my mother, Zaida; my late father, Jim; family and friends; and to you, Dear Reader.
My deepest gratitude.

# 1.

**THE BOY WAS A BIT THIN AND HIS HAIR** a bit long, his sandy bangs having to be routinely swept aside with an absent flick of the hand from his bright and intelligent blue eyes but for a stubborn cowlick which always seemed to stand at attention, floating above his head like a lazy cattail. His rumpled clothing was secondhand and outgrown, offering the illusion the boy might be tall for his age when, in fact, he was of average height, if not a bit small.

His name was Delbert.

Delbert walked home from school beneath a gray autumn sky, a backpack flung over a narrow shoulder. He was ten years old and in no particular hurry. He splashed in gathering puddles. Stooped to examine drowning worms. Pushed out a tongue to catch the falling rain. Cold and silty in the back of his dry throat.

He was surrounded by a world of gold, copper, bronze, orange, and vermilion. The autumn colors had first appeared in mid-September on the high ridges overlooking the small foothill town of Shady Creek with the turning of yellow birch and American beech alongside their high elevation cousins mountain maple, hobblebush, the hickories, and the oaks. These vibrant brushstrokes of motley watercolor had followed in a wake of descending cold air, slowly moving down from the steep passes and into the small town by late October, setting ablaze sugar maple, scarlet oak, sweetgum, red maple, and buttery poplars.

The town itself was hidden from the world in the foothills of western North Carolina, built around a rug mill a century before and only existing because of it. The rug mill sat perched on a modest hill behind the Methodist church, its rusted whistle a shadow behind the church bell tower and spire. If the wind was favorable, the eye-watering sting of dyes and treating chemicals were absorbed into the thick woodland rising to the west. If not, the miasma seeped into the town, silently searching out every corner, lurking in every crevice, settling like rot.

The mill whistle pierced the stillness this gray afternoon, signaling a shift change. Its shrill cry no longer startled Delbert. In fact, Delbert hardly heard it anymore. No more than he heard the faint rumble of freight trains passing on the outskirts of town or the somnolent hum of crickets outside his bedroom window at night or, for that matter, the mild thump of his sneakers hesitating before a small white clapboard house at the end of a dead end road now. He regarded the white clapboard house from the road, his young pale face wearing an expression that might best have been described as weary disappointment. The cross-planks were decayed and in need of fresh paint and the front porch was crooked, sliding off its foundation like an old man with ill-fitting dentures. The driveway was a muddy mess and the yard overgrown with wild things. Delbert sighed softly, circumvented the deeper mud, and entered the house, dodging moving boxes. Some unpacked weeks ago. Others gathering dust in encroaching shadows.

He trekked to a lone light upstairs.

A moth to a flame.

He found his mother, Lillian, hunched in a robe before a large antique vanity mirror. Delbert had once heard a heartbroken man in a trailer park outside Des Moines describe his mother as a winter rose. Her beauty frozen but dying on the inside, he'd said.

Delbert dodged more boxes and dumped his backpack on the floor. It made a small gunshot noise on the hardwood, earning an almost imperceptible frown from his mother. He settled on her bed, sinking into the mattress, getting comfortable, bed springs whining beneath him before falling quiet again with a final gasp. His mother paid him little more notice than Delbert had paid the mill whistle. He stared at her for a long spell before speaking.

"Holly wants to see you," he said.

A mascara brush glided over her cold eyes.

Like a magic wand. Thick and dark.

"Who's Holly?" she said.

"My teacher."

"Holly. You call your teacher by her first name."

"Yeah. She likes it."

"Well, I don't. It's weird, Delbert. Don't do it."

She expertly smudged the eyeliner with a tissue.

"Parent-teacher conferences were last week," he said. "You didn't go."

A sigh. "We just got here." A dismissive wave at unpacked moving boxes. "She doesn't know you from Adam, yet, kiddo. And I don't need a stranger telling me about my own son."

"She knows you," he said, and his mother looked at him for the first time, finding him in the cold flat mirror glass. Suspicious now. "Says you went to high school together."

Rain pattered on the window.

"Holly. . ." his mother considered slowly with deeper suspicion, her eyes turning blank for a moment before dilating and blinking hard. "Holly Sherwin. . ." she guffawed. "Marmalade." A sarcastic snort. Her head shaking ruefully. "Regular backseat drive-in cheerleader slut."

Delbert's eyes grew wide.

"We called her Marmalade on account that dumb post somehow thought a handful of jelly--" Her voice hitched and she thought better of continuing. She returned to her face in the vanity mirror before adding: "Suffice to say, her daddy took her on a long drive down to Bedford to visit a doctor friend late one spring night, but you didn't hear that from me."

Delbert wasn't sure what he'd just heard.

"She said you were good at math."

Another sigh. "I was good at lots of things."

A half hour later Delbert was sitting in the front window. The rain was falling harder, blurring the outside world. Car headlights splashed across the window's flimsy curtains. His mother, a hazy reflection in the rain-beaded glass, hustled down the narrow staircase behind him. A short skirt. Tight blouse. Cleavage.

A lot of purposeful jostling.

Delbert spoke without turning around.

"What time will you be home?" he said.

His mother made a last check in the wall mirror.

"I'm not having this conversation," she said.

A quick air kiss and she was out the door beneath an umbrella. Delbert remained in the front window long after the headlights and the car engine faded into the distance.

He trudged into the kitchen after a spell. Peeked into the fridge. A barren place. He used condiments to construct a sandwich. A Delbert special. Bread. Mayo. Peanut butter. A forgotten slice of baloney (cutting off the green moldy edges) and the dredges of an old corn chip bag. He ate while playing a game of checkers in the soft glow of a small flickering TV with bent rabbit ears.

The rain drummed sleepily on the roof.

He woke in his bed upstairs sometime after midnight beneath a squadron of model airplanes hanging from the ceiling and dull headlights bouncing about the bedroom, glancing off the bombers and fighter jets and apache helicopters. For a moment, though, in his confusion, he had the impression the squadron was actually moving. Descending in formation, preparing to drop their payload on him. He could almost hear the guttural roar of their engines before realizing it was only the idle of a car in the driveway outside. The idle punctuated with the muffled pop of a car door opening. Closing. His mother giggling like a schoolgirl in the rain.

Sounding impossibly young.

Delbert heard the front door open and close downstairs. The car engine faded along with its headlights. The curtain of darkness descended once again. There was no moon. The overcast sky revealed no stars, either. The world fell still, but for the rain and the muffled click of his mother's heels rising on the staircase in the hall before pausing at his door. She stood at the threshold. She looked wrinkled and tired. Like a doll left out in bad weather.

"That man your boyfriend?" he said.

His voice seemed to startle her.

Perhaps she thought him asleep.

"I'm sure his wife might have something to say about that," she said. She lit a cigarette. The butt glowed and jumped up and down in the dark hall like a dancing firefly, turning his mother into a silhouette. Hiding her from his scrutiny.

"He's married?" Delbert said.

"They're all married, Delbert."

She slipped away into the darkness like Peter Pan's shadow. To bed. The slight groan of the bed springs at the end of the hall and a satisfied exhale signaling her landing.

Delbert turned to a clock radio on his nightstand. A flick of the switch and gentle classical music floated about his bedroom like a warm mist. He rolled toward the window, peeking past curtains and the dreary rain. Staring at a lighted window next door.

There was a girl.

Allison. Fifteen. Pretty.

She was lying on her bed.

Talking on the phone.

The girl hid the phone beneath a wool blanket when her father poked his head in her bedroom door.

Harlan Winslow.

Delbert winced at the sight of the man. A cheap brown suit and a receding hairline. A salesman in a bad slump. He told his daughter goodnight. She hid behind a textbook, offering only a sullen nod. Her father hesitated in the doorway. Awkwardly hovering. She ignored him. Like he was no longer there.

Eventually her father was no longer there.

As if the man had been erased from existence by the supernatural. The bedroom door having closed in his aftermath without sound or any discernible movement as if the door had never been opened in the first place. Time reversed.

Allison pulled her phone out from the wool blanket.

Talking as if uninterrupted.

Mid-conversation.

Delbert pushed closer to the window until his tiny nose was touching the cold pane. Mesmerized by her. Puppy love. Breath catching in his throat as she inexplicably rose in an intoxicating exhibition of contorting arms and legs before plopping down again, her head suddenly and queerly at the foot of the bed, her long blonde tresses spilling in a wave off its edge.

She lifted her coltish legs into the air above her head and while still on her back allowed her thin cotton nightgown to fall about her waist while she painted her toenails, the nail polish defying gravity as she continued to gab on the phone, handset propped between her slender shoulder and rosy cheek, the spiraling cord wrapping like a snake around her slim arm and narrow waist.

The portrait of innocence transforming into womanhood.

The butterfly trapped in the claustrophobic cocoon.

Delbert remained transfixed until her bedroom light blinked out a quarter hour later. A silly smile on his young pale face, he settled into a pillow, falling asleep completely and peacefully this time to the soft classical music floating about his bedroom.

The composition embracing him in its own cocoon.

# 2.

GALLOWS RIVER STATE PRISON WAS ONE of the oldest operating prisons in the country. It was built on a former mining camp in the Smoky Mountains, occupying fifty-two acres along the Gallows River seventy miles northwest of Shady Creek. The river was so-named for the hanging of horse thieves and other such reprobates in the late 19th century. Its namesake was constructed of large granite slabs dynamite-blown and ripped like giant rotten teeth from the hard, unforgiving earth by the first prisoners at a nearby quarry. A temporary wooden stockade was constructed around the original warehouse of cell blocks until thick granite walls could be erected. It took decades to complete the prison, including tall granite watchtowers rising like medieval turrets at strategic intersections along the outer wall, their bright yellow spotlights roaming about the haunted grounds like playful ghosts, illuminating soft, foamy whitecaps on the otherwise deep and dark Gallows River flowing silently below.

The river had seduced more than its fair share of hearty souls over the past century. Desperate men who had managed to escape the institution and mistook the river for a more amenable path to freedom than the jagged peaks rising to the northwest. The black water appeared lazy, inconsequential on the surface, but below the current was strong and pitiless with swirling eddies like black holes, each eager to gather an ill-informed man into its clutches, spinning him around slowly at first, lulling him into a drowsy complacency like a mother rocking a child, the shore often only an arm's reach away, before suddenly, and quite heartlessly, yanking the startled fool down into the river's icy belly and everlasting darkness.

The prison interior was a honeycomb of stone cells and stone walkways. Prisoners and guards alike found the labyrinth cold as a meat locker in the middle of summer after returning from hot, sticky days laboring in the nearby quarry and hot as Hades in the middle of winter when the boilers ran day and night and fresh air was at a minimum as bodies upon bodies of bored, lethargic men waited out the snow in exhausted, mind-numbing inertia.

Each stone cell measured six foot by eight foot with a stainless steel toilet and stainless steel sink opposite narrow bunk beds. The small cells were secured by thick cast iron boiler-plate doors which only amplified the cacophony of prison noise. Each boiler-plate door had been outfitted with a narrow eight inch by two inch eye-slit (the sliding metal flap only accessible from outside the cell) and small air holes drilled into the base. Unfortunately for the earliest residents, the addition of the air holes had only been added in the early 1940's after a series of unfortunate asphyxiations.

The bedtime whistle pierced the prison din this late autumn evening as it did every late evening and all the lights blinked twice, replaced by eerie blue nocturnal lights in the corridors and complete blackness inside the cells. A blackness like the bottom of that black river. Freddy Jackson sat on a bottom bunk in a cramp cell on the top tier. His face was pale because Freddy had been there long enough to earn regular kitchen duty and avoid hard labor in the quarry mines. It also meant he very rarely saw sunshine but for an hour or two a week in the exercise yard, though it was a small sacrifice to broken bones and a broken back. His hair was long and scraggly. His eyes nervous. He had an assortment of tics, including a mild twitch below his right eye and a stubborn spasm in his left hand. Freddy wore these maladies without shame. They were an invention of this dark hole in the world. He supposed in time he might have eventually gone blind like a mole rat burrowing deep in the earth or deaf like an earthworm.

Eventually. If time had really stood still.

If this world had been allowed to consume him.

But it would not.

He had not let it.

Freddy drifted his unsteady left hand toward a cheap transistor radio. The radio sat on a shelf beside a pile of old magazines gathering mildew, a small cracked coffee cup with a threadbare toothbrush resting inside, and his allotment of toilet paper for the week. He flicked the power button to ON.

There was an initial burst of static like alien speech from a distant planet before an agreeable oeuvre of classical music drowned out the clamor of the prison. Freddy sighed and leaned back on his pillow, his hands folded behind his head.

A prison guard making rounds stopped outside the cell, the staccato echo of his hard-soled boots and his shadow passing through the air holes at the bottom of the thick boiler-plate door revealing him even before the eye-slit slid open, the flaky, oxidized metal flap offering a protesting whine. The guard's bluish-gray visage appeared in the narrow slot, the blue darkness hiding weary eyes Freddy knew to be slightly jaundiced. The faint waft of cheap drugstore aftershave accompanied the man. "You know that shit gives me a headache, Freddy," the guard said.

"It helps me sleep," Freddy said.

Knowing he wouldn't sleep.

Not tonight. Not tomorrow night.

Not a wink.

His cellmate on the bunk above him, however, snored softly.

"Just turn it down," the guard said eventually, completing a familiar repartee between the men. "This ain't Carnegie Hall."

Freddy turned down the radio for the moment.

The eye-slit screeched shut, the sliding metal flap now offering a rusty farewell. The guard's shadow moved off with the telltale click-clack of the guard's hard-soled boots. Freddy sighed again and stared at the stone wall pushing against him. Taped prominently above the radio on the wall was a newspaper cutout.

An obituary.

The short newspaper article was still crisp with the faint aroma of ink tickling the otherwise stale air. A thin short headline read: GERTRUDE MARGARET OLSEN: FRIEND OF THE CHURCH. The obituary article was accompanied by a small black and white photo. A pious face beneath a bird's nest of gray hair. Hard eyes. No smile.

A Polaroid was also taped to the wall.

Yellowed and tattered. Frayed at the edges.

It revealed Lillian in her early twenties. Baby-faced. Eyes twinkling. Cheeks flushed. Pregnant. The world still a magical place with a yellow brick road in front of her. A much younger Freddy sat beside her, his arm thrown casually over her shoulder.

Caught in the middle of a laugh.

Frozen and now soundless.

# 3.

DELBERT WOKE TO NOISY TRAFFIC reports from Bedford down in the valley. By comparison, there was only one traffic light in the town of Shady Creek and it blinked red after nine in the evening. The shopfronts, apart from the twenty-four hour diner on Main Street and the bar on the corner of 1st and Maple, closed at six each night and the sidewalks rolled up shortly thereafter.

Delbert turned off the clock radio and yawned, stretching, toes reaching for the knotted pine ceiling. The rain outside his window was gone, but the sun remained hidden behind another gray sky. He dressed for school in the morning dimness, eyes puffy with sleep, then took a moment to fight that stubborn cowlick in the mirror before conceding defeat.

The elementary school was kitty-corner to the Methodist Church and across the street from the city library which was only open on Mondays and Thursdays from 10am until dark. The schoolhouse was the third building raised in the town after the factory and the church and sat on land donated by the factory. It was composed of dusty red brick with chipped mortar and fronted by a large aluminum flag pole on a circular front lawn surrounded by a bed of Allegheny Onions -- a native plant with bright umbels of purplish flowers which had an odd, distinctive nodding habit, an evolutionary trait which protected them from all intruders but bees as other flying critters were supposedly disinclined to hang upside down to collect nectar.

The school had begun life as a three room building with slate blackboards and small wooden desks bolted to the floor, but it expanded quickly with the factory and town. At mid-century, for a short while, it also housed an orphanage to accommodate factory misfortunes. Sterile young couples would venture up from the valley to adopt. Factory modernizations and new rules limiting spouses from working near each other on the assembly line made the orphanage obsolete in time and it was closed and forgotten like a bad dream. The orphanage was converted into a basketball gymnasium, including a stage used mostly for annual Xmas performances and school plays. Still, it was whispered amongst the schoolchildren (as well as their parents and grandparents and great-grandparents who had attended the school over the passing generations) that the oldest buildings were haunted by the misery visited behind these dusty brick walls during those low and dreadful years. Mistreatment. Sickness. Death. Still evidenced in black and gray detail in the small cemetery hidden in the woods behind the cafeteria. Small thin plots. Smaller crosses with no names.

Dark little terrible mysteries.

Delbert stared out toward those dark woods this late morning, back pressed firmly against a brick wall. He stood amongst a nervous, jostling scramble of other schoolchildren facing a throwing-line fifteen feet away and a big red plastic ball that left welts.

Dodge ball.

The game always began with laughter and good-natured banter before devolving into a viscous affair in which unspoken rivalries were settled. Holly Sherwin, the teacher, sat beneath a tree, oblivious. A home dye job. A romance book. A cigarette.

Ollie, a big-boned country boy with a jiggling gut and the first sprouts of chin hair, dominated the brick wall this morning, manhandling smaller classmates, using them as body shields, tossing them like rag dolls into the path of the big red plastic ball.

A child with buck teeth and a laugh like a hyena and a perpetually runny nose (that managed to stain both shirt sleeves and often his shirt collar) closed his eyes tightly. His head flipped up toward the gray sky. His arm rotated in a long sweeping arc and he hurled the ball with every ounce of his seventy-five pound being. The ball whistled through the cold air, arcing away from Delbert until a crushing Ollie forearm created a predictable intersection. The heavy plastic ball struck Delbert in the stomach. Delbert crumpled to the wet ground, making a wheezing noise -- not unlike a balloon spilling air out a narrow opening.

Ollie hooted. Grinning madly.

Proud of himself.

Delbert's mouth moved, but his lungs refused to work properly. Certainly not in the manner the Good Lord had designed them. His lungs felt glued shut and it took several long unnerving moments of pounding on his narrow chest with a closed fist before a rush of that wonderful cold morning air managed to suck back down his collapsed windpipe.

The sudden rush of air made him dizzy.

He grimaced. "That's not fair. You pushed," he whined.

"Life's not fair, vomit breath," Ollie said, still grinning.

Holly Sherwin, the teacher, sitting under the tree, never looked up from her romance book, but spoke in a monotone. Well-practiced. "Watch the language, Ollie."

Ollie bobbed and weaved along the brick wall, preparing for the next onslaught by the big red plastic ball. "Gee whiz. Just sayin', Holly. Get him a tic tac already."

Holly Sherwin peeked over her paperback this time, a bushy brown eyebrow raised. "Careful, twinkle toes, or I'll tic-tac-toe your dodge ball privileges," she said.

Delbert picked himself off the ground, angry. "You pushed."

"No do-overs, doofus," Ollie said as the game resumed.

Delbert trudged over to the throwing-line. Five minutes later the throwing-line had doubled and the brick wall was nearly empty. Only Ollie and a small fragile girl with big glasses remained. Ollie was the target. The small girl with glasses ignored.

Ollie was deceptively light on his feet for such a big kid. He laughed hysterically as he duck and dove and slid and skipped from the ball's offending path, frustrating the children. At least until the big red plastic ball rolled to Delbert. Delbert scooped it up, still angry. He raised the ball in one hand. His arm rocked forward, but the big red plastic ball never left his hand. A fake throw. Surprised, Ollie slipped in the grass, falling clumsily on his butt.

An easy target.

Delbert took advantage, rifling the ball. The big red plastic ball full of compressed air struck Ollie in the knee with a deep, hollow drumming noise -- before rebounding with even greater speed into the face of the small girl with glasses. Her glasses made a horrible cracking sound. One lens splintered into a series of spider webs, reminding Delbert of a Xmas in Little Rock when his mother had tried to cook a roast for the first time. In a clever, if misguided and misremembered attempt to imitate a chef she'd seen on the TV, she had poured cold white wine straight from the fridge on the roast after removing it from the oven. The searing hot oven dish had shimmered, almost seeming to levitate, before shattering along invisible fault lines. As for the small girl with glasses, the other lens exploded, a large shard diving and sinking into the muddy grass beside her foot while smaller pieces tinkled against the bricks behind her. Time slammed to a screeching halt, the Earth no longer turning on its axis, the schoolchildren holding their collective breath, staring in wide-eyed wonder, frozen before the dusty brick wall. The lungs of the world glued shut before -- in what felt like a sudden shrieking and bone-jerking motion -- the world began to spin again with the little girl bursting into tears.

Holly Sherwin dropped her romance book. Rushed over.

The child with buck teeth and that perpetually runny nose considered Delbert with a mixture of profound horror and shocked amusement. "I think you broke her face," he said.

Ollie glared at Delbert. Furious.

"You're dead," he said.

"It's his sister," Buck Teeth said.

Ollie charged like an angry bull, the big red plastic ball tucked under his brawny arm. Delbert ran. The chase zigged and zagged around the schoolyard. Delbert had never believed himself capable of running so fast and Ollie quickly flagged. Delbert looked sure to make his escape, but when he peeked a final time over his shoulder, he failed to notice a hole hidden in the grass. Perhaps a ground hog. His right foot landed in the hole and twisted. Badly.

Corkscrewing Delbert into the ground.

Ollie loomed over him. "Choke on it, doofus," he said and rifled the ball from close range. Ollie had a strong arm and the ball struck Delbert's head like a sledgehammer and the world swam from view, the Earth tilting right off its axis this time, gravity destroyed. Delbert slid behind a curtain of darkness full of exploding stars and angry buzzing static, his fried brain shorting out like the town's electric grid had done during the terrible windstorm the previous month. Eventually, though quite unhurriedly, his shorted brain came back on-line. One tiny neuroreceptor at a time.

Click. Buzz.

Buzz. Click.

Delbert saw only hazy images at first.

Then--

Holly Sherwin.

She appeared over Delbert, leaning forward, peering down at him, heels sinking in the mud. She was holding the hand of the little girl now without glasses. The glass frames dangled from her trembling grasp. Bent askew. An uncomfortably odd angle.

Like hot plastic.

The little girl whimpered softly.

The other children were crowding around, too.

"Maybe you should apologize to Betsy Sue, Delbert," Holly Sherwin said. Her voice sounded funny. Faraway. An echo.

Delbert held his injured ankle. Hurt and embarrassed.

'You apologize, Marmalade," he heard himself say.

The words, spoken in haste and humiliation, more a reflex than conscious thought, nevertheless stunned Holly Sherwin with no less force than the big red plastic ball that had ricocheted off Ollie's knee and struck his little sister in the face and had made like a giant sledgehammer against Delbert's temple.

Hot tears filled the teacher's eyes.

*Marmalade.*

Delbert was still trying to process and comprehend how that single strange word had elicited those hot painful tears while sitting in the nurse's office a half hour later. It baffled Delbert even as it filled him with remorse. Ollie's little sister sat on the room's examination table, holding an ice pack to her face, short legs and sneakers dangling in space, thick tissue paper crinkling beneath her bottom, broken glasses lying beside her, peering blindly.

The nurse, a young, short, fat woman who also taught in the kindergarten, examined Delbert's swelling ankle. The ankle was already turning a dull shade of blue and it appeared twice its normal size. Delbert tried to stand. Walk on it. He grimaced. Limping.

"Hurts," he said.

Ollie's little sister smiled with satisfaction.

"Should hurt," the nurse said. "You popped a ligament."

"Popped a what?"

"A ligament."

"What's that?"

"Like a rubber band," the nurse said.

"Oh," Delbert said.

Ollie's sister squinted for a better look.

Delbert favored the lame foot, scowling with each step, as he dragged it through the dirt away from the schoolhouse after the final bell, lugging his backpack with a disconsolate grunt, when Ollie rolled up beside him on a bike several sizes too small for the big country kid.

"Hey, doofus," Ollie said. "You want to fight?"

Delbert frowned. Exhausted.

"Well…?" Ollie said.

"How many times you been in the fifth grade, Ollie?"

Other children followed expectantly at a distance.

"You want to fight or not?" Ollie said.

"Only if you promise not to hit back," Delbert said.

Ollie's broad forehead furrowed. "But that's not fair."

"Life's not fair," Delbert said.

Repeating Ollie's line from dodge ball.

Ollie's broad forehead furrowed even more.

"I'm kidding," Delbert said.

Ollie contemplated this, then his face broke into a big harmless smile. He shrugged. "That's okay, Delbert. We don't got to fight. I only wanted to if you did." The bike frame sagging beneath his weight, he watched Delbert hobble on the bad ankle through the dirt. The bike's rusty chain was loose and jangled noisily with his every heavy-push on the squeaky petals. "It broke?" Ollie said after a brief spell. "If you have to get a cast I'll sign it."

"Ain't broke. Just popped a ligament is all."

Neither boy seemed to know what this meant.

"Your name really Delbert, Delbert?" Ollie said.

"Yep."

"Your daddy named Delbert, too?"

"Don't know."

"Don't know your own daddy's name, doofus?"

An old Pontiac Firebird with a rattling muffler and a broken taillight passed by on the road. Holly Sherwin was behind the wheel. She noticed Delbert. Her face turned red. Her hands gripped the steering wheel tighter and the Pontiac sped forward, muffler rattling and belching and a dented back bumper jumping up and down with each pothole in the road.

Ollie's voice dropped to a conspiratorial whisper. "Saw her blubbering in the principal's office," he said, broad shoulders shrugging again. "Like a racoon face." Delbert watched the Pontiac turn, sending up dust and a pile of fallen leaves before sliding around a corner -- but not before passing a Shady County sheriff cruiser sitting lazily in the shadows of a tall elm tree.

The sheriff cruiser paid the Firebird no attention. Still, it offered the impression of an alligator waiting to ambush prey.

Ollie spotted the cruiser, too.

He turned pale. Voice suddenly jumpy. "Want a piggyback?" he said, motioning to the bike's skinny handlebars.

"Better not," Delbert said, nodding at the ankle.

"Suit yourself, then," he said. "See you 'round, doofus."

Ollie turned and pedaled off. Huffing and puffing down a side street in the opposite direction of the slumbering cruiser, swaying dangerously on the small bicycle.

"And he calls me doofus," Delbert said beneath his breath.

The other children scattered, too, disappointed.

Meanwhile, Delbert found his eyes drawn back to that cruiser sitting silently in the shadows. A large silhouette sat alone in the back seat. Perhaps that was what held Delbert's attention. It was strange to see someone sitting in the back of a cruiser like that, the front seat empty. More to the point, though perhaps it was only a trick of the absence of light, it was the manner in which the dark silhouette seemed to be *watching* Delbert with a particular interest limp along the sidewalk before Delbert ducked through a hole in a chain-link fence and out of sight. Like whoever was sitting in the back of that cruiser had been sitting there waiting for just him to appear. The eerie sensation sent sharp, cascading prickles up and down Delbert's narrow spine as he passed through the chain-like fence and onto the high school athletic field and stood there for a moment beneath the overcast sky. Alert. Disquieted. But resisting the inclination to peek back through the hole in the fence.

Instead, he shook it off, assuming he had imagined the entire exchange. Of course he had, Delbert decided now, as he shuffled past football practice before pausing briefly to observe the large high school kids on the athletic field.

What interest would he be to anyone in this town?

Especially anyone with the law?

The high school football team echoed the economic pulse of the town, cresting and tumbling with the wide fluctuations of factory business. Lucrative industrial contracts somehow seemed to coincide with state playoff berths versus long losing years when the town subsisted primarily on the factory's core business, specialty items, the most popular orders being hand-hooked and hand-tufted rugs. This year's football team was limping to the finish line at a four and eight record dovetailing with recent layoffs at the factory. Folks were now discussing the merits of the upcoming basketball campaign this winter, including much conversation about a muscular six foot five sophomore who was still recovering from a fractured tailbone sustained during an ATV accident over the summer. Delbert himself wasn't aware of any of these small town intrigues, however. He was merely captivated by the clattering clash of the shoulder pads, the dull bell-tone of colliding helmets, the soft screech of the earth torn by spiked cleats. Less interested in the incomprehensible rules and unfathomable strategy of the ballet performing in front of him than the raw naked violence of it. The flinging of mud and sweat and the bloody rashes and snorting and snarls and all that screaming and whistle blowing. It all somehow seemed in holy contradiction to the attendant smiles and pats on the backs and butts.

He shook his head. Kept moving.

Gratefully unnoticed.

Passing by like a soft brush of wind.

He limped from the noisy gridiron and snuck in the back door of the high school gymnasium. A back door which he knew would be unlocked. He was careful, however, to hide beneath empty pulled bleachers, knowing he would otherwise be conspicuous in the confined space. He peered from between the hollow steps at a small stage where his neighbor, Allison, an angelic figure in a pale shaft of intruding sunlight, was standing in a choir.

Delbert had no idea where the pale sunlight had come from. He had abandoned a gray world outside only a moment before and he was certain it would still be gray and dreary if he peeked his head back out the door behind him -- yet somehow that pale shaft of sunlight had managed to penetrate the gray haze and find Allison, slipping through a dusty skylight high on the gymnasium ceiling and spilling like an arrow through the murk to single her out from all the other choir members, her transcendent voice rising and falling in spiritual wonder amongst the comparatively gray backdrop of the other voices around her. And for a moment Delbert felt his dirty sneakers lifting off the gymnasium floor, floating inside a weightless bubble created by her divine singing. His eyes flitted closed and that heavenly resonance lifted him from the floor toward the gymnasium rafters, past the cloth banners of past athletic achievement, through the dusty skylight, and into that tunnel of pale sunlight -- seeking what made it beyond the low-hanging overcast sky. The pale light blinding him. Embracing him. Promising to reveal the secret of its creation in a final hypnotic crescendo of gravity-defying psalm when suddenly the beautiful enchantment evaporated as the chorale fell silent in an abrupt conclusion and the gray hand of the world snatched him back into its uncompromising grip and Delbert found himself once again hiding behind the hollow steps of the pulled bleachers.

Delbert was still blinking when he exited the auditorium later and slunk along its brick wall and watched Allison meet her football boyfriend at the locker room entrance. Her boyfriend had a severe crew cut, splinters of harsh black hair standing at attention amongst white patches of scalp. Denuded trees in patches of dirty snow. He was somehow both big and skinny -- skinny big. A walking contradiction of teenage physics. All shoulders and elbows and bony kneecaps with impressively large hands and large feet and large ears. Alternately athletic and strong yet gangly and cumbersome, suggesting he could sprint like a deer on the football field but might as easily trip over his own shoelaces negotiating a short flight of stairs. He was an uncoiling spring with a tottering jack-in-the-box head bouncing in coordinated discord. A constellation of welt-like, blistering red pimples dotted his upper arms, back, and neck like smallpox.

His name was Bobby Joe.

But everybody called him Trigger.

Allison was a foot shorter.

Trigger hugged Allison into a concaved chest and under an arm where dark hair spurted like black weeds. His long folding embrace swallowed her head whole, leaving only a thin torso and matchstick legs dangling beneath him. Her face was red and hot when he released her and she carried his helmet and shoulder pads to his truck in the parking lot, tossing them into the bed of a large rusted Chevy with a thick black roll bar, deep-tread tires, and steel wire mesh cages encasing oversized headlights and taillights. A tattered bumper sticker shouted ROBIN BUCK HOOD with a large bulls-eye superimposed over a twelve point stag. A compound bow rested sleepily in a gun rack just inside the dirty rear cab window. The silhouette of a naked woman in a cowboy hat smoking a cigarette peeked from the driver's side mirror.

Delbert frowned.

Hugged the brick wall.

Trigger opened the passenger door for Allison. As Allison jumped into the truck he smacked her small round bottom with the back of his hand. A quick flat strike. Playfully, but a little too hard, too. Allison squealed, offering Trigger a wounded smile, her eyes watering. He circled behind the truck, his cleats scraping noisily on the pavement, and hopped behind the wheel, slamming the door shut with a dull thump, revealing a nasty dent in the sidewall. The truck's engine roared to life. A big grumbling beast waking from a nap. The muffler spat out black soot and the beast was in sudden accelerated motion, peeling backward, grinding treads kicking up smoke and muddy dust before the monster of rusty aluminum and steel jolted into Drive with a loud shuddering hitch and howled off, reaching an excessive speed in seconds, perilous in the crowded school parking lot, screeching around a scattering group of loitering students and bouncing onto the road.

Fading away in a cloud of more dust.

Delbert took his usual route home, including a narrow side road behind the high school. The side road was bordered by short chain-link fences guarding small square blue-collar homes. All the homes looked the same on this side of town. Raised quickly and efficiently at cost. Two bedrooms. One bathroom. A family room facing the quiet desolate street. Delbert would soon find pyramid-shaped Fraser fir Xmas trees in each of these front windows. Hand-cut from the nearby hills or dragged home from hastily raised lots in the town with strings of bright, obligatory Xmas lights hanging from the gutters. Wreaths on doors.

Delbert struggled on the swollen ankle.

His backpack felt as if it were filled with river stone.

The gray light had begun to fall behind the high ridges to the west and Delbert found himself drifting into a world of inky shadows untouched by the fuzzy home lights or a dull street lamp on the corner. Something stirred in the darkness behind Delbert, startling him as it melted out of the gathering murk like a specter before its headlights flipped on suddenly, blinding Delbert in a flash of white light -- revealing its true identity as it slowed beside him. It was the Shady County sheriff cruiser from that afternoon. The cruiser slowed to a crawl. Content to keep pace with him, radials kicking small rocks in the road.

Delbert stopped.

The sheriff cruiser braked.

Also coming to a stop.

The front driver window slid down.

A soft electronic whine.

A large fat-bellied lawman with cold, penetrating gray eyes and a slippery grin peeked from the interior darkness. His face was ruddy and gray-grizzled and pock-marked from adolescence. The enormity of him stuffed behind the steering wheel somehow reminded Delbert of Paul Bunyan.

Or maybe Paul Bunyan's demented brother.

An illuminated dash placard offered a name.

Sheriff Charlie Snodgrass.

A bitter wind rose from the northeast. The cold wind seemed to cut right through Delbert's clothing as if he were wearing none at all and Delbert shivered.

"You're Lillian's boy, ain't you," the sheriff said.

The sheriff's voice startled Delbert all over again. Delbert had expected a deep voice. A voice to match the massive figure seated before him. Instead, he found it deceptively soft and mesmerizing. Not unlike a down comforter concealing a bed of sharp nails.

"Don't look so surprised, boy," the sheriff said, those cold, penetrating gray eyes digesting the boy frozen on the sidewalk, chilling him like the bitter wind. "This is my town. I know everything. Knew you were here before you did," the sheriff said.

Delbert discovered himself moving again.

The cruiser inched forward.

"That foot. Looks 'bout ready to fall off," the sheriff said.

"Popped a ligament," Delbert said.

"That can be serious. Serious, indeed," the sheriff teased with a smirk. "Infection. Gangrene. Maybe amputation. Better get in, hop-along," he said, pumping the brakes and pushing open the passenger door. The cruiser idled softly, purring.

Delbert stopped.

Stared at the open door.

"C'mon. I don't bite. Not today," the sheriff said.

Delbert blinked with uncertainty, but found himself sliding through the open door. Like he had been cast under a spell. The vinyl seats squeaked softly beneath him. Delbert closed the door and the cruiser abandoned the roadside shoulder, moving forward again, rolling at a snail's pace past the blue-collar boxes and their short chain-link fences and fuzzy lights.

"You at Margaret's place, then?" the sheriff said.

Delbert hunched his shoulders.

"Your grandmother, boy."

"She died."

"Course she did, son," the sheriff said with a whiffling sigh. "Dropped a hot iron into her own tub water, didn't she?" he said and reached for a fat expensive cigar burning in the ash tray. Delbert noticed a gold watch adorning a thick hairy wrist and gaudy rings glimmering on thick hairy fingers. "Told you once, didn't I?" the sheriff went on with a slight drawl. "This is my town. I know everything." A dramatic pause, then: "Knew your daddy, too."

He said it in a whisper.

As if saying it out loud might tempt an awful curse.

Delbert sat up. "You knew my father?"

"Took the animal down myself."

The statement was like a punch to Delbert's gut.

"What my daddy done?" Delbert said quietly.

"The worst kind of business."

The cruiser reached the end of the road. Turned.

"I just wonder how far that acorn fell from that rotten tree," the sheriff said, offering Delbert a sidelong glance and a troubled frown. "You look just like him, you know," he said. "Yep, you do. Like a stray dog after a good beating. Nothing more dangerous."

Delbert digested this in silence. Wounded.

"But I tell you what, Delbert," the sheriff said.

Delbert reacted to the sound of his own name.

To the sheriff knowing it.

"I'm a fair man. What that means is you got a clean slate with me," the sheriff said, nodding to himself. "How 'bout we just keep it like that, you think?" The sheriff offered a hand. Full of all those gaudy rings. Glimmering in the fading light.

Delbert stared at the hand.

At those rings. Some with diamonds.

"C'mon, son," the sheriff grunted like his feelings might be hurt. "You come to an understanding with a man and he offers you his hand, you shake it."

Delbert reluctantly offered his own hand.

It disappeared into the sheriff's.

The sheriff squeezed.

A bit too tightly before releasing it.

Delbert didn't make a sound.

The sheriff parked the cruiser at the end of the muddy driveway before the white clapboard house. Delbert tried to open the door, jiggling the handle, but found it locked. He tried pulling up the door lock manually, but it was a futile exercise.

The sheriff just sat there. Staring out.

"Look here, Delbert," the sheriff said after Delbert stopped fiddling. The sheriff had become only a dark amorphous shape in the deepening blackness, a blackness disturbed only by the blinking panel of colorful police lights on the long dashboard. "I never knew my daddy neither, you got me? That man, if you can call him that, run off on us and that was that," the sheriff revealed listlessly in the dark. "What I'm saying is, we've met, you and me, so don't be a stranger. No reason to be in a town this small."

The sheriff toggled a switch.

The door locks popped open.

Delbert nodded. Hobbled out of the cruiser, pushing the door closed behind him, almost slipping in the mud with the effort, his injured ankle betraying him. The front driver window rolled down for the second time that night with its soft electronic whine.

The sheriff smiled.

That slippery grin.

Full of small teeth around that cigar.

"And tell your momma somethin' for me. Tell your momma that old Chuck says welcome back. Tell her I'll come by and say howdy nice and proper one night."

Delbert noticed for the first time a brown sedan parked in the driveway shadows. A small piggish man with a pale balding dome and a blue banker's suit was seated inside the brown sedan. Face slick with sweat. Blinking like a mole caught by a flashlight.

"Say, yes sir," the sheriff said.

"Yes sir," Delbert said.

The sheriff offered the balding man a half-hearted salute. The balding man nodded sheepishly. Stenciled on the side of the brown sedan was SHADY CREEK SAVINGS AND LOAN. The sheriff cruiser melted away into the night. Delbert, his swollen foot suffering the uneven muddy ground, took a wide berth around the brown sedan. The balding man, sipping from a brown bottle tucked in his lap, watched him with small fleshy eyes.

Delbert limped into the house to find his mother primping in front of the hall mirror. Another short skirt, tight blouse, and a pound of make-up, transforming her once again from his mother into one of those women in the fashion magazines stacked in the bathroom. A beautiful, if sad foreign species.

"Where you been?" his mother said, looking at him without looking at him, still primping. "I've been worried sick."

She didn't look worried sick.

She didn't notice his limp, either.

"What time will you be home?" Delbert said.

"I'm not having this conversation," she said.

An impatient honk was heard outside.

"I don't like him," Delbert said.

"Jack? He's a marshmallow."

She grabbed her coat.

Delbert frowned. "Why'd we come here, anyway?" he demanded to know. "I hate it here."

"The wicked witch is dead," his mother said with a sigh, a final glance in the mirror, dabbing at lipstick with a middle finger, puckering, "and we had no place else to go."

"Is my daddy dead, too?" Delbert said.

The question caught her off guard.

"Which one?" she said.

"Is he dead?" Delbert said.

She adopted a coy, defensive smile. A barrier.

"I told you, Delbert," she answered him. "Your momma's always had lots of boyfriends. You got lots of daddies."

Another honk. Louder.

"He kilt somebody, didn't he?" Delbert said.

His mother finally looked at him. Studying Delbert in the cold flat mirror glass. Her voice became cross. And suspicious. "Who you been talking to? Did Marmalade put that nonsense into your head?" she said, her eyes sinking into him like teeth.

"The sheriff," Delbert said.

She froze. Not little by little like the creek outside Delbert's trailer window back in Hendersonville last winter, but all at once like his mother had been dipped into a tub of liquid nitrogen. Delbert wasn't sure she could move. Eventually she did move.

Kneeling beside him. Still looking at him.

But not really seeing him any longer.

Those eyes were somewhere else.

"Listen to me," she said grimly, voice barely above a whisper. "What your daddy done ain't got nothin' to do with us. Nothin'. And it ain't never gonna be our fault."

A final sustained honk from outside.

The front window shivering.

"Ain't never gonna be, Delbert. And that's all you got to know about that business," she said in a breathless hush, then gave him a quick cold peck on his cheek, leaving an imprint of red lipstick. "And you just let that sheriff alone. Promise me."

The words hung in the air. Forebodingly.

"Promise me," she said again, shaking him.

He nodded. Stubbornly.

She slipped out the front door, her eyes still vacant. A strange and disturbing juxtaposition against the ridiculous fake smile on her face offered for the marshmallow sitting in the brown sedan with that brown bottle tucked between his legs.

Delbert stood in the front window, favoring the ankle.

It was really beginning to smart.

He watched the marshmallow's headlights.

Watched them bleed off into the night.

# 4.

**THE PRISON SETTLED INTO A FAMILIAR** nightly routine. An ebb and flow of echoing sound. Like waves crashing and receding on a dark beach. Rising and falling voices. Clanging metal. Droning radios. The collective sigh of bodies coming to rest. But unlike his cellmate lounging lazily in a white T-shirt and blue undershorts in front of a small black and white TV on the bunk above him, the bunk's thin mattress sagging heavily beneath his considerable weight, Freddy was fully dressed behind the thick boiler-plate door, sitting rigidly on the bottom bunk, prison-issue boots firmly planted on the hard granite floor.

A packed duffel bag beside him.

Prison-issue denim jacket buttoned.

A telltale click-clack stopped outside the cell. The eye-slit slid open with its protesting whine and revealed the guard. His slightly jaundiced eyes viewed Freddy with mild amusement.

"You gonna sit like that all night, Freddy?" the guard said. "You ever heard of a watched pot not boiling?"

"You ever heard it's always darkest before the dawn?"

"Fucker has an answer for everything, chief," the cellmate said to the guard. A sleepy yawn. Never taking his eyes off the TV.

A noisy sitcom.

An hour later, after the prison whistle had blown and the lights had blinked twice, replaced with the dim blue nocturnal lights, Freddy was still sitting in the same position. Still fully dressed, prison-issue denim jacket still buttoned, prison-issue boots still firmly planted on the hard granite floor while the prison slept around him. His cellmate snored softly three feet away while soft classical music hushed from the cheap transistor radio. The stone wall was now empty, however. The obituary article gone. The yellowed, tattered photo with the frayed edges also removed.

Leaving a small faded rectangle on the stone.

The yellowed, tattered photo with the frayed edges hung from Freddy's pale fingers, trembling with the spasm in his left hand. Freddy stared at the photo of his younger self and a pregnant young Lillian in the dim blue lights reflecting off the hard granite floor through the air holes in the thick boiler-plate door before tucking the photo gently into a pocket of the denim coat.

He sighed. And waited.

Waited for the stone wall to warm.

For the first hint of sunrise.

# 5.

**DELBERT SAT IN FRONT OF THE TV,** watching nothing in particular. The crumbs of another Delbert special sprinkled across a dinner plate on the coffee table in front of him. The remnants of bread, mayo, an expired can of black olives, and the last of the whipped cream.

His swollen ankle was propped on a couch pillow beneath a bag of frozen broccoli (the ice maker had suddenly stopped spitting out ice cubes last week and its internal coils had frozen solid). The initial shades of blue had added strange, unnatural colors in the intervening hours. Yellow, orange, bronze, and vermilion. An odd symmetry with the colors in the trees outside the window. The distension had only grown worse, too. Delbert could just barely see the faint outline of his ankle bone. Even his toes had become grotesquely large and an unsightly hue of purple. The foot itself felt constricted and heavy. As if encased in a block of drying cement or crushed beneath the suffocating squeeze of a Burmese python like the enormous serpent he'd seen crushing an unfortunate baby fawn on the TV earlier. And it throbbed. A dull, nauseous pain which flared into hot needles of agony if he twisted it only slightly.

He sighed. Tried not to think of gangrene.

Unfortunately, once Delbert tried not to think of such a horrible thing, it was the only thing he could think of. How his foot might become like something out of a zombie apocalypse film. A gray dead piece of meat hanging on ribbons of decomposing muscle and ligaments. And the smell. He could only imagine what it might then smell like. Putrid rotten eggs.

He fished a couple pink tablets from the children's aspirin jar above the kitchen sink and tossed them into his mouth, relishing the bitter taste on his tongue before washing the pills down with the last of the lemon lime soda. The soda was suspiciously flat and didn't leave a sticky residue on the corners of his mouth or bullfrog belches in his belly and he thought perhaps his mother was watering it down again to extend its life. He would have to start marking the plastic jug with a felt pen. Catch her in the act. Of course it might only embolden her, this defiance.

Delbert sighed again. Tried not to think of flesh-eating disease. Immersing himself in a game of solitaire checkers.

At least until he found it difficult to keep his eyes open.

The clock on the wall suddenly reading after midnight.

He contemplated the steep staircase. Grimaced.

An hour later the ankle was still protesting the climb to his bedroom. It felt like a sharp poker yanked from a stream of flowing volcanic lava had been shoved into the sole of his foot. Delbert hid the offended ankle beneath the bed sheets and tried to ignore it, but the undulating waves of grief discovered a fiendish harmony with the classical music on his clock radio.

Trebling with the woodwind instruments.

Rising and falling with the stir of violins.

Hammering with each bellowing horn.

Pounding with the percussions.

Pale headlights splashed across the wall.

Delbert peeked out his bedroom window. It was not his mother, but it was interesting nonetheless. A welcome diversion. A familiar rusted Chevy truck made a shallow U-turn and parked on the sidewalk curb next door beneath a dull street lamp. Delbert sat a little higher in the bed, wincing at the groan of his ankle beneath the sheets. He watched with fascination as Allison and Trigger embraced in the cab, kissing. But it wasn't like the kissing Delbert saw on the TV. It was more frantic. Less practiced and less romantic. Somehow reminding him in an unsettling way of that thick Burmese python and the unfortunate baby fawn.

Allison fell backward.

Against the passenger window.

Trigger fell over her.

Delbert felt his breath turning whispery in his chest, then locking in his narrow throat when Trigger's large pale hand groped, then slipped beneath Allison's shirt. Allison seemed to freeze before glancing over her shoulder at the dark house behind her, slight alarm in her eyes. Still, she didn't resist him and his eager fingers danced more deliberately beneath the fabric of her shirt, disturbing a couple buttons, peeking open the blouse and then her undergarment. Exposing a pale breast. A pink nipple.

Delbert blinked with disbelief. Enthrallment. Shame.

Unable to take his eyes off any of it.

Even though he knew he should.

Until, flushed and befuddled, he noticed another swelling problem beneath the bed sheets. Horror gripped his young pale face. He threw back the linens. Eyes growing wide.

"Oh my god in heaven," he said.

The whispery breaths were back. Gasping.

Threatening hyperventilation.

"I think my dick just popped a ligament."

Later, Delbert would be unable to recall if he'd actually said those words out loud to the empty room or if they had only echoed nonsensically in his numb head. The only thing he would be able to remember with any true clarity about his first erection was stumbling down the steep staircase on his screaming ankle like the house was on fire, hopping madly through the dark living room, just avoiding what might have been a messy collision with a wandering end table, stumbling into the dark kitchen, and popping open the freezer -- avoiding the ice maker coils entombed in ice and yanking out the re-frozen bag of broccoli, shoving the bag down on his nether regions. In his frantic haste, Delbert never noticed his mother at the kitchen table, smoking in the darkness.

Not until her voice startled him.

"What's got into you?" she said.

She had come home while he was asleep.

Her voice sounded uneven. Rough around the edges.

"I popped a ligament," he said.

"You popped a what?"

He held out his discolored ankle.

"Aw fuck, Delbert."

"It wasn't my fault."

"You know we don't got no health insurance. Better not be broke. Shit," she said. Then confused, she blinked and motioned with the glowing cigarette at the crinkling bag of frozen broccoli pushed against his crotch. "What else you done to yourself?"

"Nothing," he muttered, humiliated.

Delbert peeked beneath the frozen bag.

Blood rushed to his face. Burning his cheeks.

"Don't make me come over there," she said.

He found himself unable to move.

"Fuck, I mean it, Delbert."

He slowly removed the bag.

"Jesus, Mary, and Joseph," she said, sitting forward.

Delbert slammed the bag back over his crotch.

To her inebriated laughter.

"Guess I'll have to worry about you going blind now."

"Blind?" he said. A mysterious new worry.

"Get yourself a cold shower," she said, laughing. Her throaty laughter ended in a coughing fit. She bent forward into the moonlight to clear the congestion--

--revealing for the first time a black eye.

"Your eye," Delbert said.

"Just a love scratch."

"The marshmallow do that?" Delbert said.

His mother managed a smile, then nodded at the bag of broccoli and sighed. Suddenly very tired. Like it was an effort to defeat gravity any longer. An effort to simply keep herself from sliding from the chair and onto the floor. "You think you're a man now, that it?" she said. "You think you can protect me?" A colder, more cynical laughter followed. Delbert could still hear the derision in that laughter as he stood beneath a cold stream of water in the shower later. He glanced nervously below his belly button. Fortunately, it appeared everything was back to normal with the exception of his ankle. It now looked like a messy shovel of clay unceremoniously dumped and still waiting to be molded before it dried. Shivering, Delbert toweled off and headed to bed -- trying to ignore the siren lure of the window.

He peeked out anyway.

Unable to help himself.

Harlan stood in a robe on the front porch next door. Hands on his hips. Sniffling with growing impatience. Stamping a slipper like a child having a tantrum. A comb-over flapping in the breeze like an injured bat wing. Or like his scalp might come clean off, reminding Delbert of those unlucky pioneers in the black and white westerns on the TV where Indians hooted and hollered in war paint and rode spotted ponies and twirled stone hatchets.

Allison exited her boyfriend's truck and marched into the house past her father, still buttoning her blouse, chin tucked into her chest. Harlan barely gave his daughter a glance, choosing instead to stare down Trigger. Trigger stared right back at the man in his robe and slippers on the porch, a goofy smile pulling across his face, before turning over the ignition.

The grumbling beast roared to life. Revved.

Then peeled from the curb.

Burping and convulsing.

Harlan watched the truck gain speed, tossing aside a mound of wet, moldy leaves congregated over a storm drain, leaving a strip of rubber when it ran a stop sign and took the corner without braking. Harlan shook his head. Comb-over tickling his opposite ear.

Allison's bedroom light blinked on upstairs.

Her curtains were open.

Delbert silently scolded himself, but propped his dimpled chin on the windowsill, helplessly watching Allison undress and slip into her nightgown. Her father eventually appeared in her bedroom doorway. Apoplectic and interrogating.

There were heated words.

His voice became louder.

More imprudent. Reprimanding.

Allison didn't try to defend Trigger as much as she attempted to defend herself. At least that was the impression Delbert had from this distance. It was a fruitless exercise and she finally turned her back on her inconsolable father, slipping below the bed sheets and a warm comforter, staring out the window toward the heavens. Her eyes desperate and yearning. As if wishing for wings to fly away. Delbert became lost in that sad, vacant stare. Until he sensed someone watching him. A chill shook him like the cold shower water earlier. His gaze lifted. He found Harlan's aggrieved stare.

Glaring past the window glass.

And the curtain of night.

Into his bedroom.

At him.

Delbert ducked beneath the windowsill, his breath coming in short, desperate, gasping pants once again. The world became silent, too quiet, at least until the big plastic number flaps inside his clock radio turned suddenly with a shuttering click. He waited, staring at the knotted-pine wall beneath his bedroom window until he heard five such shuttering clicks. He then slowly lifted his head. Allowing his eyes to slip back over the windowsill.

Millimeters at a time.

Only to find Allison's curtains now shut.

A moment later her bedroom light blinked off, too.

# 6.

**B**UT FOR THE OCCASIONAL FLUSH OF a toilet and the quick rush of water running through corroded pipes behind the thick stone walls, there was an almost perfect silence. It was a rare early morning treat. An impermanent magic spell which would soon be broken by men rising from bed -- shuffling feet, a growing symphony of flushing toilets, running sink water, noisy TVs, and scratchy radios. But for those brief moments before the world inside this gloomy dungeon woke from slumber to waking nightmare, there was an almost perfect silence. It was interrupted for Freddy very early this particular morning by the click-clack of a guard's hard-soled boots in the blue-tinted darkness outside the boiler-plate door and the ensuing screech of the eye-slit. A whispering voice said: "You ready, then, Freddy?"

The guard with slightly jaundiced eyes peering through the narrow eye-slit at the end of his night shift found Freddy still sitting like a statue on the edge of his lower bunk just as he had been at last check the night before. Still fully dressed. Prison-issue denim jacket still buttoned. Prison-issue boots still firmly planted on the hard granite floor. Packed duffel bag still at his feet.

Freddy rose stiffly in the cell blackness. His knotted muscles and his frozen bones unlocking in stubborn fits and starts from their self-imposed curse. Freddy stood for a brief moment in the darkness, listening to his cellmate toss and turn but not wake in the shadows beside him before gathering his duffel bag and tossing it over a shoulder. The guard led Freddy through the narrow catwalks past more boiler-plate doors and a guard station and down a maze of narrow stone tunnels constituting the bowels of the prison before climbing a series of stone stairs. The dim blue lights slowly gave way to bright white fluorescents and wired windows filled with the first bands of cold pale sunlight.

Shortly thereafter, Freddy stood in a processing center.

A prison clerk with sleepy bags drooping beneath his eyes like a basset hound stood behind a short counter in a small office completely enclosed in a steel wire cage. The wire cage offered the impression of a chicken coop, but for the shelves and drawers and dusty stacks of paperwork to be processed and filed. Freddy stood as he had been instructed behind a double yellow line. The guard who had escorted him to the surface stood beside him. The prison clerk blinked his sad-looking basset hound eyes and pushed a form toward Freddy through a small square opening in the cage and past a half-eaten jelly donut sitting on top of a duck hunting catalogue advertising an end of the year clearance on duck hunting boats.

"Listen up now," the clerk said, preparing to recite a litany of humorless directives. There was a fresh jelly stain on his tie amid a hodgepodge of older, more permanent stains. "No booze on the outside," he said drearily. "No drugs. No unauthorized pharmaceuticals without written permission from this processing center. Not even aspirin." He tapped the form. "Initial here."

Freddy initialed the form.

A pen attached to a metal string.

"You will phone this processing center at ten p.m. each and every night, including tonight," the clerk said. "And nine a.m. each and every morning. Not ten-oh-five. Not nine-I-couldn't-find-change-for-the-pay-phone-oh-five," the clerk cautioned with a tiresome sigh. "You will call this processing center at your designated times." Another tap of the form. "Initial here."

Freddy initialed.

"You will remain in Shady County for the duration of your release," the clerk said. "Understand you are participating in a graduated early release study program for the next five months prior to your scheduled parole hearing date. You've been selected for this early release program based on your good behavior in this institution and by conditional recommendation of the parole board," the clerk continued, wiping accumulated wet from his nose with the back of his hand. "This program is designed to ease re-entry into society, but it is not mandatory. It is a privilege." The clerk's voice momentarily dropped any pretense of formality. "In other words, convict," he said pointedly, "your parole looks solid gold, so don't fuck it up." He tapped the form again. "Initial here."

Freddy did as instructed.

"You will check back into this processing center no later than five p.m. Monday afternoon the eighteenth of November," the clerk continued. "Any questions?"

Freddy shook his head.

"Sign here, then."

Freddy signed the form.

The clerk examined the form, back to front, then back to front again, then sighed and rummaged through a drawer before sliding a gray envelope through the square opening in the wire cage and across the counter to Freddy.

The gray envelope contained money administered from his prison account. "My advice," the clerk said, his basset hound features tugging down his wrinkled face in the bright and buzzing fluorescents, his large sad eyes blinking, "stay away from women of questionable virtue if you want bus fare back up the hill."

Freddy considered the crumpled bills in the envelope.

The money was a mere pittance.

He stuffed the envelope into his denim coat.

"You can take that off now," the guard said. "The shirt."

Freddy nodded and temporarily removed the denim coat in order to remove his prison work shirt with his prison ID number stenciled on the breast pocket. He placed the shirt in a heap on the short counter extending from the wire cage before pulling the denim coat back over a plain white prison-issue T-shirt and prison-issue denim jeans. He had no clothes of his own.

The guard smirked. "You look like James Dean, Freddy."

"There goes the bus fare," the clerk muttered, dragging the prison work shirt through the square opening in the wire cage and retreating to his jelly donut and duck hunting catalogue.

The fluorescents buzzed and blinked.

Blinked and buzzed.

# 7.

**DELBERT WOKE FROM A FEVER DREAM** on the precipice of a scream. In his nightmare he had imagined the closet door opposite his bed niggling open while he slept and something stirring in the cave-like darkness. Something scaly with a narrow snuffling snout and blinking yellow eyes and sharp claws and long jagged teeth. A golem. He had dreamt the golem had considered him only briefly, however, before slinking off down the dark hallway, dragging its reptilian belly to his mother's bedroom. His mother had been asleep on her bed. A foot dangling off the mattress, hanging in space over the dark hollow beneath her bed, her chest rising and falling heavily as if she was lost in her own night terror as the prehistoric creature born from Delbert's closet slid silently beneath her box spring.

Delbert had tried to scream -- to warn her -- but nothing would come out as the demon's jaws flashed swiftly in the murky dimness, seizing his mother's foot and wrenching her down into the hollow darkness. Delbert could still hear the awful wet sound of her flesh being stripped like banana skin and the echoing crack of her fragile bones and his mother, now awake, screaming his name over and over again from the blackness.

He woke drenched in sweat. Panting.

The real world swam into view.

The closet door was open and gray sunlight exposed its shallow interior, revealing only a growing pile of dirty laundry and old secondhand clothes hanging limply from hangars while traffic reports droned noisily from the clock radio beside him. Everything was as it should be. Still, Delbert found it difficult to push aside the terrible dream and even more difficult to resist a primordial urge to shout out his mother's name just to hear her voice.

He closed his eyes. Inhaled.

Opened them again. Exhaled.

Inhaled. Exhaled.

He remained there on his back for a few long moments, staring at the ceiling, allowing galaxies of dust motes swirling silently in the gray morning light around him to wash away the macabre of his sleeping mind. There was no need to pull back the bed sheets to know his ankle had not miraculously healed overnight. The tight knot of pain greeted him, throbbing, as surely as the dust motes swirling about the room. Like it was a thing separate from himself. A thing with its own hammering heartbeat. And once again Delbert helplessly thought of his mother's foot dangling in space and the silvery flash of that miscreation's salivating jaws.

He rubbed the sleep crud from his eyes.

Yawned. Stretched.

And listened to the birds rustling in the trees outside his window, calling out to each other in their shrill, excited voices. He then cautiously rose on skinny elbows. And peeked over his windowsill. Allison's curtains were open. But did not reveal Allison.

Rather, her mother.

Delbert blinked with surprise. Ducked.

Inhaled. Exhaled.

Lifted his head again. Peeking.

Allison's mother was a pale, willowy woman with an expressionless face and long, unkempt curly hair. She was sitting on Allison's unmade bed. Just sitting there facing the window. Alone. Staring at nothing. Unmoving. Unreal. As if in effigy.

She was gone by the time Delbert finished dressing.

The bed neatly made in her absence.

Delbert hobbled downstairs, gritting his teeth with each painful step, to find his mother had slept on the couch, the frozen bag of broccoli over her black eye. He flipped on cartoons, turning up the volume loudly on purpose, then resuming an unfinished game of checkers from the previous evening.

His mother peeked with irritation from the vegetable bag.

"How is that fun, Delbert?" she said after a beat, sighing, her voice raspy from a lack of sleep, frowning as he rotated the checkers board. "You always win."

"I always lose, too," he said.

"Jesus Christ in heaven above, you're going to give me a worse headache than this hangover," she moaned and hid again behind the vegetable bag with an exasperated grunt. "What I need is ten more hours of sleep and enough aspirin to kill a small dog."

"Maybe you shouldn't drink so much," he said.

"And lose my sanity? I'm self-medicating."

She peeked out again. Warily.

Earning a sanctimonious stare from Delbert.

"You're going to drive me crazy today, aren't you?" she said with another sigh. She grabbed a small notepad from an end table, scribbling with a pencil. "Want you to go to the corner for me," she said, handing Delbert the note before ducking again behind the bag of broccoli. "The hair off the dog that bit me. Get it. There's money in my purse."

Delbert opened his mother's purse.

Found a wad of money. Damp and sweaty.

Delbert proceeded out into the gray morning. He tried not to favor the ankle and he thought maybe it had begun to loosen as he rounded Magnolia Street and turned onto Main. Ten minutes later he was piling grocery items next to the cash register in the country general store on the corner of Main and 2nd. A small bottle of aspirin, a can of whipped cream, a half dozen pixie sticks, a liter of root beer, a jar of peanut butter, Wonder bread, a box of cheese crackers, a plastic carton of tomato juice -- and a large bottle of vodka.

A grocery clerk with silver hair and silver eyes and a long white vendor apron that swished at his ankles like a reversed cape stood behind the register. "Need to see some ID, sir," the grocery clerk said with wry amusement, a silver eyebrow lifting.

Delbert handed him his mother's note.

"You forgot Tabasco sauce," the grocery clerk said after reading the note, gesturing to the condiment aisle.

Delbert hobbled over to the condiment aisle, searching the shelves with neat rows of ketchup and mustard and mayo and relish and tartar sauce and a colorful assortment of salad dressing brands. "Bottom shelf, partner," the grocery clerk said.

The bell over the front door jingled.

Allison stepped quietly into the store.

Reluctantly. Like she wasn't sure where she was.

Or if she should even be there.

Delbert's face flushed, but Allison didn't appear to notice him. She appeared to stare right through him before vanishing to the back of the store. Delbert located the Tabasco and proceeded back to the front counter, searching out Allison, but she was hidden amongst the back shelves.

"How 'bout some celery, kiddo?" the grocery clerk remarked, a silver eyebrow raised. "Or you gonna stir this Bloody Mary with those pixie sticks?"

"She don't like anything green," Delbert said.

"Course not." Chuckling dryly, his silver head shaking, the grocery clerk handed the note back to Delbert. "Pretty decent forgery, kiddo. Least that's what I'd say if I didn't know your momma. Unfortunately, I do know your momma and this has gone far enough 'fore you start taking the long way home or never get home at all with a bottle of nonsense to occupy your afternoon. Next thing I know they're scraping you like a June bug off the tracks," the grocery clerk contemplated, scooping the vodka off the counter and placing it on a shelf beneath it. Simultaneously, he was watching Allison in a security mirror.

She was loitering in the drug aisle.

Unaware she could be seen.

Stuffing something beneath her shirt.

The grocery clerk's silver eyes narrowed, lips pursing. His voice remained calm. Unrevealing. "Still want the Tabasco sauce and tomato juice, chief?" he said to Delbert, drifting out from behind the counter, turning the dead bolt on the front door.

The lock slid home with barely a whisper.

"Tabasco sauce, tomato juice, yes or no?"

"Tomato juice," Delbert said, flustered.

The grocery clerk returned behind the counter.

Rang up the sale.

"Doesn't like anything green," he repeated, chuckling again, though his laughter no longer bore any resemblance to amusement. He was still monitoring Allison in the security mirror. The narrow security mirror ran the length of the store above the drug aisle and the sundries, tilted downward, revealing every last corner and crevice. "Word to the wise, next time take the celery, partner."

Allison tried to sneak out the front door.

Found it locked.

The grocery clerk grunted, somehow both satisfied and disenchanted. He stepped out from behind the counter for the second time in the last minute, hand extended from his long white apron swishing at his ankles, his palm turned toward the ceiling. "Either you're with child, Miss Allison Winslow," he said, "or you're trying to steal from me." Allison's entire body seemed to collapse into itself like a dwarf star. She looked everywhere at once and nowhere in particular as if wishing she could melt into the hardwood floor beneath her sneakers and disappear between the odd gaps in the splintered old planks. When she realized such an escape simply defied the laws of nature, her round young face crumbled inward and her chin fell into her narrow chest. She lifted her shirt--

--and a pregnancy kit fell out.

She burst into tears.

"Oh no," the grocery clerk said.

Ashamed, Allison desperately reversed course and ran past the sundries and the drug aisle and below the tilted security mirror to a back door propped open with a wet mop and bucket, disappearing into the gray morning. The grocery clerk stared at the back door, then slowly bent over, back and knees cracking, and scooped up the pregnancy kit with a sad, grandfatherly sigh. "If I had a flat nickel every time a teenager got herself pregnant in this godforsaken town," he said to no one in particular, "I'd be a Rockefeller."

He finished ringing up Delbert's order. Still sighing.

"That, too," Delbert said.

He pointed at the pregnancy kit.

"Best you run home and get another note," the clerk said.

"Sell it to him, pops," a voice said. A woman's voice. It came from a narrow staircase beyond the frozen foods. It led to an office upstairs. The voice belonged to Holly Sherwin, Delbert's teacher. She had a pencil behind her ear and paperwork in her hand.

"Miss Holly," Delbert said. Surprised.

"Hello yourself, Delbert. Your foot better, is it?"

Delbert shrugged. Speechless.

"Don't worry," his teacher said, standing on the narrow staircase, the wooden steps beneath her worn to a slick, polished nub in the middle where foot traffic had concentrated for decades. "We're still friends. What happened yesterday, not your fault, anyway."

Delbert nodded. Relieved.

His teacher motioned to the pregnancy kit.

Imploring her father.

The grocery clerk relented. Stuffing it into a paper bag with the other grocery items. "You're still not getting the pickle juice, though, chief," he said with a grunt.

Delbert exited the general store. He juggled the grocery bag, trying to find just the right spot above his hip where it wouldn't dig into his hipbone. He noticed Holly Sherwin standing in a small attic window above him. He silently nodded his thanks.

She nodded back.

Delbert adjusted the grocery bag again. Somehow it kept finding that hipbone. And shuffled off down the street. He only got a few short steps before noticing the sheriff cruiser parked outside the Shady Creek Savings and Loan across the road. Sheriff Snodgrass was loitering on the front steps chatting with Jack the Marshmallow. Delbert scowled at the marshmallow.

He had half a mind to march across the road and--

Well, truth be known, Delbert wasn't sure what he might've done if he had done so, but he supposed it wouldn't have ended well for the marshmallow if he could have just figured it out. He would have put the hurt on that fat tub of cowardly dog shit in his silly banker's suit stretched like stale taffy to accommodate his nauseating girth. He was sure of it. Unfortunately, all Delbert found himself capable of at the moment, while the grocery bag dug deeper into his hipbone, was consider what a crackling campfire might do to a soft, gooey marshmallow neglected for a few moments too long on the end of a sharp stick. It was during the throes of entertaining the image of such a marshmallow turning sooty black and sliding off that stick to be devoured into nothingness in the fire when Delbert realized the men had noticed him, too.

He ducked his head low (as if frightened they might be able to read his thoughts) and quickly limped away, his lame foot bouncing like an over-inflated tire over the uneven sidewalk.

He could feel their eyes on his back, tracking him, as he hobbled around the corner and out of sight.

His mother was still reclined on the couch, watching a game show on the TV, when Delbert finally pushed through the door with the grocery bag. "You break another ankle, Charlie Brown, or were you hoping I would die of thirst?" she said.

Delbert handed his mother the tomato juice.

"Hey, forgetting something?" she said.

Delbert put the liter of root beer in the fridge, then headed for the staircase with the grocery bag. He crumpled his mother's note and tossed it in a wastebasket along the way, speaking to her without turning around: "Get your own dog hair, mom," he said.

A few minutes later he was in his bedroom.

He dumped the remaining grocery items on the bed. He sat on the bed with his back against the wall and sucked down the tart pixie stick candy with healthy squirts of whipped cream and read the pregnancy kit package with bewilderment and wonder.

The curtains were again drawn over Allison's window.

Beyond them was only darkness.

# 8.

THE BUS SPENT LESS THAN EIGHT minutes in the small foothill town of Shady Creek. Five minutes were spent parked in front of the bus station on Bus Depot Lane and 4th Ave. A few passengers made use of the toilets and the vending machine inside the station before trudging back onto the old Greyhound, the factory town around them already forgotten in their travel-weary minds even before the brakes released with the quiet hiss of a dragon and the bus continued down the highway, disappearing into the green curtain of forest.

Only a single passenger remained behind.

Freddy Jackson.

Freddy reflexively swallowed a gulp of the cold morning air like a drowning victim might take in a mouthful of brackish water in an instinctive, if ill-conceived spasm to survive. The cold morning air stung his lungs and he shivered and found himself staring up at the gray sky. The sky seemed impossibly large and impossibly vast. A dizziness washed over him. A world without stone walls was proving overwhelming to his stunted sense of proportion and space. The sky a bottomless chasm into which he might himself be swallowed. Freddy grabbed a handrail. He grabbed the handrail as much to steady himself from fainting as to prevent himself from simply floating off like an un-tethered balloon into those infinite gray heavens where he might drift and disappear from all existence below. When the dizziness finally subsided, more or less, he willed himself to release the handrail, gradually unlocking his fingers from the cold aluminum. He still felt the weight of that endless expanse tugging at him like a magnet, but further willed himself to remain on the ground, pulling his prison-issue denim jacket tighter around him and shouldering the duffel bag.

He walked slowly into town.

His back hunching more than before.

His head bent low.

As if into a headwind.

A stranger might have been startled by the sudden and piercing whine of the mill whistle on the hill, but not Freddy.

Freddy wasn't a stranger and he paid the mill whistle no more attention than he did the muffled click-clack of a freight train passing on the outskirts of town or the soft whispering shuffle of his prison-issue boots on the sidewalk pavement.

# 9.

**DELBERT SPENT THE AFTERNOON** staving off an otherwise certain sugar crash with cheese cracker sundaes. Cheese crackers topped with healthy dollops of canned whipped cream and a dusting of pixie stick candy. He sat at his desk beside his bedroom window, popping the cheese cracker sundaes into his mouth and occupying himself with the construction of a model airplane. A WWII German Messerschmitt BF109 from the North African theater -- distinguished by its leopard spot camouflage and an ominous black iron cross on the rear fuselage. Unfortunately, a tray of model airplane parts had been misplaced during the move and Delbert spent a good hour searching through cardboard boxes marked DELBERT'S BEDROOM before he finally found the lost tray under a pile of dirty Tonka trucks and an old pitted baseball bat.

The tray of airplane parts was crushed.

Leaving the plane only half-finished.

Delbert dropped his head on the desk beside the incomplete model and stared at it morosely until he realized the Messerschmitt might have looked much like this if it had been shot down in mid-flight by an Allied fighter jet and allowed to tumble in a death spiral from the brilliantly blue North African sky to smash in a cloud of gravel dust on the sunbaked African tundra. This satisfied him immensely and Delbert got back to work with a renewed purpose, forehead furrowed with concentration, fashioning the Messerschmitt BF109 into a casualty of war. Even having the inspiration to use a lit match to create realistic burn patterns on its fuselage and wings and twisting pieces of plastic metal to imitate a horrible concussion. Eventually, the task complete, Delbert sat back with satisfaction, the world now turning dark outside his bedroom window, and admired his clever work for a long moment. Then, tickled with the results, he placed the Messerschmitt on a shelf along with a debris field of crushed airplane components. He could almost hear the screaming engine choking and spitting as the front propeller wound down for the last time, the airplane listing in death.

"Cool," he said.

That done, Delbert leaned to the left as he had done intermittently most of that lazy afternoon and peered at Allison's bedroom window. The curtains were still drawn, but there was now a dull light behind them, offering tantalizing shadows. Delbert scrunched his eyes, trying to make sense of the odd shadows when a larger shadow grew on his bedroom wall. His mother blowing into his bedroom in her usual chaotic frenzy.

Short skirt. Make-up. Skintight blouse. High heels.

She checked her appearance in a mirror.

"I should be an artist," she said. Primping.

Her black eye was expertly concealed.

She eventually considered Delbert in the cold flat mirror reflection. "Aren't you going to ask me what time I'll be home?" she said. "You're usually a broken record."

"I'm not having this conversation," he said.

"Little smart ass," she said.

She sat on the bed, facing him.

It was only then Delbert noticed with alarm the pregnancy kit sitting in an open desk drawer beside various knick-knacks, including a yo-yo and the last of the model airplane glue -- a tightly scrunched, dimpled plastic tube. Delbert sucked in a startled breath and slapped the drawer closed with the back of his hand, the resulting bang earning a frown from his mother. But she was otherwise too busy untangling a small knot in her necklace, lost in her own thoughts, to have apparently noticed the drawer's contents. "I told the marshmallow he could stick it where the sun don't never shine," she said proudly after a beat, finishing with the necklace, turning to adjust her hair again, this time in the dark reflection of the bedroom window. "I got a new friend tonight. A dentist."

Delbert didn't pretend to be impressed.

"If I had a flat nickel every time you got yourself a new friend in this godforsaken town," he said, "I'd be a Rockefeller."

The words stunned her. Like a slap.

First with surprise. Then hurt.

Like Marmalade.

She became mean, spine stiffening, her shadow falling over him. "You wanted to know about your miserable father the other day, didn't you?" she said, staring off into the distance now. "I think you did. Well, Delbert, you just reminded me of him."

Headlights splashed across the window.

A honk. A sports utility vehicle.

His mother left the bedroom without another word, just the hollow click-clack of her heels marching down the hall and descending the staircase. Delbert stared drearily at the empty doorway after she had gone. Frozen with guilt and curiosity.

Each emotion gripping him in equal measure.

Paralyzed by the inherent mystery of her rebuke.

The headlights splashed away from the window.

The car engine faded into the night.

Delbert turned back to Allison's window.

Her window was now open, allowing the flimsy curtains to be teased by the evening breeze, offering brief glimpses of the young girl standing in a bathrobe, brushing her hair before a vanity mirror. Absent, zombie-like strokes. The soft bristles tugging through her long hair in stuttered and staggered grabs. Pull. Repeat. Pull. Repeat. Soft clouds of steam from a warming shower forming an ephemeral mist outside her open bathroom door.

A few moments later Delbert stood before the vanity mirror in his mother's bathroom. The vanity counter was a collision between a drug store and a beauty parlor. Delbert studied himself in the mirror, then sat down to get to work. A giant brush to allay his hair. A mist of hairspray to knock down that stubborn cowlick. A cotton ball and rubbing alcohol to clean the model airplane glue from his fingers and a rim of black filth from beneath his fingernails. He then sniffed at his mother's perfume bottles. Wrinkled his nose. Sniffed others tucked beneath the counter. Settled on something. Something that wasn't too floral. Something adorned by a purple bottle resembling a genie lamp. He positioned the bottle's spigot just below his jaw line like he had seen his mother do a hundred times before. Unfortunately, he lacked his mother's deft touch and the trigger-sensitive lever unloaded a barrage of abrupt squirts, producing a sweet acrid cloud of fragrance, doubling him over in a coughing, sneezing fit. He was still coughing and sneezing when he exited the white clapboard house. He cleared the noxious phlegm from his throat a final time, spitting into the bushes, before slipping from the weak porch light into the darkness, hobbling on his ankle between his house and Allison's bedroom window. His sneakers quickly became damp in the wet grass. A grocery bag dangled from his right hand, making a soft crinkling noise.

He paused in the darkness.

And faced a giant Maple tree.

The tree stood outside Allison's window like a monstrous sentry from a fairy tale, its crown hidden in the darkness above. It had a wide and sturdy trunk, bark dark gray and deeply furrowed, with thick wandering roots and a playground of rising limbs offering a crude ladder cloaked in brilliant orange and yellow foliage.

A rusty bike leaned at its base.

The bike startled Delbert. Its presence.

"If you was a horse, I'd have to put you down," a voice said. It was a familiar voice. Belonging to something rustling in the nest of orange-yellow leaves. Delbert blinked his eyes, adjusting them to the darkness after the weak porch light, and discovered the voice belonged to Ollie hidden amongst the autumn colors.

Ollie pointed a stick like a rifle.

"Turn you into dog food," he said. Bang, bang.

"Ollie, that you?" Delbert said stupidly.

"That's my name, ask me again I'll tell you the same."

"What's your name?" Delbert said more stupidly.

"Ollie. That's my name, ask me again I'll tell you the same."

"What's your--?"

"Shut up, Delbert."

Ollie was standing on a thin branch. The branch extended out from the wide and sturdy trunk to within four feet of Allison's bedroom window, allowing the large country bumpkin to use the rifle stick to peek open Allison's bedroom curtains.

"What're you doing?" Delbert said more stupidly than ever.

"Ain't you never seen a peepshow?" Ollie said.

Running water could be heard beyond the curtains.

A small waterfall behind the closed bathroom door.

The shower. Allison was in the shower.

Delbert felt his face getting hot.

"They climb trees where you're from, doofus?" Ollie said.

Delbert regarded the tree. Gritted his teeth. Reached for a low thick branch and swung a leg over it. Then his body. He stood up carefully. Reached for another branch. Pulled himself up. Belly. Butt. Feet. Ollie watched. Bemused. Not offering to help. Content to watch Delbert's awkward ascent into the orange-yellow heart of the magnificent old Maple tree made more challenging by his swollen ankle and the crinkling grocery bag in his right hand.

"What stinks?" Ollie said suspiciously, sniffing the air.

"I don't smell nothin'," Delbert said,

He scrambled beside Ollie. Out of breath.

Ollie sniffed the air again. Spat.

"What's in the bag?" he said.

"Nothin'," Delbert said.

"Show me," Ollie demanded.

"Nothin', I said."

"You buy her perfume?" Ollie said.

Maybe a bit jealous.

Delbert struggled to find his balance on the thin branch. The branch danced up and down and back and forth with the slightest movement of the big country boy, shooting fresh splinters of pain from Delbert's swollen ankle into his leg.

"You bought her perfume," Ollie surmised.

"Did not."

"Did too," Ollie said.

"Did not."

"You're sweet on her," Ollie said.

"Am not," Delbert said, his face getting hot again.

"Are too."

"Am not," Delbert said louder.

Ollie put a finger to his lips. Pointed his rifle stick at a downstairs window. Allison's father, Harlan, and Allison's mother could be seen watching TV. Harlan was drinking a beer, slunk down on the couch, slippers on a coffee table littered with the day's newspaper. Allison's mother sat on the far end of the couch, pushed stiffly against the arm, staring blankly at the flickering TV lights. Like maybe she was watching and maybe she wasn't.

"Are too," Ollie repeated, whispering. "No take backs."

"You're the one in the tree, doofus," Delbert said.

"Don't call me doofus, doofus," Ollie said and punched Delbert in the arm, causing Delbert to wobble precariously on the branch, ankle screaming. Ollie took advantage of Delbert's incapacitation and grabbed the grocery bag from his hand. Delbert protested with alarm, but the branch bounced even more wildly beneath him, forcing him to forgo the grocery bag and instead grab a bushel of spidery branches to keep from tumbling from the tree. Ollie, meanwhile, rode the branch like he was glued to it. Hips and knees moving in different directions. The ground jumping and retreating. Sliding back and forth. The world an earthquake.

Eventually the branch settled again.

Ollie opened the grocery bag like it might contain the treasure of the Sierra Madre. Eyes blissfully wide, his mouth slanted in a crackerjack smile, his greedy hand dug into the crinkling brown bag and pulled out the pregnancy kit. He stared at it dumbly at first. "One Minute Pregnancy Kit," he read. Then stared at Delbert.

Bewildered. Impressed.

"Give it back," Delbert said.

"This ain't perfume," Ollie said.

"She wants to be knocked up."

"Knocked up?"

"That's what the man at the store said. She tried to swipe it."

Ollie grunted with amusement and jiggled the one minute pregnancy kit in front of Delbert's nose. "You don't need a preggars kit to get pregnant, doofus," he said.

Delbert absorbed this with fascination.

One mystery replaced by another while the shower water continued behind the closed bathroom door.

"You swipe this?" Ollie accused.

Delbert realized there was no good answer.

But shook his head.

"You spent money. You are sweet on her, then."

"Am not."

"Are too."

"Am not."

"Are too," Ollie hushed, putting a fat period on the matter and reconsidering the pregnancy kit with disdain now. "But you ain't the only one neither. Not if she was trying to swipe this. Not 'less you got a super duper penis, Delbert, and she was unconscious."

"She got a boyfriend," Delbert said.

"I know. A real dickweed."

Delbert digested this, too. Frowned.

"Pound your skinny ass when he finds this."

Ollie smiled. That crackerjack smile. Then flung the pregnancy kit through the open window. The pregnancy kit wobbled and twirled like a hockey puck, then slid across the hardwood floor like it was on ice before cleverly vanishing beneath the bed.

Delbert was mortified. "You doofus…!!" he shouted.

"Said don't call me doofus, doofus," Ollie said.

He socked Delbert's arm again for good measure.

The branch shuddered. Delbert danced with it. Cringing. Rubbing his arm only when the branch finally settled down again.

Only a corner of the box stuck out from beneath an overhanging comforter. Ollie whistled softly with admiration at his own serendipitous heave. Then said in ominous forewarning:

"Bet dimes to donuts her mom finds it the next time she changes the bed sheets."

"No," Delbert said lamely. Horrified.

"So go get it," Ollie said.

After several tense moments of back and forth conversation and accusation devolving into double dares only two young boys could understand, it was decided Delbert should crawl through the window and rectify the misdeed before Allison got in serious trouble. Really serious trouble.

Grown-up trouble.

With Ollie gripping Delbert's shirt collar to anchor him, Delbert sucked in a deep gulp of that cold, sobering autumn night air and stretched out his good foot from the tree, the branch trembling beneath his bad foot, tempting a steep drop onto the thick root-rippled lawn and thorny hedges below. His sneaker stretched and stretched and landed on the windowsill--

--only to promptly slip in a slime of dew.

Nearly tumbling him head over butt.

But for Ollie's sure grip.

Delbert tried again. This time landing his sneaker more fully on the sill. He leaned forward with determination and felt Ollie's fingers release his shirt collar. He was now fully committed. And using his good foot like a pole vault, jumped through the window, soaring through the swishing curtains as if appearing from thin air and landing awkwardly and quite heavily on the bedroom floor. Legs and arms going in all sorts of directions.

All of which made a loud and horrible thump.

Ollie threw up his hands.

"Don't move. Jeez," he said.

From the tree shadows, Ollie stared at the downstairs window revealing the TV room. "Her daddy got up," he said, hands still in the air as if their machinations could keep Delbert frozen in place or somehow fling him back into the Maple tree, if necessary. Fortunately, the shower water continued behind the bathroom door. Meanwhile, down in the TV room, Harlan scowled. Stared up at the ceiling. Then walked slowly toward the stairs.

Ollie held his breath.

Delbert tried to read Ollie's face. He felt nailed to the floor. Like a deer in bright headlights. He doubted he could move unless Ollie's hands proved magical after all. The thump he'd made seemed to echo about the bedroom and into the bones of the house itself like a tuning fork. Announcing his trespassing even as his body failed to heed its warning.

Harlan paused at the staircase. Listened.

Then wandered into the kitchen.

Collecting another beer from the fridge.

He then wandered back into the front room and stared up at the ceiling a final time before plopping back down on the couch beside his wife who hadn't even blinked.

Ollie's hands gradually lowered.

"He sat back down," he whispered.

"Honest to god?" Delbert said.

"On my mother's soul," Ollie said.

Delbert found himself moving. Crawling.

Toward Allison's bed.

Delbert pulled the pregnancy kit out from its mischievous hiding place beneath the overhanging comforter and placed it on top of the bed in plain view.

It was then the shower water cut off.

Inviting a sudden and terrible silence.

Frantic, Delbert hobbled toward the window. Certain he could hear his lame foot bouncing like a stone on the hardwood floor. The window seemed to recede with his every step. Like he was moving in slow motion and the distance between himself and that small opening was somehow growing like something in a funhouse mirror. He tripped. Fell toward the window. Hands grasping for it dumbly. Grappling. Then pulling himself up.

Only to have Ollie block his exit.

His large frame filling the void.

"Lemme out," Delbert hissed, pleading.

It was met with the crackerjack smile. And a finger jabbing at a pile of clean folded laundry on a dresser all the way back across the room. "Panty raid, doofus," Ollie said, eyes gleaming, crackerjack smile pulling wider. As if in that funhouse mirror.

"Lemme out," Delbert said again.

A struggle ensued.

Ollie playfully shoved Delbert away from the window and then snapped the window closed from the outside, trapping Delbert inside the bedroom. Delbert could no longer hear the big mischievous country boy, only read his moving lips beyond the shimmering glass. "Panties, doofus," the lips said.

A pair of flowery underwear sat on top of the laundry pile. Pink and yellow and blue. Head shaking ruefully, Delbert hobbled back across the room and snatched the undergarment from the laundry pile just as the bathroom door opened with a large escaping cloud of steam. The window was no longer an option.

It was now on the other side of all that steam.

Delbert squealed without making a noise--

--and dove into the closet--

--pulling the shutter doors closed behind him--

--just as Allison exited the bathroom.

She was wrapped only in a bath towel. Wet hair matted on her narrow shoulders. She played with her wet hair, standing in the middle of her bedroom, staring at nothing in particular, running long fingers through the long wet curls, her mind elsewhere. She seemed to come back to herself with a deep lonely sigh and adjusted her towel, pulling it tighter around her naked torso, before gasping with surprise. Eyes wide and utterly disbelieving.

Unable to comprehend what was in front of her.

The pregnancy kit on her bed.

What happened next, happened very slowly, then very quickly. Like a roller coaster clicking and clacking up the initial steep rise before hesitating at the zenith of the loop like it might freeze there, before dipping and diving into space with greater and greater speed. Allison glanced at the closed bedroom door, but it held no obvious answers. Then instinctively turned toward the closed bedroom window. Her dark pupils dilating and locating--

--Ollie paralyzed in the tree.

Startled, Ollie hiccupped violently--

--and fell from the grand old Maple.

Thump…

Thump…

Thump…

All the way down to the root-riddled ground.

Thump…

…Splat.

Even behind the closet shutters, Delbert could hear the fall and the subsequent rusty metal clicks of Ollie's bike racing off into the darkness, the bike swaying perilously beneath the large country boy as Allison watched with shock from her bedroom window. A moment later the bedroom door slammed open. The roller coaster in full and glorious descent now, barreling down the tracks at a hundred miles an hour, whistling and clanging.

It was her father. Harlan.

"What in the blazing hell is going on up here?" he said.

His voice was thick. Tongue cottony.

Delbert could smell beer. A sickly, sour smell.

Delbert pressed the flowery panties to his nose and mouth to prevent himself from making any sound and through the closet shutters, eyes round and afraid, observed Harlan passing before him, moving gruffly to the window, pushing Allison aside for the moment and in his agitated state never noticing her stuff the pregnancy kit beneath the towel.

The branch was still swaying outside.

Allison cowered in the corner by the window.

Pulling the towel even tighter.

"You think I'm a fool, don't you," he said.

He loomed over her.

She shook her head.

"You think your old man is a rotten old fool," he said again.

She didn't bother to shake her head this time.

Harlan's eyes narrowed and trembled. His nostrils flared. Sniffing the air. Snorting. Cottony tongue swiping at dry lips. The pores on his slender nose and forehead large and pronounced. Like dark craters on the moon. His nostrils flaring again.

"I can still smell the prick's cologne," he said.

Delbert felt a panicky chill.

Pushed the flowery panties harder against his nose and mouth.

His face began to turn shades of blue.

Meanwhile, Harlan's voice softened, but the softer tone only made the menace in his voice more apparent. Pushing back his thin oiled hair with a pale shaking hand and looming even more heavily over his daughter cowering in the bath towel in the corner of the bedroom with the last wisps of shower steam evaporating around them, he murmured with that sticky, cottony tongue:

"You don't need a boyfriend, sugar. You're only fifteen."

"I'll be sixteen in April," she said, barely audible.

"Only if I say so," he said.

He reached out with the trembling hand. Almost hesitantly. Like a nervous schoolboy. Before letting it fall on her warm bare shoulder. She shrugged from his touch with revulsion, almost dropping the pregnancy kit hidden beneath the bath towel.

"Christ, Allison," he moaned, "you always were a little flirt."

Delbert realized only too late he was holding his breath. He had once tried to hold his breath for three minutes at a public pool in DeWitt, Arkansas. He had been determined to make the time because he had heard on the TV Navy Seals had to be able to hold their breath for at least three minutes to qualify for Seal training. He could remember sitting on the bottom of the pool, lazily watching air bubbles exit his nose in a steady stream, parading toward the surface past the thrashing arms and legs of noisy children swimming above him, certain he would make the time. The big red second hand on the giant clock shimmering beneath the Lifeguard station above the undulating waterline had nearly completed its second long rotation -- just one more revolution and he would be a Navy Seal. It was at the end of this second revolution a final bubble had suddenly and unexpectedly popped out from his right nostril. A large lopsided bubble. That bubble had presented a lonely, wounded apparition rising slowly toward the dappling sunlight before hanging just beneath the surface, unable to break it, gliding along the underside of the water, riding the undercurrent of waves created by the boisterous children.

Delbert had felt his lungs glue shut.

His eyes grow larger. Rounder.

His chest suddenly leaden.

Yet his extremities light as air.

But he had been determined.

Determined to make that third and final revolution.

The chlorinated water sloshing in his ears had faded, replaced by a hollow, eerie silence. Then, gradually, a distant crackling noise had entered into that silent void, initially at a great distant, then slowly becoming louder and louder. The underside of his eyelids had filled with twinkling lights. An exploding fireworks display of expanding stars and flashing orbs before a crash of darkness. The next thing Delbert could remember was waking beside the swimming pool, the lifeguard kneeling over him, a pretty girl with a whitehead on her chin, telling him to breathe you stupid little brat, fucking breathe. Delbert had spit up a stomach-full of the foul-tasting chlorinated water and spent the remainder of the afternoon in the emergency room with doctors and nurses warning his mother about secondary drowning.

She had been drunk. His mother.

Someone had called child protective services.

He and his mother had left Arkansas the next day.

Standing in the closet, with the flowery underwear shoved over his nose and mouth, Delbert was suddenly overcome by that familiar distant crackling noise in his ears and that familiar fireworks display flashing and exploding behind his closing eyelids. He might have guessed what was coming next, but in the end it all happened too quickly and he wasn't consciously aware he was falling even as he was actually falling--

--not forward--

--but backward into Allison's clothing.

The sudden horribly loud jingle and jangle of the disrupted hangars woke him from his fainting spell like a sniff of smelling salts and Delbert heard himself suck in a ragged breath as he crumpled to the closet floor, clothing falling in a heap around him.

The voices in the room stopped.

Delbert blinked. Reorienting himself.

Ears still buzzing softly.

Soft lights still flashing before his eyes

He sucked in another ragged breath and clamored to unsteady feet, hands palming desperately up the slick closet drywall, spilling more hangars. Through the narrow shutter slats, Delbert witnessed a fresh explosion of rage in Allison's father's eyes. The man actually snarled before snatching at the closet door handle. Allison stepped back, alarmed and confused, as her father flung open the closet doors and Delbert tumbled out, spilling to the hardwood floor. Still inexplicably holding the flowery underwear. Harlan stumbled backward with surprise, taking a seat on the bed. The pregnancy kit fell out of Allison's towel. Delbert took advantage of the ensuing mayhem and rose, lurching frantically toward the bedroom window, accidentally stepping on the pregnancy kit with his lame foot, squashing the box beneath him.

"C'mere, you little worm!" Harlan said.

Delbert could hear confusion in the man's thick angry voice. Unable to comprehend why in the world it might be that a small boy had been disgorged from his daughter's closet. Delbert threw up the window. Unwilling to provide him with any answers.

Allison kicked the pregnancy kit beneath a dresser.

Harlan grabbed at Delbert's collar, ripping his shirt as Delbert threw himself out the window and into the wide and outstretched arms of the Maple tree. He tumbled down the giant tree like a falling acorn, bouncing off increasingly thicker limbs -- before meeting the unforgiving root-riddled ground with a terrific bone-jarring smack that stole the air from his lungs for the second time in only minutes. Wheezing, his lungs glued shut like that lazy afternoon in the bottom of that pool in Dewitt, Arkansas, he peeled himself off the earth, hobbling away.

Harlan burst out his front door seconds later.

Chasing him. A deranged man.

"You! You get back here!" he shouted.

Delbert, still unable to draw any air, feeling like he had an anvil on his chest, glanced back over his shoulder to find Harlan was quickly gaining on him. Delbert tripped. Fell. Skinning his knee on the sidewalk. Found his feet again somehow. Gasping. Wheezing. Like an asthmatic. Staggering like his very young life depended on it. And never noticing the man in denim--

--melt out of the night shadows on the sidewalk.

A duffel bag thrown over his shoulder.

A cigarette hanging loosely from the corner of his mouth.

Delbert was still searching back over his shoulder, consumed with terror, the world spinning dizzily around him--

--full of electric stars and crackling static--

--when he ran smack into the man in denim--

--on the sidewalk outside the old white clapboard house.

He promptly fell again. Arms and legs flying in different directions. In a scattered heap like those clothes on Allison's closet floor. His bones jingling and jangling raucously inside his numb, oxygen-deprived head like so many hangars.

The man stared down at Delbert.

Delbert stared up at the man.

The man in denim with the duffel bag thrown over his shoulder and the lit cigarette hanging loosely from the corner of his mouth could as easily have been fifty-five years old as thirty-five. He was thin, but running into him was like running into a wrought-iron fence. He stared at Delbert with hard but welcoming blue eyes. Daunting, but also familiar. Smelling of dried sweat and the earth and highway exhaust and the cold and Delbert would remember later how time had halted dead right in its tracks that night like the big red second hand on the clock beneath the Lifeguard station beside the pool in DeWitt, Arkansas when his starving brain had locked up like a car engine without a spit of oil and how those hard blue eyes above him in the night had spoken silent volumes even before the man in denim had laughed dryly and said:

"Went and caught you in the hen house, did he, son?"

Harlan, panting with red-faced temper and the effort, charged up the sidewalk, but he stopped dead in the dark when he saw that man in denim. The color drained from his face in an instant. Like a TV switched from warm color to cold black and white.

"Hey, Harlan, old boy," the man in denim said.

The man Delbert would come to know as Freddy.

Harlan blinked hard. Unnerved. Frightened.

"You look like you seen a ghost," Freddy said.

Harlan took a shaky step back.

"Been a long time, Freddy," he only managed.

"Suppose it has," Freddy said. Freddy stood a little taller than before and he was already a good four inches taller than Harlan. He flicked his cigarette to the sidewalk. Crushed it with a boot.

Delbert found his feet.

Still clutching the panties.

"Boy was in my daughter's closet," Harlan said, though suddenly the whole incident seemed apropos of nothing and unimportant. "Peekin'." His voice had lost all authority. Gone hoarse. Like he wasn't even sure if what he was saying was true.

Freddy lit another cigarette with a match.

A burst of blue flame in the darkness.

"That right, Delbert?" Freddy said.

Delbert blinked, startled.

"How you know my name?" he said.

Freddy pinched out the match.

"Cuz I gave it to you," he answered simply.

This simple bit of information short-circuited Delbert's still fuzzy brain. Buzz. Poof. Short-circuiting it like too many electrical plugs in an outlet. He might have even fainted again if Freddy hadn't placed a strong hand on top of his head, steadying him in the darkness before reaching down and removing the panties from his skittish grasp. As Freddy did so, he made a point to notice Harlan's daughter standing in her bedroom window in her bathrobe. She was framed neatly by the border of the window and backlit by the soft bedroom light. Her mother stood behind her in the shadows. Like a wraith. A frightened and bewildered expression on her normally vacant countenance.

"She is a peach," Freddy said after a long moment in a manufactured sunny voice, meaning Allison. He tossed the panties at Harlan. "A real peach," he said.

The underwear landed on Harlan's shoulder.

Harlan snatched blindly at the panties with the cutesy flowery design and placed them behind his back. His lips pulled back from his gums and his long teeth gritted like a territorial dog, his voice falling low. Trembling. A growl. "I don't know what you're doing here, Freddy," he said, struggling to find that authority in his voice once again, but only sounding more hoarse. "I don't know why they let you out of that cage. I can't even fathom it." He pointed at Freddy now as he said this, only realizing too late he was pointing with the panties, looking ridiculous. "But you stay away from her," he warned. "That goes for you, too, boy, and I damn well mean it." Harlan appeared interested in saying more, but his feet had other ideas, backpedaling across his neatly trimmed lawn to his front door as if afraid to put his back to Freddy.

Time then seemed to skip rudely forward.

Like a rusty needle over a scratched record.

Jolting from that odd, if slightly wonderful image of Harlan backpedaling across his neatly trimmed lawn to Freddy sitting on Delbert's front stoop. Delbert was sitting beside the man in denim without any memory of the transition. The short porch steps and Freddy's skinny grasshopper legs had Freddy's bony knees bumping up under his bearded chin.

"You really my daddy?" Delbert said.

Freddy blew smoke. "Yep, 'fraid so," he said.

And then sighed tiredly.

To Delbert's addled mind all the answers to all the unanswered questions in the entire world seemed to be contained somewhere in that one tired sigh if only he could decipher it.

Freddy punched out his cigarette.

Tossed the butt into the nearby bushes.

Sighed again. "You gonna invite me inside, Delbert," he wondered out loud, "or we gonna sit out here and freeze?"

"Momma don't let me have strangers in the house."

"I ain't no stranger than the next guy," Freddy said thoughtfully, rubbing his hands against the deepening cold. "Not no more. And you need to get somethin' on that ankle."

Delbert led Freddy into the house. Freddy stood in the front room and seemed to glance everywhere at once and Delbert realized the man had been here before. In this house. The thin walls like a time machine, offering memories. Pleasant and perhaps not so pleasant. Evidenced by a soft smile. And a frown.

Freddy followed Delbert into the kitchen.

Delbert popped open the freezer and dragged out the now frostbit bag of frozen broccoli. He plopped down in a chair at the kitchen table and applied the bag to his smarting ankle. It might never heal after the fall from the tree.

Freddy opened the fridge like it belonged to him. He wrinkled his nose at the meager contents before grabbing a bottle of beer and snapping the fridge door closed with his foot. He twisted open the beer bottle using his teeth, something Delbert found both exotic and fascinating, and spat the bottle cap across the room and into the open garbage can in the corner.

He took a long pull on the beer.

Studied Delbert.

Then turned his attention to a series of photographs on the fridge beneath a drab series of magnets. Including a recent photo of Delbert and his mother at an amusement park.

Freddy whistled softly. "Your momma got old," he said. His soft smile returned. He leaned in for a closer look, his eyes squinting to mere slits. "Still pretty, though. Always too pretty for her own good. She always stay out all night, does she?"

"Sometimes," Delbert said.

Freddy removed a tattered photo from his denim coat. The photograph that had once occupied space on the hard stone wall inside his prison cell. A younger Freddy from a not so distant yesterday with an arm thrown casually over the shoulder of a pregnant young Lillian. He placed the photo beneath a fridge magnet.

Delbert stood up. Limped over for a closer look.

Freddy pointed at Lillian's pregnant belly.

"That's you, kiddo," he said.

Delbert became transfixed by that magical window into the past, unable to pull away, almost certain the people populating that happy scene would begin to move and perhaps live again. It seemed impossible to believe that *that* was really him inside his mother. That he had been that small and that his mother had been on the precipice of that smile, cheeks blushing like a little girl.

Delbert stared at her hand caressing her swollen belly like what was inside her contained all the treasure worth having in the entire world. Him. Delbert.

"Now let's see 'bout that ankle," Freddy said.

He sat Delbert back down. Rifled through a few cabinets before snatching out a jar of pickled eggs and beets. An artifact of the house. Delbert flinched as he unscrewed the lid and released a pungent vinegary, moldering smell. The eggs and beets had turned a grayish brown inside and looked slimy. Freddy used a fork to remove a snarl of beets and smashed them to a pulp in a bowl. The vinegary, rotten smell filled the kitchen, causing Delbert's stomach to hitch. Freddy dug into more cabinets before settling on something with a frown. "Suppose this'll have to do," he said, removing a dusty bottle of murky castor oil from the shadows. He dumped a couple tablespoons of the oil into the beet bowl. Delbert held his nose in disgust. Delbert had once found a moldy can of Fisherman's Delight cat food beneath a motel bed in southwest Texas. The can had been so old it had begun to disintegrate, releasing the most awful fragrance. The cat food had been a brown mush inside with a green lawn of stomach-churning fuzz. That science experiment hadn't smelled any worse than the concoction Freddy was mixing with glee in the bowl on the kitchen counter now -- but before Delbert could offer any real protest, Freddy, without ceremony, scraped out the foul stuff with a spatula and slathered the warm, slimy paste directly onto Delbert's discolored ankle.

At least he wasn't going to make Delbert eat it.

"Think I'm gonna puke," Delbert said anyway.

His stomach hitching again.

"Should bring down the swelling," Freddy said, "'specially the beets."

"Think I'm gonna puke. Serious," Delbert said again.

"So there's the sink," Freddy said.

"Totally serious."

"And I'm serious. Hit the sink."

Delbert swallowed hard, instead. Tasted warm bile.

He pulled up his sock.

If only to contain the dreadful smell.

And felt the warm paste sink into his skin.

Loosening the muscle and the ligaments.

"Might work," Delbert said.

"Sure as hell," Freddy said.

"Still might puke," Delbert said.

"Sink still ain't going nowhere," Freddy said.

Delbert swallowed again.

Felt his stomach settle. A little.

"Okay?" Freddy said.

"Okay," Delbert said.

"Sure?"

"Yeah. Maybe."

"Don't maybe on the floor or my boots."

"Yeah. Sure."

"Good boy."

"Where you learn to do that?" Delbert said.

Meaning the paste.

Freddy washed out the bowl in the sink. Didn't answer.

Headlights hit the kitchen window, startling them.

"She's back early," Delbert said.

Freddy dried his hands absently on his denim pants despite the fact there was a dish towel on a hook above the sink. His eyes suddenly had that faraway look from earlier when he had first entered the house and that flood of memories, pleasant and unpleasant, had overcome him, and for a moment Delbert had the peculiar and ridiculous sensation Freddy might vanish into thin air right in the middle of the kitchen. As if the universe would never allow his mother and father to coexist in the same time and place. That it might just be a paradox to the natural order of things. Delbert would blink and the man would simply not be there, but reduced to a figment of his overactive imagination. A hallucination conjured, perhaps, from his fall from the tree outside Allison's bedroom window. The product of a whack to the head by a thick tree root. To watch it happen -- to watch Freddy simply disappear into nonexistence before his blinking eyes suddenly became too unsettling a proposition -- and Delbert turned toward the small kitchen window above the sink, instead. Staring past Freddy's ghostly reflection in the dark window glass amongst the bright halo of kitchen lights for the shadows moving outside in the darkness.

His mother was exiting the sports utility vehicle.

Slamming the door.

Angry and exasperated. And drunk.

Blouse ripped.

"I've met a lot of disturbed assholes--!" she said.

The dentist, her date, sat behind the steering wheel of the sports utility vehicle. The dentist was a nerdy, reed-thin man with thick glasses. A slender beak-like nose and a small doll-like slit for a mouth. He was wearing a blue windbreaker and an orange tie.

"But you--" Delbert's mother continued, voice shrill, stumbling in her heels on the muddy driveway. "You should be tied in a fucking strait jacket."

"Sounds fun," the dentist said dryly. "Maybe next time, sweetheart." He offered a perverse wink and punched the gas.

The sports utility vehicle quickly backed out of the long driveway with a high-pitched whine, thin all-weather tires digging aggressively into all that muck, kicking up moist, exploding dirt clods in Delbert's mother's direction.

"Asshole," she said again.

She staggered to the porch and peeled off her muddy heels at the front door like they were mud boots before stamping into the white clapboard house, her hair hanging in her face. She dumped the mucky heels and her purse on the floor by the stairs and examined herself in the mirror. She sighed at her haggard appearance and the crow's feet etched in deep grooves beside her eyes.

Delbert appeared in the mirror reflection.

Then Freddy.

First only his silhouette. Then him.

Delbert's mother's eyes jittered about her skull, bouncing back and forth and up and down and out of her eye sockets, trying to process the apparition in the living room shadows beside her son. Finally her mouth fell open in a wide, unnervingly silent, inebriated scream before those restless eyes fluttered and rolled up into the back of her head--

--and she fainted.

Arms and legs falling limp like a puppet.

Knocking over things as she slid to the floor.

Crumpling beside her mucky heels and purse.

"Same old Lillian," Freddy said.

Freddy crossed the small room, squatted down with a small grunt, and gently lifted Delbert's mother from the floor and into his arms, her lolling blonde head falling against his thin shoulder and bearded chin. He held her like a child for a short spell in the soft light of the front room, gazing down at her gathered in his arms, before placing her on the couch.

Delbert covered her with a blanket.

Freddy and Delbert exited the small white clapboard house without a word spoken between them. The man and boy sat on the front porch steps side by side.

"She'll be fine," Freddy said eventually with an unconcerned shrug, reading the disquietude on Delbert's young pale face. "Just a small bump on the head. Suppose we were just lucky that lamp and coffee table broke her fall."

Delbert smiled. A sense of humor.

Freddy lit a smoke. It sizzled in the darkness. Like a sparkler. The world fell silent around them afterward. Just the crickets in the high grass across the road before Delbert found the courage to ask eventually: "You come back cuz you knew I was here?"

"Guess you could say that."

"But you done somethin' bad," Delbert said.

He said it reluctantly.

Kicking rocks from the porch steps.

"Somethin' to make this town and my momma hate you."

"Guess you could say that, too." Freddy said, shrinking with the admission, staring past curling cigarette smoke.

That faraway look in his eyes again.

This time pained.

"What you done, then?" Delbert said.

Freddy only sighed.

Delbert kicked more rocks.

The crickets continued to buzz in the high grass.

"You like fishing, Delbert?" Freddy said finally.

Delbert offered a shrug in the moonlight.

"You don't like fishing or you don't suppose you know?"

"Never been."

A deep puff on the cigarette. Contemplating this.

"Truth is I was giving some thought 'bout trying my luck off Shady Creek Bridge in the morning," Freddy said after a moment. "Thinking on it, anyhow."

There was a rustle in the bushes beside them.

Then a small voice:

"Won't catch nothin' but a sunburn off Shady Creek Bridge."

It was a familiar voice. Ollie.

Ollie's voice startled Delbert, but not Freddy. "Thought maybe you'd grown roots and sprouted leaves," Freddy said.

Ollie stepped out of the bushes. Sheepishly.

"Ain't no water 'neath Shady Creek Bridge on account of the rug mill," Ollie said, brushing leaves from his hair and clothes before taking a seat on the bottom porch step.

"That's Ollie," Delbert said.

Freddy nodded, unimpressed, flicking white hot cigarette ash. The ash scattered like a shower of meteors in the night. "Saw him fall from the tree yonder," Freddy said. "Make a run for it on that bike." The bike lay in a heap in the bushes. Spokes tangled in the brush. "The accomplice," Freddy said wistfully after a beat. "Always an accomplice."

Ollie studied Freddy and Delbert.

Back and forth. Curious.

"So you're his daddy, then, mister," Ollie said finally.

Freddy punched out the cigarette on the top porch step, grounding it down like a bug. "You can call me Freddy," Freddy said. "You, too, Delbert, if it makes things easier." He then stood. Stretching off the cold. "In the morning, then," he said in conclusion. Then offered a parting nod and walked off into the night. Duffel bag over his shoulder. The two young boys on the porch steps watched him vanish into the surrounding blackness like a man disappearing into a sea of endless black water.

"That man really your daddy, doofus?" Ollie said.

"That's what he said," Delbert said.

Delbert was still trying to digest the enormity of that simple statement when he settled into bed later that evening, his mother still passed out on the couch below him. Classical music floated about his bedroom from the clock radio on the nightstand, offering a soft, poignant score to the fantastic images floating before his mind's eye from that incredible evening. The images still seemed otherworldly to him. Impossible to believe.

He found he could not sleep.

He sat up in bed and stared out into the darkness. The darkness where his father had disappeared an hour earlier. His father was out there in that darkness somewhere. And not an abstract father tempting the corners of his boyish imagination as had been the circumstances before this evening. But a real man of flesh and blood. A man who smoked and drank beer. A man with a photo of Delbert's pregnant mother. Of Delbert himself before his birth. A man who had named his son. Delbert was his son. And that man was his father. Freddy. His father's name was Freddy.

Delbert shook his head.

Overwhelmed. Ebullient. Apprehensive.

Filled with so many new questions.

He was contemplating all these questions, the questions spinning around in his head, faster and faster still like a hurricane rising in warm tropical waters, when he noticed Allison's window. The curtains were parted. Allison was standing behind the glass.

In her nightgown.

Ostensibly waiting for him.

Delbert sat up in bed.

She held a small ink board.

She lifted it high for him to see. The ink board had a flourish of handwriting. Allison's handwriting. In erasable magic marker.

The sign read: THANK YOU

She smiled. A tender, sad smile.

Delbert blushed.

The curtains closed.

Delbert slipped back down beneath the bed sheets. He felt like he was floating on a weightless cloud in the night sky. Floating along with the classical music in the darkness, mind and body at the gentle mercy of the wind currents pulling and tugging and drifting his feathery cloud this way and that until all direction was lost.

# 10.

**FREDDY DRIFTED THROUGH THE SMALL** town of Shady Creek, initially past small square homes with lighted windows, then dark sleepy storefronts, before crossing the intersection at 1st and Maple beneath the town's lone blinking stoplight to avoid a noisy, crowded bar made of gray-gunmetal brick that in another life had been a mortuary.

The cold seeped into his bones.

Freddy shook himself like a dog trying to shed its coat of water, but the effort only seemed to settle the cold deeper inside him and he stooped beneath the weight of it.

He eventually found himself back at the bus station.

The bus station was empty at this time of night, but warm. The only light was in the foyer. The ticket counter and three rows of benches beyond it were pitched in darkness.

He locked his duffel bag in a locker against the far wall, then stood in the intervening dimness smoking a cigarette. He glanced at a clock behind the ticket counter. It read 9:56pm.

A sign read OPEN FOR BUSINESS 6AM.

He proceeded to a pay phone.

Dumped change in the slot.

It echoed loudly in the silence. He dialed.

A voice answered on the other end.

"Yeah, this is Freddy Jackson," Freddy said into the phone receiver, staring at his shapeless reflection in the change slot, then quickly reciting his prison ID number. "I'm supposed to check-in." A beat. Listening. Then: "Sleep? I got a place," he said.

A hard wooden bench waited for him.

Freddy tried to sleep on the bench, denim coat spread over him like a blanket, head resting against the hard wooden armrest, but it was just too quiet. The only sounds were the mechanical tick-tick of the clock on the ticket counter wall and the high-pitched hum of the compressor kicking on and off below a vending machine in the bathroom alcove around the corner along with the gurgling flow of refrigerant through its cooling coils.

Freddy sighed.

Closed his eyes, anyway.

Eventually and mercifully exhaustion stole the tension from his overworked body and mind. His breathing began to slow and he was on the precipice of much needed slumber when a shadow fell over him and the hard rounded-toe of a black boot with thick rubber outsoles and tumbled leather splitting at the creases kicked the bench beneath him. Rap. Rap. Rap.

A hollow sound in the stillness.

Freddy opened his eyes and for a moment he was confused, certain he was back inside the cage. Back behind those abysmal stone walls and behind that suffocating boiler-plate door in a world of dim blue lights, his sabbatical to the world outside only another foggy and tattered dream already beginning to dissipate with the resurgence of the dark underworld nightmare.

"Can't sleep here, friend," the shadow said.

Freddy blinked.

The bus station swam back into focus.

The shadow belonged to a security guard.

"Not 'less you have a ticket for the morning bus."

Freddy sat up tiredly and pulled on his denim coat, silently praying he would not be recognized. This was a small town after all and ten years was probably only a blink of an eye outside the stone walls. Fortunately, he did not recognize the guard standing over him and the guard didn't appear to recognize him. Freddy made no pretense about having a morning ticket. He simply thanked the guard with a quiet mumble and trudged slowly out again into the cold darkness, hugging himself, shuffling past the guard's idling patrol car in the station's loading and unloading zone designated with double yellow lines. The patrol car's exhaust fumes produced a vapor cloud in the cold, obscuring Freddy like a magic trick.

Before poof.

He was gone.

# 11.

LILLIAN SAT IN A ROCKING CHAIR ON the front porch with a cup of coffee and a cigarette, warming herself in the pale morning sun, the sagging wooden planks beneath the chair causing her to lean like the Pisa tower over in Italy until she found a cruddy old rubber doorstop by an empty planter and shoved it beneath a rail of the rocking chair to prevent it from listing. A worn groove running the length of the doorstop suggested the use had occurred to her mother long before her.

She sighed bitterly, brushed away dust motes, shielded her eyes from the sun, and watched a man materialize from the morning haze on the road. He approached on foot. A denim jacket. A slanted walk reminding her again of that leaning Pisa tower.

He looked rumpled. Tired and dusty.

"You're not on the run," she said. "I checked the morning paper." A newspaper sat folded on her lap.

The man paused just below the porch steps. He carried a brown paper sack and a rusty fishing pole with a handwritten price tag dangling from the reel. $3.50 USED.

"They let you out, did they?" she said.

"Something like that," Freddy said.

"Something like what?" she said.

Upstairs Delbert woke to the sound of Freddy's voice in the yard below and traffic reports mumbling inanely on the clock radio.

He hopped out of bed and dressed quickly, only stopping to fight that darn cowlick in the mirror before promptly conceding.

He glanced at Allison's bedroom window.

The curtains were drawn.

He limped down the stairs and exited the house for the porch and immediately felt conspicuous. Both Freddy and his mother were staring at him. An uneasy truce.

"Hey Freddy," Delbert said.

"Hey yourself," Freddy said.

Lillian made a face, wrinkling her nose.

"You smell like sour milk, Delbert. And pickles."

"How's the ankle?" Freddy said.

"Better. A little maybe," Delbert said.

"Okay, then," Freddy said.

"Yeah," Delbert said and stepped off the porch, trying not to favor the ankle. He considered the rusty fishing pole like it was a mysterious artifact.

"I want you back before dark," Lillian said.

"I'm not having this conversation," Delbert said.

"Get some new material, Delbert," she said.

Freddy winked. "Well, c'mon then."

Delbert looked to his mother.

She shrugged. Go on if you must, it said.

The man and boy turned into the pale sunlight and walked out of town. The dead end street led them to the train tracks. The train tracks skirted the edge of town and the man and boy plodded contently along the ties, listening to the Methodist church bell at the center of town calling the God fearing to worship. The long walk loosened the boy's ankle.

Freddy often stopped along the side of the tracks, stooping to collect railroad spikes lying in the weeds. He explained to Delbert the discarded spikes had once held the rail ties together and were made of soft steel, allowing them to bend without breaking. Freddy handed Delbert a corroded old railroad spike. It was thicker and longer than Delbert's index finger and it was bent in a severe L-shape, its large rounded head folded like a mushroom, silky smooth to the touch after so many years exposed to the harsh and changing weather. "Could be a hundred years old," Freddy said.

"Cool," Delbert said.

He pocketed the nail.

Eventually, Freddy left the tracks, hiking up a steep embankment. Delbert followed cautiously, his bad ankle and worn sneakers slipping in loose rocks. Freddy sat on top of the embankment beneath a grove of white ash trees turned burgundy and stuck a long grass stalk between his teeth, chewing it thoughtfully. Delbert sat beside him. Indian style. Stuck grass between his teeth, too. It tasted of the earth. Loamy and bitter.

The embankment overlooked the town landfill.

Piles of garbage and rotting junk.

"This is where I grew up," Freddy said.

Delbert frowned. "You grew up in the dump?"

Freddy pointed to the northeast corner. "My folks place was right there. Heard they moved, my folks and my sister. Don't know where. Don't suppose it much matters now. The town took the land. Razed the house. Extended the dump out over it."

Delbert stared at the trash in the northeast corner.

A burnt out car frame. A couple rotten tires.

A moldy old freezer. Scraps of decaying wood.

Indistinguishable trash. Plastic bags and flies.

Freddy lifted his head and watched large seagulls slowly pinwheel in the sky, outnumbering the turkey vultures. "Pa used to tell me some of these birds, the big gray ones there, come all the way from the sea just for this town's garbage. Imagine."

Freddy nodded his head after a spell. Stood.

Delbert nodded, too. Stood.

The man and boy, the grass stalks still clenched between their teeth like pipes, side-stepped down the steep, rocky embankment and continued following the tracks along the edge of town. The tracks eventually led to Old Stump Road below the rug mill.

The road was paved until Shady Creek Bridge.

It then turned to dirt, disappearing into the woods.

The bridge was a simple truss design, extending fifty feet across a narrow gorge. It was constructed of thick wooden beams and iron tension members, the beams designed to jump and vibrate like rattling teeth when logging trucks, heavily-loaded with timber, passed over them from the hills.

Ollie sat on his bike in the middle of the bridge.

A fishing pole. A split-willow creel bag.

"See," Ollie said. "No water."

The thick wooden beams echoed softly beneath their trespassing footsteps, somehow reminding Delbert of the fairy tale *Three Billy Goats Gruff* and the troll with eyes as big as saucers and a nose as long as a poker who lived beneath the bridge in that story.

*Trip trap trip trap. . .*

*Who's that tripping over my bridge?*

*Now I'm going to gobble you up. . .*

Delbert pushed to the railing and glanced beneath the bridge. The creek was an anemic black sludge trickle, seeping out slowly from a pair of large culverts behind the rug mill. Dark smokestacks spewed gray filth above the mill, creating a black cloud.

"I know a good place, though," Ollie volunteered, tapping his sneaker with mild impatience, "if you don't mind walkin' a bit. You got crawlers?"

Freddy peeked open the brown grocery bag for the boys, revealing a carton of night crawlers. A bag of peanuts. Root beer. And a tall brown bottle of whiskey.

"That Wild Turkey?" Ollie said.

"Don't suppose it should matter to a boy your age."

"Tell that to my daddy's belt," Ollie said and lifted his thin black bangs, revealing a decent scar on his wide and pale forehead. "The buckle," he said.

Freddy and Delbert followed Ollie across the bridge and further down the logging road and into the forest. The road grew narrower and dark beneath the tree canopy and turned back on itself before climbing a slight rise. Ollie straddled his bike, dirty sneakers shuffling in the earth, tire chain spinning freely about the spokes, hitching and rattling and clanging.

A clearing appeared in the trees.

"Here," Ollie said.

Ollie dumped the bike beneath a large Black Willow and led Freddy and Delbert into thigh-high grass populated with lazy Black-eyed Susans. The wild grass and swaying Black-eyed Susans painted yellow, orange, copper brown, and russet red by the failing season seemed to acquiesce with each step of their forward progress, bowing and parting like a crowd of dutiful worshippers. Small scampering birds squeaked from the nearby brush. Crickets buzzed. And a creek could be heard bubbling beyond a curtain of tall reeds and cattails swaying in the breeze. A tributary of Shady Creek unaffected by the schemes of the rug mill in the town below.

"Lemme have them crawlers," Ollie said.

A few minutes later Freddy was sitting on a tree stump in the middle of the clearing, cradling the open whiskey bottle in his lap in a shaft of slanted sunlight and watching with amusement as Ollie led Delbert with baited fishing poles into the tall reeds.

"You look like you're taking Normandy Beach, boy," he said.

Ollie was on hands and knees, crawling deliberately through the stalks of reeds and cattails, belly low to the moist ground, sneaking up on the bubbling creek. "Tell your daddy to hush up," he said. "And stay low, doofus. You'll darn near spook the fish."

Delbert hunched down, too, elbows in the mud.

He could feel the wetness soak his T-shirt. His shins.

"Thought fish were stupid," he said.

"Not half as stupid as a dumb flatlander like you," Ollie said.

The boys disappeared into the reeds and cattails.

Freddy remained alone sitting on the tree stump in the middle of the clearing. The amusement faded from his face. His expression turned blank and sad. The surrounding forest seemed to push closer, dark boles like so many watchful eyes, rustling leaves and limbs a congregation of condemning whispers and pointing fingers. A wind gathered, chilling him. He drank from the whiskey bottle, but the bitter drink failed to warm him as a young girl's voice slipped into the gathering wind. Distant and forlorn. Begging for mercy.

Freddy blinked. Haunted by the memory.

*A teenage girl. Lucy Caldwell.*

*Terrified. Dress ripped. Blood on her mouth.*

*Backpedaling. A shadow falling over her.*

*The teenage girl screaming. Lucy.*

The scream merged with another scream.

In the here and now.

Freddy blinked again. Suddenly awake. Startled.

It came from beyond the thick curtain of swaying reeds and cattails. Delbert. Creeping only a moment before beside the bubbling creek beneath a reddish purple grove of Flowering Dogwoods. The creek high and clear, frothing beneath an undercut bank. One moment he had been right behind Ollie and the next moment he had lost him in the thorny brush and made the mistake of trying to stand. A misstep on the bad ankle -- and the undercut bank had collapsed beneath his weight, sending Delbert screaming and tumbling into the icy water. Ollie appeared from the brush.

Just a round face at first. Irritated, then breaking into a huge grin. Thc grin pulled across his face like silly putty before he was overcome with a hysterical laughing fit, doubling him over. Unable to help himself. Unable to help Delbert. Delbert grabbed at an exposed hanging tree root to keep above water.

To keep from drowning.

Soaked. Ego bruised.

"Stupid flatlander doofus," Ollie said, happy tears in his eyes.

His laughter died when a siren was heard from the dirt road.

"Ah, shit," Ollie said, his grin fading. "My pops."

Delbert climbed out of the cold water. Dripping. He followed Ollie back through the swaying reeds and cattails to the small clearing. Just beyond the wild grass and Black-eyed Susans the boys could see a sheriff cruiser blinking beneath the Black Willow.

A cloud of dust was still settling behind it.

"Your pop's the sheriff?" Delbert said with surprise.

"Step-pops," Ollie said.

The blinking light bar fell dark and a moment later Sheriff Snodgrass slowly heaved himself out of the cruiser. The shocks depressed with his shifting weight on the driver side, then sprung upward again with an exasperated sigh when the sheriff finally lifted himself free of the sedan.

The sheriff adjusted a round patrolman hat with a silver star and bright gold trim, then organized himself, hitching his considerable belly over a creaking leather utility belt and gun holster, and stepped out from beneath the shade of the Black Willow into the forest clearing, a fat expensive cigar protruding from his colorless lips beneath mirror sunglasses. The sheriff removed the sunglasses, stuffing them into a breast pocket, and surveyed the frozen tableau before him in the forest clearing before barking out with a deepening frown, his large hands planted on his hips: "Thought I told you to clean out the shed. This mean it's done?"

This was directed at Ollie.

Ollie shook his head. Ruefully.

"Well, c'mon then," the sheriff said.

Ollie trudged toward the cruiser.

"Don't give me that sour look, boy," the sheriff warned, biting down on the cigar. A large hand glittering with all those gaudy rings smacked at the back of Ollie's passing head.

"Doofus," he said.

The sheriff regarded Delbert's wet clothing.

"You tryin' to grow gills?"

"I fell," Delbert said.

"Course you did," the sheriff said, staring up at the sky for a beat. "Ground funny that way out here. Real funny." Without turning around he sighed and reacted to Ollie stuffing his bike into the back of the cruiser. "Careful now. Don't scratch that vinyl, boy."

His gaze then finally settled on Freddy.

Freddy was frozen on the tree stump in the middle of the clearing. The whiskey bottle gone. Disappeared. Concentrating instead on the bag of peanuts. Jittery. Body shrinking into itself while blue cigar smoke circled above the sheriff's head like an ill-boding halo. "Heard you might be around," the sheriff said, mumbling around the cigar clenched between his teeth. "Them books say the perps always return to the scene of the crime." His large hand now swept through the cool foothill air, those gaudy rings glinting again, the gold watch catching dull sunrays. "But there ain't no absolution for you here, Freddy," he said peevishly, head shaking with callous melancholy. "Not for what you done anyhow."

Freddy blinked. The past again returning.

Like a rumbling train without brakes. Shrieking.

*A teenage girl. Lucy Caldwell.*

*On the ground. Dress ripped.*

*Head bloodied. Eyes closed.*

*A shadow falling over her. Freddy.*

*A tire iron clutched in his trembling right hand.*

*He poked at her with the tire iron.*

*But she was lifeless.*

The sheriff frowned past the cigar, his large shadow falling over Freddy, eclipsing the sun. "Got themselves a regular old revolving door up there on the hill, do they?" he accused. "Crazy liberals." A snort. "A dog turns rabid," the sheriff said, cold, penetrating gray eyes narrowing, "you shoot it. Common sense. You don't let it go off the leash. It's gonna bite."

Delbert shivered in his wet clothing.

"Got any bite left, Freddy? Sure you do." The sheriff leaned closer still. His voice dropping to a venomous whisper not overhead by either boy. "You maybe have them fooled up on the hill," he hushed gleefully to Freddy, "but you don't fool me. Not for a New York minute. They think they might want to parole you in a few months, but that won't do. Won't do at all. I'll be at your hearing, sure enough, Freddy, and I got me a long memory even if those crazy liberals don't. You ain't never getting out, Freddy Jackson. And that's a promise."

The sheriff dropped his cigar.

Crushed it underfoot.

It made a soft sizzling noise in the wet grass.

He put his sunglasses back on. The mirror lenses reflecting the forest. His voice rose again. Loud and authoritative and directed as much at Delbert as Freddy. "Just make sure and get yourself back up that hill 'fore dark come tomorrow night," he cautioned. "Don't make me come looking for you, boy. You don't want that," the sheriff said, hitching up that creaking utility belt, palm coming to rest on the butt of the revolver. "I shoot rabid dogs." The sheriff tipped his hat and marched back to the cruiser. He climbed inside, the car sinking toward the dirt, shocks gasping. He flicked at Ollie's ear with a thick nimble finger like a cruel older brother might do, then rolled down the window, tilting his sunglasses and winking at Delbert standing in the tall grass and Black-eyed Susans. "Tell your momma Chuck still comin' by to say howdy nice and proper one night. Nice and proper."

Delbert just stared.

"Say, yes sir, boy."

"Yes sir," Delbert said.

The sheriff nodded and the cruiser pushed off, making a quick three point turn on the narrow dirt road, kicking up a cloud of fresh dust before vanishing down the road in a swirling cloud of it. The tornado of dust settled around Delbert and Freddy.

Freddy pulled the whiskey bottle out of the weeds.

Took a long pull on the large brown bottle.

Delbert shivered in his wet clothing.

"What's absolution, Freddy?" he said.

Freddy considered the question, staring absently toward the swaying reeds and cattails hiding the bubbling creek and colorful dogwoods. "Absolution?" he began softly. "It means not having to say you're sorry, Delbert. Not no more. Not for nothin'."

"What's on the hill come tomorrow night at dark?"

Freddy took another pull.

A burning sip. Eyes glazed.

"A place to feel sorry," he said.

The man and boy contemplated this and contemplated each other until colors filled the sky above them. Pink, orange, and red. The colors faded and dusk found them walking back over Shady Creek Bridge and along the train tracks bordering the small town.

Delbert struggled on the ankle.

Swelling again after his misstep into the creek.

Freddy noticed him shivering in his still damp clothes. He removed his denim jacket. Handed it to Delbert. The jacket was too big and it hung like a dress on the boy. They exited the woods at the end of the dead end road near the white clapboard house.

And froze.

Froze right in the middle of the road.

A small mob of angry townsmen had congregated on the porch of the small white clapboard house. Harlan. Jack the Marshmallow from the bank. The skinny dentist. Others with equally unfriendly faces and unsettled dispositions. Firearms and baseball bats. And pacing anxiously in front of them was Delbert's mother. Pale. Afraid. Chain-smoking.

None yet aware of Freddy and Delbert in the night.

"You boys-- You ain't got no right to play the law," Delbert's mother pleaded, her trembling voice carrying out into the darkness. "You just don't," she said.

The mob rippled in agitation. Like a pack of wild animals. Harlan was in the forefront, sitting on the railing with a shotgun. "He ain't got no right, Lillian," he scowled. "Not to this town. Not here. Not no more. Best he understands that now. Best he does."

Allison stood in her bedroom window.

Eyes large. Nervous. Mesmerized.

The marshmallow stood, gripping a Louisville slugger.

The first to notice Freddy and Delbert in the dark.

"Here he comes," the marshmallow said.

The mob piled off the porch, moving forward like a black wave into the night from the white clapboard house. A malevolent shadow heading toward Freddy and Delbert.

"What you done, Freddy?" Delbert hushed, awed.

A light bar flashed behind Freddy and Delbert.

The sheriff. Arriving from a side street behind them.

The mob hesitated. Except for Harlan.

"C'mon, boys. Sheriff's just here to clean the mess."

The mob continued forward.

Sheriff Snodgrass exited the cruiser, hitching his creaking utility belt, planting a boot firmly on the cruiser's rear bumper and regarding Freddy with that slippery smile. "What'd you expect coming back here, anyway, huh, Freddy?" he said with a ruminating sigh. "A fucking parade? Well, shit, boy, here it comes now."

Freddy eyed the woods at the end of the dead end road.

Thought for a moment about maybe running.

"They remember what you done to that little girl," the sheriff said, his head nodding. "In spades."

Freddy sighed and, instead, regarded the denim jacket falling to Delbert's knobby knees. "Keep it, Delbert," he said in a somber whisper. "Grow into it for me."

"Don't leave," Delbert said, bottom lip trembling.

"Don't got no choice," Freddy answered.

A sad, defeated nod and Freddy began walking toward the woods at the end of the dead end road beyond the sheriff's idling cruiser and silently flashing light bar. Not running. Just walking. Slowly. Chin buried into his sternum. Shrinking into himself. Prison-issue boots echoing softly on the asphalt.

The mob followed him into those dark curtain of trees.

Delbert tried to follow at the last moment.

But the sheriff held him back.

"Sorry, kiddo," he said. "Damn sorry, frankly."

# 12.

**DELBERT DIDN'T SLEEP A WINK THE** entire night. Lillian found him at dawn. The boy was sitting on top of his bed sheets. Still dressed from the previous afternoon's fishing. Clothing soiled and badly wrinkled from his tumble into the creek. He was staring out the window at the still dark woods where he'd last seen Freddy. A cold mist hung over those woods like a sticky spider web, its frayed edges flapping and buffeting in a cold wind. The cold wind tunneled beneath the eaves of the white clapboard house, too, making a forlorn screeching noise while traffic reports droned on the clock radio.

Lillian hovered in the bedroom doorway.

A robe. Cigarette. Dark circles under her eyes. "Heard they took him to the hospital down in Bedford," she said

"Can I see him?" Delbert said.

Only the gloomy wind offered an answer. At first.

The gloomy wind and all that meaningless radio buzz.

"Don't suppose you can," she said eventually.

He put his back to her. End of conversation.

Lillian found the boy in the same position several hours later. She hadn't bothered arguing with him about going to school. The cold morning mist had melted from the woods, dissolving with the retreat of the night darkness. The cold wind, however, continued to howl beneath the eaves. A lonesome voice speaking in desperate tongues. Lillian hovered again in the bedroom doorway. Still in her robe. Another cigarette. Queasy taste of bile in her mouth. "You going to mope there all day?" she said, apprehension creeping into her voice. Delbert ignored her. "Don't waste your tears on that man, Delbert," she demanded crossly of him, stamping her foot. "That man made his own bed 'fore you was even born."

Delbert continued to ignore her.

Staring out at those woods.

The sun moved around the boy.

So did the shadows.

The sun eventually fell beyond the ridges and the shadows slowly crept out from the corners and fell over the boy, consuming the last of the light. The wind rose and fell, causing the white clapboard house to tremble and shake and creak and moan.

Classical music floated from the clock radio.

Lillian appeared in the bedroom door a final time.

Tight blouse. Short skirt. Heavy make-up. A surly attitude.

"I've had enough of this shit, goddammit, Delbert."

The boy hadn't moved but an inch the entire day.

"Don't you go fruity on me," she said mulishly.

After the echo of his mother's heels had taken her downstairs, Delbert turned to the denim jacket hanging at the foot of his narrow bed. He pulled the denim jacket to his chest. Felt a warm tear slide heavily down his cheek. Drip off his chin. The tear left a round water stain on the collar of the denim jacket. More tears followed. Once they started, Delbert couldn't stop them. Stinging his eyes and salty in the corners of his mouth. Meanwhile, cruel voices haunted his thoughts, echoing from the darkness:

*Took the animal down myself.*

*There ain't no absolution for you here, Freddy.*

*Not for what you done. I shoot rabid dogs.*

*What your daddy done ain't got nothing to do with us.*

*And it ain't never gonna be our fault.*

*That man made his own bed 'fore you was even born.*

A knot the size of a walnut settled in Delbert's throat.

Delbert swallowed hard. The knot burned. Delbert let out a quiet bubbling sob and slipped beneath the denim jacket, curling into a fetal position below the enveloping fabric, wiping tears on its sleeve before his tears were interrupted by a blinking light.

From Allison's bedroom window.

Delbert lifted his head and found Allison in her nightgown framed in her bedroom window like the other night, flicking a light switch on and off to get his attention. She was holding up the ink board scribbled with the erasable magic marker.

The sign read: YOU OKAY?

Delbert nodded. Not convincingly.

She wiped the ink board clean. Scribbled again. Lifted it.

The sign read: YOU DON'T LOOK OKAY.

Delbert shrugged. Wiped away more tears.

This was met with more scribbling from Allison.

And a sympathetic shrug. The sign read: ME NEITHER

Her round flushed face then went pale as bright headlights turned from the road onto Delbert's muddy driveway below. It was the sheriff cruiser. It parked in front of the white clapboard house. The engine idled for a moment, then went silent. Ticking.

Allison hid behind her curtains.

Her eyes plaintive and concerned for Delbert.

Sheriff Snodgrass slowly hauled himself out of the cruiser, the cruiser dipping, then snapping back up like a yo-yo on its shocks. A ubiquitous cigar hung from his mouth. Blue smoke floated above his head, vanishing with him beneath the sagging porch roof.

His heavy knocks shook the small house.

The wind rose and fell, whining softly.

Allison disappeared. Curtains drawing closed.

Delbert limped from his bedroom out to the staircase landing to find his mother peeking past the window curtains downstairs. Wired. A bit drunk. She whispered at Delbert without turning around. "Get back to your room." A quick flick of the hand.

But Delbert stayed put.

"I said get," she said more urgently.

More heavy knocks. The front door rattling noisily in its frame. She backed away from it. The only light in the front room was from the muted TV set.

"Lillian, I can smell your perfume," the sheriff said eventually outside the door, slightly amused.

Delbert's mother fretted. Exhaled.

Finally unlocked the door. Opened it.

"Been a long time," the sheriff said.

"Not long enough," she said.

"Play nice," the sheriff said, removing his hat. His greedy eyes slid up and down Delbert's mother, deliberately soaking in every detail. The revealing blouse. Short skirt. Heavy make-up. "Only thing that outfit needs is a meter running," he said.

"I'm expecting company."

The sheriff made a show of checking the glittering gold watch strapped on his thick hairy wrist. "At this hour?" he said. A slippery, knowing smile. "Of course you are."

The sheriff entered the house, uninvited.

"This is harassment," she said, hugging herself.

"Keep your pantyhose on, sweetheart," the sheriff said, his voice suddenly without humor. "Afraid this is official business." The sheriff noticed Delbert standing in the shadows on the staircase landing. "Those city slickers down in Bedford couldn't guard a kitten. Freddy went and punched out a hospital window, don't you know. The crazy bastard. Jumped three stories. At five o'clock this evening he officially became a fugitive of the law."

Delbert's mother hugged herself even tighter.

"Got any idea where he might turn up, boy?" the sheriff said.

"He don't know shit," Delbert's mother said.

"You'd tell me if you did, wouldn't you, Delbert?"

"Nope," Delbert said, surprising himself.

The sheriff smiled. Intrigued.

Delbert stood a bit taller.

"Delbert, go to your room," his mother said. "*Now.*"

Something had crept into her voice.

Something primal. A scream without screaming.

It sent a chill up and down Delbert's spine.

Delbert vanished into the dark of his bedroom.

"Lily, I'm just trying to make things easier on Freddy," the sheriff said.

"Careful, Chuck, your nose just grew three inches," she said.

Delbert sat on his bed and stared at Allison's bedroom window. The curtains remained closed. He sighed softly. Stared into the night instead. Into all that blackness.

"Where you at, Freddy?" he said desperately.

In the front yard his mother led the sheriff from the house.

Their voices muffled beyond the windowpane.

From the yard Lillian stared up at Delbert's window and flicked her hand at her son, insisting he withdraw from the dark glass. She continued to stare, hand in the air, until she was certain he was gone. Meanwhile, headlights slowed on the road beyond the driveway. A sports utility vehicle. The dentist. But upon noticing the sheriff, the headlights turned down the side street, vanishing around the corner and back toward town.

"Looks like I'm bad for business tonight, sweet pea," the sheriff said. A leering wink. "Maybe you should take out an insurance policy. Pencil me in for tomorrow night."

"I don't think that's a good idea, sheriff," Lillian said.

"Why not?" he said.

"'Know what they say about mixing business with pleasure."

The sheriff chuckled.

"*They* don't need to know nothin' about it, sugar."

He plopped himself down heavily in the cruiser. It sank beneath his weight, nearly bumping against the muddy ground. Lillian stood with hollow defiance. Arms crossed. "Listen, sheriff," she said, "what Freddy done, it don't have nothin' to do with us."

The sheriff chuckled again. Started the cruiser.

"I think your pretty nose just grew three inches, Lillian."

From behind his bedroom window Delbert watched the cruiser slip into the night. His mother stood in the middle of that long muddy driveway for a period of time, unmoving. Just frozen there, thin arms wrapped around her increasingly gaunt torso and Delbert realized just how emaciated his mother had become, staring at her in the moonlight. How hollow her cheeks. How sunken her eyes. How prominent the bones in her forehead. Tendons like papier-mâché flexing in her elbows and ankles.

Eventually she plopped down on the porch steps.

Her head falling into her hands.

Delbert thought about going down to her, but Allison's curtains parted. Delbert lifted himself, expecting to see her. But it wasn't Allison. It was her father. Harlan. Standing there barechested in the window. Boxers over skinny legs. Opening the window for air. It startled Delbert. The half-naked man standing in the girl's window. Harlan noticed Delbert, too. He glared at the boy with tired, hooded eyes for a long unnerving beat -- before finally pulling the curtains shut again.

# 13.

EARLY THE NEXT MORNING DELBERT hid behind the thick trunk of the large Maple tree standing tall and proud outside Allison's bedroom window. The morning was cold and wet, turning everything in the world slick and shiny. The dew in the grass seeped into Delbert's sneakers, dampening his socks. He found the usually coarse bark of the Maple had turned temporarily soft and spongy beneath his touch. A breeze shook gathered moisture from the orange-yellowish leaves, sending sporadic cold sprays softly down on his head like rain.

Delbert ducked further behind the tree when Harlan exited the house in a customary brown suit. Allison's mother, dressed for work in a long skirt and matching blazer, followed a minute later. They climbed into Harlan's car and drove off into the hazy morning. Delbert watched the car stop, then turn the corner at the stop sign and vanish from sight. Only then did he step out from behind the tree. He collected a handful of small rocks strewn about the lawn at the base of the grand old Maple and stuffed them into a pocket, then climbed the tree. He carefully straddled the thin wandering branch leading to Allison's windowsill.

The curtains were tightly drawn.

He considered a neighboring house. The road.

The house windows were dark.

The road empty.

He swallowed a mouthful of the cold morning air to focus his mind, but it was like ingesting ice cream too quickly and it gave him a brain-freeze. Groaning, sniffling back a runny nose, he shook his head to clear it, then began lobbing the small rocks at Allison's closed bedroom window. The pebbles made soft *ping-ping* noises as they bounced off the glass. The curtains parted.

Allison appeared in a nightgown.

Her face was drawn and tired. Confused.

She lifted the window. Peered at Delbert in the tree.

"Why aren't you in school?" she said.

Delbert shrugged. "Why aren't you?" he said.

Allison considered this thoughtfully for a beat before motioning for Delbert to crawl inside the window. Delbert scooted down the thin wandering branch and, mindful of his ankle, cautiously stretched and lowered himself into her bedroom. Allison was sitting on the edge of her bed, facing him. Unlike the recent and terrible night when Delbert had found himself trapped inside her closet, or in the past when he could only longingly appraise her from a frustrating distance, he could now really take her in. He felt dizzy being this close to her. His knees uncertain and weak. He could not imagine a more perfect creation. To Delbert, even this close, especially this close, the young girl was absolutely lovely. He would have never guessed Allison thought her nose a bit crooked and her feet a size too large. Or the slight dusting of freckles on her forehead freakish and off-putting. Her eyes bulbous and her hips too round. Her brows too thick and tangled and wild. If he had thought to ask she might even have directed his adoring attention to the moon-shaped mole on her thigh and the small cleft on her small round chin. Not that Delbert would have been swayed.

He found each feature faultless.

Indeed, perfect.

Like her long golden hair. Uncombed this early morning and falling in untamed waves around her endearing face. Or the tease of her small breasts beneath her cotton nightgown. Or how her long legs curled effortlessly beneath her on the comforter and the swan-like gesture of her neck when she cocked her head to consider him standing there in her bedroom.

Rather, it was Delbert who felt conspicuous.

Small and homely. His hair too long.

Freddy's denim jacket hanging to his knees.

Allison blinked, her large blue eyes beneath those bushy brows twinkling to life with a playful mischief, her cute off-center nose wrinkling like a bunny, that constellation of light brown freckles jumping up and down on her forehead. "That's not your jacket, is it?" she said eventually, smiling. "It's too big for you. It looks like a moo moo." Delbert shrunk. Embarrassed. She giggled gently at his tortured embarrassment. "Aw, I didn't mean to hurt your feelings, Delbert," she said. "It's cool, though. Really."

Delbert reacted to the sound of his name.

His name on those soft, plump, pinkish-red lips.

Never had it sounded so lyrical. So poetic.

He felt dizzy again. He bit down on his lower lip and glanced around the bedroom, taking in her private things. A short bookcase crowded with well-read, dog-eared paperbacks. Mostly fantasy novels with mysterious sounding authors like Madeleine L'Engle and Piers Anthony and more familiar collections from stalwarts like L. Frank Baum and Lewis Carroll. There were also many science fiction selections. Glossy covers featuring pretty young heroines in distant star-filled galaxies. Meanwhile, across the bedroom was a tall antique armoire with a spooky congregation of Ginny dolls. Miniature hard plastic toddlers incongruously dressed in stylish adult clothing. Taffeta, velveteen, brocade, and cotton with frilly lace trimmings. Tiny designer shoes. Decorative handbags. Jointed legs. Large lifeless eyes as if under a spell. On the bedside table was a Tiffany lamp. Stained glass featuring swirling pond green and blue violet dragonflies with scarlet eyes that refracted the sunlight coming through the window. Below the lamp was a framed photograph. A younger Allison cradling a fluffy poodle like the pooch was the most precious thing in the whole world. Delbert had never seen the dog before. He wondered what had happened to it. Was it dead? Buried beneath the large Maple? Had it run away? The question seemed important somehow. But impossible to ask.

A soap opera played on a small TV.

Inane, melodramatic dialogue.

"My soaps," she said, self-conscious. "They're stupid, but they make me feel better somehow." She muted the TV with a remote. Patted the bed beside her. "Sit," she said.

Delbert remained standing. Unsure.

"You know your ears turn red when you blush," she said.

"C'mon already," he said.

She smiled softly. Patted the bed again.

"I don't bite," she said.

"Not today, right?" Delbert said, recalling the sheriff's line.

He limped to the bed. Sat down.

"What happened to your foot?" she said.

"Popped a ligament is all."

"Looks like it hurts."

Delbert shrugged, embarrassed again.

An awkward silence followed.

The soap opera on the small TV gave way to a commercial. A baby in a diaper sitting in the middle of a car tire.

Allison's fingers absently traced her slight belly.

"You like babies, Delbert?" she said.

He wasn't sure. Nobody had ever asked before.

"Well?" she said, blinking.

"Kinda noisy, I guess. . . You knocked up, are you?" he said solemnly.

Allison shrugged. Scared. "Don't know."

"How come you don't know?"

"How come you were in my closet the other night?"

Delbert's ears turned red again. Poker-hot. Like they might burn a pair of giant holes in the sides of his head. "The pregnancy kit I got you. I wanted you to have it," he said.

"You left that on my bed, Delbert," she said, smiling softly again. "Doesn't exactly explain you in my closet, now does it?" As she said this she reached for a Kleenex box on the bedside table and began to dump heaps of unused tissue from the box onto the bed. "I was in the shower and you wanted to see me without my clothes on, didn't you?"

"Gosh, no," he protested quickly.

"You don't think I'm pretty?" she said.

Delbert felt like he might faint.

"There go your ears again. Like a four alarm fire."

At the bottom of the tissue box was the pregnancy kit.

Well-hidden until now.

She pointed at the pregnancy stick on the shiny box display.

"You hold the stick in your pee," she said.

Delbert frowned, fascinated. "How does your pee know?"

"Just does."

The box was unopened. Shrink wrap still intact.

A few minutes later Allison was inside her bathroom, the door closed. Delbert, his damp sneakers dangling above the floor, remained on the bed, watching the muted soap opera. The breeze tickled the window curtains and Delbert glimpsed his bedroom across the yard. His window looked impossibly small and dark from even this short distance.

"Can't go," Allison said from the bathroom.

"Run the faucet," Delbert called back.

She stuck her head out the door. A questioning look.

"Sometimes I run the faucet."

"Okay," she said.

She ducked her head back inside the bathroom. Closed the door. A moment later the faucet was heard running. Simultaneously, on the small TV, the soap opera was abruptly preempted by a flashing red banner scrolling across the screen.

-- SPECIAL NEWS REPORT --

A serious-looking anchorman with perfectly combed hair that somehow looked unreal and oddly plastic appeared at a news desk in a Bedford TV studio. Above his left shoulder an old mug shot of Freddy appeared. Tangled hair. Dirty clothing. A wild expression.

Delbert gasped.

Restored the TV to full volume with the remote.

*"A model furlough program at Gallows River State Prison turned sour yesterday evening,"* the anchorman reported, *"when state inmate Freddy Jackson somehow escaped custody at a local hospital here in Bedford and then failed to report back to the prison on schedule. Freddy Jackson remains on the run this morning."*

The anchorman and TV studio disappeared. Replaced by old footage of Freddy's arrest a decade ago, including Sheriff Snodgrass and state police troopers leading Freddy in handcuffs into a courthouse before TV cameras. Freddy walked stiffly toward the courthouse steps, offering the public a thousand yard stare.

*"Freddy Jackson was convicted ten years ago on rape and murder charges,"* the anchorman voiced over the old footage, *"stemming from Mr. Jackson's involvement with a pregnant, under-aged girl in the foothill community of Shady Creek."*

The bathroom door opened, startling Delbert. He muted the TV. A reflex as Allison exited the bathroom. She held the pregnancy stick forward like a magic wand. Reminding Delbert of the pretty young heroines on the glossy covers of her sci-fi novels.

She noticed the TV screen.

The anchorman in the TV studio was back.

And the mug shot.

"That man your daddy, is he?" she said.

Referring to the mug shot.

Delbert nodded. Ashamed.

"He really done those things they say, did he?"

A noncommittal shrug.

The TV studio vanished again, transitioning to a live shot. A Barbie Doll reporter stood outside the stone walls of the Gallows River State Prison beside a tubby man with a walrus mustache. A caption indicated she was interviewing the prison warden.

"I suppose if he didn't, then why'd they go and put him in there for, right?" she considered after a beat, still holding the pregnancy stick.

"Suppose," Delbert said, discouraged.

"Doesn't mean I think you're a crazy killer, though."

Delbert nodded. Grateful.

He was even more grateful when the soap opera resumed.

"Doesn't mean that at all," she said.

She placed the pregnancy stick on the windowsill.

"We have to wait three minutes," she explained to him, her voice hollow. "If it turns blue--" She couldn't finish the thought. "You want to hold my hand?"

He nodded again.

She sat beside him on the bed.

Took his hand.

The girl and boy stared alternately at the pregnancy stick on the windowsill and at a digital clock on the bedside table beside the empty Kleenex box and beneath the extravagant Tiffany lamp with the swirling dragonflies with scarlet eyes.

"What's rape mean?" Delbert said after a spell.

Her eyes became misty. "When you love someone and they don't love you, I guess," Allison said quietly, and held Delbert's hand tighter than before.

Three minutes slowly ticked off the digital clock.

Allison squeezed Delbert's hand a final time.

Stood and went to the windowsill.

Lifted the pregnancy stick.

"It blue?" he said.

Her shoulders slumped. Sobs overcame her. She collapsed into Delbert, hugging him desperately, crying into his denim jacket. The denim jacket absorbed her tears just as it had absorbed Delbert's tears only the night before. Delbert sat there frozen, unsure what to do. Unsure what to say. This beautiful, cheerless girl weeping in his small thin arms.

"Ollie wanted your underpants," he heard himself mutter.

The heavy waterworks stopped. Replaced by sniffles.

Her head lifted. She stared past damp hair, eyes wet.

"He dared me. That's why I was in your closet."

More sniffles. "My underpants? What for?" she said.

A discomfited shrug.

"You weren't going to wear them, were you?"

His ears went absolutely crimson.

She was laughing and crying now.

Delbert stared down at the blue pregnancy stick still in her hand. "You gonna tell your boyfriend?" he said.

A flushed cheek found his shoulder.

"We broke up," she said.

"You should tell him."

She closed her eyes. Pained. "The baby ain't his."

As the subsequent hours passed the hazy morning sunlight was intruded upon by afternoon shadows. The shadows moved unhurriedly about the small bedroom -- creeping in and out of corners -- before finally falling over the young boy and girl playing checkers in front of cartoons on the small TV. The shadows deepened, growing bolder as late afternoon became early evening, pushing out the last of the diminishing daylight.

"You cheat," Allison said, frowning at the board.

"I take no prisoners," Delbert said.

Headlights bounced off the wall. A car engine. Her parents.

"You better go," she said, rising from their unfinished game.

She stuffed the pregnancy kit back into the bottom of the Kleenex box before shoving fistfuls of the tissue over it and setting the box neatly back on the bedside table.

Delbert moved to the window.

She grabbed his hand. Squeezed it. Eyes sad.

"Play hooky again with me tomorrow, okay?" she said.

He nodded. Okay. Smiled.

She lifted his hand and made him cross his heart. Delbert laughed nervously without making a sound. Allison squeezed his hand a final time, regarding him with those sad eyes, then let go. Delbert scrambled into the Maple as the front door was heard opening below the porch roof. He remained hidden in the orange-yellow foliage until he was sure both her parents had entered the house, then slid down the giant tree. Soundlessly. Its bark rough and coarse again, the morning dew only a distant memory. Delbert hung in space for a moment from the final branch before swinging to the ground, landing gently on his ankle.

"Delbert, wait," a voice whispered from above.

Allison was there, leaning over the windowsill. When she was sure he would wait, she ducked back inside. Delbert could not see her clearly in the fading light, but her shadow on the wall gave everything away. She was lifting her nightgown. Above her waist.

A moment later she reappeared.

Nightgown back in place.

"Here," she said, giggling softly.

She threw something out the window.

It see-sawed in the air. Seeming to float.

Delbert grabbed the flimsy object before it could hit the ground. As if instinctively knowing such a thing would be a terrible sacrilege. He examined the object in the darkness. It was soft, falling about his hand, forming to the contours of his palm and fingers. His eyes grew large and disbelieving.

His first instinct was to drop it after all.

It was a pair of underwear.

Little Bo-Peep and her lambs.

"Still hot from the oven," she hushed and watched Delbert, red-eared, grinning wider than ever, shove off from the tree and vanish into the sea of darkness, stuffing the underwear in a deep inside pocket of his low-hanging moo moo denim jacket.

Allison closed the window. An audible snap.

And sighed as a shadow fell over her. Her father.

His brown suit wrinkled. A long day.

"Hey beautiful," he said.

She ignored him. Climbed into bed.

"You feeling better?" he said.

Harlan entered the bedroom. He sat on the edge of her bed, the mattress sinking sideways beneath him. He smiled. An empty smile. Tried to feel her forehead with the back of his hand. She shrank from his touch. He frowned. Eyes wandering. Over her. Across the unfinished game of checkers. Across the bedroom. And settling on the pregnancy stick still resting on the corner of the windowsill. Somehow it had been forgotten.

Then again, perhaps it hadn't been forgotten at all.

She glared at him.

Her father rose from the bed.

Picked up the pregnancy stick.

Read the display. His expression sinking.

"Can't hide this, daddy," she told him with an eerie calmness, yet edged with self-righteous venom. "I can feel it growing inside me. I can feel what you did."

Her father's shoulders sagged and he slowly lifted his balding head, staring out the window at the darkening night. Suddenly looking small and inconsequential to his daughter. Like a slight, frightened little boy. As if afraid all that darkness gathering out there might at any moment suddenly grab through the thin windowpane and snatch him as if no border existed at all and banish him into its opprobrious clutches forever.

Eventually, Harlan noticed Delbert.

In the corresponding bedroom window next door.

This time the boy returned his stare.

# 14.

A **THICK SILENT FOG SETTLED ON THE** town of Shady Creek that night. Delbert woke from a restive sleep and peered out his window with amazement. It was like being lost in a strange world of colorless cotton candy. No matter how hard he strained his sleepy eyes he could no longer distinguish any familiar landmarks in the shifting white embankment. It was as if the entire world had been expunged from existence. Allison's house next door had simply been disappeared. Along with the giant Maple. Meanwhile, tendrils of fog like ghostly fingers slipped under his open window and Delbert could taste it on his tongue, but it wasn't sweet like cotton candy. It was wet and cold and salty, hinting at the distant sea. Delbert imagined it rising over the dark ocean and pushing inland, swallowing slumbering cities and lonely small towns in its hungry embrace. Seeping through evergreen forests and autumn-hued woodlands and up and over climbing hills and tall ridges before sliding down into sunken valleys and across fissured gorges and trespassing deep canyons like a colossal pencil eraser, wiping it all clean, leaving behind nothing. Only a vast whiteness. Setting the white clapboard house adrift in space.

In nothingness.

From that vast white nothingness--

Delbert thought he heard a voice.

An eerie, low-pitched call.

At first it seemed to be calling his name and Delbert pushed his nose against the window as the inquisitive tendrils of fog crept deeper into his dark bedroom and swirled like a conjuring magic spell, trying to erase his things from existence.

The model airplanes hanging from the ceiling.

The growing laundry pile in the closet.

The denim jacket hanging from the chair.

He turned back toward the window, wondering what it would be like to see the window glass disappear. To be completely lost inside this nimbus. Floating. Untethered.

Then something wonderfully odd happened.

The fog was disturbed like cream in a cup of coffee stirred by a spoon, generating an eddy, then a whirling vortex. Spinning faster and faster still. From the eye of this vortex there appeared a bird. A great horned owl. Dark gray-brown with feathered ear tufts. Golden yellow eyes. Giant disc-shaped head with black and white patches. Large wide-spread wings. Flapping without sound.

It flew straight at Delbert, rising up, revealing its tawny breast, hovering in mid-air, considering him with those golden yellow eyes. Deeply wise and thoughtful. Sharp talons clicking momentarily on the window glass. Delbert blinked. Touched the pane.

*Hoo hoo-oo* it said.

Then it turned. A wide arc in the fog.

Head turning last. Swiveling.

Large wings rising and falling noiselessly.

The fog pushed aside. Creating a tunnel for its passage.

The magnificent bird glided silently and effortlessly past what Delbert knew to be a telephone pole. A black charcoal line in the dark. And over a crumbling split rail fence on the opposite side of the road. Hastily drawn charcoal lines running parallel to the ground. Before finally vanishing into a stand of pine trees. A thumb-smudge scribble of charcoal.

The fog settled in its wake.

Hiding the world from view again.

The world that was still there.

Just hidden.

# 15.

**THE FOG LIFTED JUST BEFORE MORNING.** Delbert listened to the traffic reports on the clock radio and watched a gradual explosion of color appear above the high mountain peaks. Violet, reddish-orange, and then a fiery yellow. As the early morning light filled the horizon, he noticed the once colorful leaves parading along the highest crests, however, were now fading and disappearing as winter hiked down the steep faces and the sheer mounts, leaving behind only skeletal tree remains standing in stark relief against the waking sky. The naked trees devoid of their vibrant fall plumage resembled an army of buried giants with only their pale hands grasping above the surface.

Delbert shivered.

The warm bed begging his return.

The air was colder, too. He could feel it. It penetrated the walls and his thin cotton pajamas and chilled his feet on the floorboards. And he could see frost on the window now. Thick and crunchy along the borders.

The Maple tree outside Allison's window had also decided to abruptly shed its first coat of leaves. The dispatched foliage lay about its base. A scattered carpet of orange and yellow already decaying to mottled brown. Iced in frost in the dawdling shadows of the previous evening. Layered in thick mildew and fungus. Surrounded by a congregation of dwarf-like toadstools.

The sun rose. The frost melted.

The world warmed a little. For now.

Delbert showered, washing his hair and teeth beneath the jet of warm water. He then spent an inordinate amount of time in front of the bathroom mirror, staring past the lingering shower steam, fighting that stubborn cowlick with a giant comb and his own spit before returning to his bedroom.

He noticed his mother's bed down the hall.

It had not been slept in.

He pushed his bedroom door closed anyway. The bedroom door was slightly warped and made a soft clunking noise as Delbert strained to push it shut. He then put his ear to the buckled wood and listened for the echo of his mother's footsteps on the stairs, but only heard a heavy silence. Satisfied, he dropped his towel and dug into the bottom drawer of his dresser.

Delbert customarily wasn't allowed to root through the bottom drawer of his dresser without her permission, but he felt no guilt as he pulled on slacks and a button-up shirt.

He studied himself in the mirror.

Fought the stubborn cowlick again. Sighed.

Fought the bedroom door again.

Tugging this time.

At first it would not give.

Before a popping noise.

Like a cork.

Delbert tip-toed down the staircase without bothering to shoulder his school backpack even for appearances. His mother was lying face down on the couch. An open bottle of vodka stood at weary attention on the coffee table beside balled-up fast food wrappers. Her head lifted a few inches. An eye opened. The black eye turned yellow. "Those better not be your church clothes, young man," she said. It was her morning voice. Hoarse and moody.

"We don't go to church," Delbert said.

And promptly limped out the front door.

He imagined her glaring at the door. At his insolence.

Then collapsing back down on the couch.

Delbert loitered on the porch behind a badly leaning post. The post had a fracture the thickness of Delbert's finger running the entirety of it. Its cubed base was pushed askew by the sunken floorboards, creating an opposing force of pressure with the sagging roof, resulting in the fracture and list. It was a small wonder the gabled awning hadn't collapsed long ago. Delbert peered cautiously around the slanted post with growing impatience at Harlan smoking on his own front porch across the yard blanketed with all those moldering Maple leaves. The man was wearing another cheap brown suit, his thinning hair oiled against his scalp.

His car was warming in the driveway.

Any minute his wife would exit the house.

Any minute they would leave for work.

Delbert suddenly realized he was leaning against the unstable post and jumped back. Not so much in alarm the awning might finally crumble down upon him in a roar of shrieking wood and a cloud of splintering dust, but with upset at discovering his church attire now blemished with a blotch of dirt and expanding dampness from the melting frost. Delbert muttered an expletive beneath his breath and wiped the offense away with the back of his hand.

Smearing the gunk on his shirt.

He was halfway through a second expletive when--

He heard the scream.

A terrified woman's scream. Spine-tingling.

From behind Allison's drawn bedroom curtains.

Delbert's eyes jumped in his skull. First to the bedroom window and then back to the front porch where he witnessed Harlan flinch. Yes, he would remember later how Harlan had unquestionably flinched, but then inexplicably taken a moment to finish his cigarette. In that moment the man's tired, hooded eyes had shifted and settled on Delbert peeking out from behind the listing post with the severe fracture running the length of it, the thickness of one of Delbert's fingers. Like the man had known Delbert was standing there all along. Their eyes met in the cold, empty, intervening space over that decaying blanket of fallen Maple leaves.

Delbert's eyes full of fright and incomprehension.

Harlan's eyes cold and aggrieved and dispirited.

Then there was another scream.

Even more desperate. More primal.

An inhuman shriek. Wailing.

Harlan finally tossed the cigarette.

And entered the house.

A few hours later Delbert stood in complete shock with his neighbors behind a state police barricade surrounding Allison's front yard. The local crowd was hushed. Ollie stood beside him. Delbert's mother, chain-smoking, stood silently bchind the boys. It was like the volume had been turned down on the world.

Even the birds had fallen silent.

The road was a parking lot of black and silver state police sedans, unmarked state criminal investigation vehicles, and local Shady County sheriff cruisers. A state forensics truck and trailer were parked in the driveway beside a state medical examiner's van.

The back doors to the ME van stood open. Ready.

State police troopers with their distinctive NC state seal collar insignias, silver long-sleeved shirts, black clip-on ties, black slacks, and round Smoky Bear hats with their diamond-shaped badges shared crowd duty with local sheriff deputies while others assigned to criminal investigations moved methodically in and out of the house like an army of ants.

At a point early in the afternoon the collection of law personnel around the front door stepped aside. Their coordinated movements mimicking a receiving line. Hats were removed, eyes pointed downward, as ME personnel rolled a black body bag on a gurney from the home. The gurney wheels clattered noisily across the porch before the gurney legs and wheels collapsed upward with a loud snap as the gurney and body bag were lifted by ME personnel and carried down the narrow porch steps to the front walkway. The legs and wheels then snapped noisily back down for the final dozen feet to the ME van. The crowd, including Delbert, his young face paler than usual and very frightened, continued to watch in muted silence as the gurney with the body bag disappeared inside the ME van, sliding and locking into place along rails.

The body bag had been designed for an adult, but the body contained beneath the long gray zipper and inside the thick rubberized plastic was small, barely offering an outline. And for a moment, just before the ME van's double doors were pushed closed with a pair of muffled popping retorts, one big heavy door then the other, Delbert almost convinced himself there was nothing inside the bag at all. Just stale air. That the whole matter was just one large cosmic mistake or a cruel practical joke being played upon himself and the town.

The media was also here. A small contingent from nearby places, including Bedford. They were gathered together in a special taped-off section. The Barbie Doll reporter who had interviewed the prison warden about Delbert's father on the small TV in Allison's bedroom only twenty four short hours ago had pushed to the front of the press congregation to lob a question at the lead investigator for the State Police Major Crimes unit.

A State Police Captain William Dwyer.

She spoke in excited, bated breath. The Barbie Doll.

It left Delbert feeling sick. That bated breath excitement.

The Barbie Doll's cameraman, his camera propped on his shoulder, set his thick legs wide apart to balance himself on the slick lawn before the Maple tree, as if any official statement might somehow blow him over like a strong gust of wind

"We don't have a cause of death," Captain Dwyer said in response to her inquiry without a hint of drama in his voice. "That will be determined by an autopsy."

The captain was a tall man with a paunch belly. Snowy white hair. Kind blue eyes. Hunched back and wide stooped shoulders as if he were carrying an invisible weight he could never quite put down. Those kind blue eyes bounced over the cameraman and media folks and seemed to scan the gathered crowd of onlookers. An absent glance surely. Then again, those kind blue eyes almost seemed to seek out and then settle on Delbert for a beat.

Delbert stepped behind his mother.

He wasn't sure why he did it. He just did it.

Meanwhile, the Barbie Doll reporter ducked under the yellow media tape without invitation, pushing closer to the miffed state police captain, lifting a microphone beneath his chin. "Doesn't your presence here suggest this wasn't a suicide?" she said.

"This is standard procedure," the captain said.

"We were told she strangled herself, captain."

"I have no further comment," he said.

The captain hiked toward the house.

The Barbie Doll reporter lifted her voice toward the captain while a trooper assisted her back behind the tape. "Isn't it true her boyfriend has already been brought in for questioning?"

"No comment," the captain repeated.

A few minutes later state troopers and sheriff deputies pushed the barricade back from either side of the narrow driveway, creating an exit lane for the idling ME van. The Barbie Doll reporter shouted at her cameraman, "On me," and quickly adjusted her blonde locks in a small compact mirror before positioning herself in the foreground of the ME van as it exited.

The shot would make the evening news.

Her honey voice fell hauntingly low.

"A teenage girl in a small foothill town," the Barbie Doll said. A dramatic pause. "Suicide or foul play? A growing mystery now in the hands of the state police."

Captain Dwyer shook his head and climbed onto the front porch, taking each step circumspectly on stiff knees. Sheriff Snodgrass was standing just outside the door, frowning around a heavily chewed cigar. The sheriff, grimacing, kept his voice low, not even moving his lips, speaking through gritted teeth and around that cigar. "Listen, captain," the sheriff said, eyes narrowing with frustration. "I don't need your boys bringing a three ring circus into my town or trampling through it like the Red Army neither."

"Trampling," the captain repeated.

"We got a language barrier?" the sheriff said.

"We got a dead girl is what we got," the captain said.

"That supposed to be clever?"

"Nothing clever about murder, sheriff."

"We can handle our own," the sheriff said.

"Not your call to make," the captain responded.

The hard truth was the state police had the legal authority and jurisdiction to take the lead on major crime investigations in rural areas lacking the requisite personnel and resources to do the job properly themselves. The investigation findings were subsequently, in most cases, referred to the county prosecutor's office for final adjudication. Of course, this didn't always make the pill any less bitter for local law enforcement to swallow.

The captain took the sheriff's hand and shook it for the benefit of the TV cameras, anyway. The sheriff smiled, but the forced smile fell lopsided on his ruddy, gray-grizzled, pock-marked face. The captain offered the cameras a restrained nod for good measure. "We appreciate the cooperation, sheriff," he said.

"Uh huh," the sheriff said.

"Uh huh," the captain repeated.

The exchange on the porch was interrupted by a young state trooper with a notepad exiting the house in a hurry. The young trooper was flummoxed and he spoke too quickly to be understood. He swallowed hard and tried again while pointing back into the house. "We have a situation, captain," he managed this time, blinking. Captain Dwyer and Sheriff Snodgrass entered the house to find Allison's mother cowering behind the dining room table near the kitchen. The poor woman was dressed for a day of work, but her once carefully coiffed hair was now falling in tangles from a bun. She was muttering half-crazy.

Troopers and deputies stood at bay.

"Not my baby girl," she moaned.

She had a knife. Allison's mother.

At her own throat.

"Lord have mercy," the sheriff sighed.

"She went into the kitchen for coffee," the young state trooper with the notepad explained, speaking more deliberately this time. "Came out with the knife," he said, the inflection in his voice rising again. "Went at him first--" he said, pointing.

Harlan stood in the opposite corner. Blank-faced.

A superficial drag mark across the jaw.

"--then threatened to cut her own neck," the trooper finished.

Sheriff Snodgrass sighed again. "Sweet Mary and Joseph." He approached Allison's mother, thick utility belt creaking. Hand extended. "Rosemary," he said softly.

Her mutterings turned into low shrieks. Animal-like.

She jabbed the knife more firmly against her neck. Sobbing.

"Gimme the knife," the sheriff said.

She sobbed harder still. Tangled hair falling in her face.

The sheriff kept his hand in the air. Palm up. Stiffly.

"Said gimme the knife, Rosemary," he said.

Her hollow eyes turned baleful behind the fallen tangles.

"Get away from me, sheriff," she hissed.

The sheriff only extended his hand further. Almost bored.

"Can't let you do this," he said. "Not in my town."

"Said get back, damn you!" she said.

The sheriff scowled with impatience. "Rosemary, please. How long we known each other? Since grade school, I imagine. Shit, I still remember when you come down here to live with your aunt after your momma got sick up in Foresthill. That mean old buzzard with the Chrysanthemums and lilacs. Your aunt, I mean, not your momma. And you, all pigtails and braces," he said, grunting with the memory. "I recall how we used to skip rocks back of the library at the pond, too. How we ran around in our bare what-to-fors with the Johnson twins after that Homecoming game. And Jesus Christ, Rosemary, don't you remember those blue-haired Nazis from thc Prayer Circle coming down from the church? My heavens alive, Rosemary, you'd have thought they'd wandered onto the Devil's own playground by their expressions."

Her guard down the sheriff's hand struck quickly.

Like the head of a poisonous snake.

Grabbing her wrist. Twisting.

Allison's mother screeched.

Like she had actually been bitten by an asp.

The knife popped free. Fell to the floor.

Clattering. Coming to a rest.

The sheriff stooped over.

Collected it.

Allison's mother hugged herself and crumpled to the floor behind him, sliding down the dining room wall in slow motion, contorting into herself like a soft pretzel, sobbing harder than ever, her breathing coming in wounded and snatching gasps. The sheriff ignored her. Instead, he turned toward the room of law enforcement personnel. Sneering, he reprimanded the young trooper with the notepad. Flashing the weapon in question.

"It's only a butter knife," he said.

He threw the knife at the young trooper.

It glittered in the sunlight.

The young trooper flinched instinctively as the knife bounced harmlessly off his uniform. "Remind me to call the bomb squad if she lights the stove," the sheriff exclaimed, frowning, before observing the Barbie Doll reporter's cameraman zooming in on the untidy scene through the open front door. "For fuck sakes," he admonished the state contingent. "Somebody get him off that porch and close that fucking door already."

A pair of troopers manhandled the cameraman.

The front door was pushed closed.

It served as the perfect distraction. Nobody noticed Allison's mother rise from her collapsed heap in the dining room corner and snatch the revolver from Sheriff Snodgrass' holster with a strident primordial scream. Not until it was too late.

The room then fell still.

Everyone staring at her.

She stood on unsteady legs.

Swinging the service revolver crazily.

Wild-eyed. Out of her mind.

Undone completely.

"Aw, shit, Rosemary," the sheriff said.

The revolver pointed first at the sheriff.

Then bounced to Harlan.

"You. . .!!" Allison's mother whined softly. Painfully. Hands shaking violently. The revolver, extended out from her lanky chest, shook violently along with her hands. Even more dangerous with a badly trembling finger bouncing all over the trigger.

"You did this!!" she said. "You *did* this--"

Harlan was frozen. Resigned.

The sheriff lunged at the gun--

--but Allison's mother dodged him this time.

The sheriff slipped. Fell.

Allison's mother took the reprieve to step back into the tight corner behind the dining room table and with a final whimper stuffed the business end of the shiny gun barrel into her own mouth, swallowing it. Her finger jerked with purpose.

Depressing the trigger.

There was a loud hollow click.

But only that.

Allison's mother stared down the bridge of her nose at the gun with an expression of confusion and grief-stricken disappointment before Captain Dwyer interceded and wrestled the gun away. Allison's mother crumpled to the floor once again.

A hysterical heap. Angry sobs.

Captain Dwyer examined the revolver.

Flipped open the gun barrel. It was empty.

The sheriff rose from the floor. Embarrassed.

"I never keep it loaded," he admitted.

"Good thinking," Captain Dwyer said.

The captain handed back the revolver.

Meanwhile, the Barbie Doll's intrepid cameraman had somehow managed to film everything through the front window this time after briefly wrestling away from his law enforcement escort on the front porch during the confusion inside.

Delbert stared with horror from the crowd.

Along with the other startled onlookers behind the barricade.

The front window a perfect viewing screen.

Captain Dwyer heaved a weighty sigh. Closed the curtains and approached Harlan. Allison's father was paralyzed against the far wall. Face vacant. Uncomprehending. Hollow eyes staring at his wife curled up into a ball across the room.

"What did your wife mean when she said you did this, Mr. Winslow?" the captain said.

Harlan didn't appear to hear the question.

Captain Dwyer asked it again.

The words hung in the air.

Invisible living things.

Harlan only responded after a hard nudge from the sheriff. In a defeated monotone, a tear sliding down his clean shaven cheek, Harlan only just managed to mumble: "The convict from up on the hill. The one on the lam. We used to run around together."

"That so," Captain Dwyer pushed.

"Testified against him," Harlan garbled.

Sheriff Snodgrass put a sympathetic hand on Harlan's shoulder. Squeezed briefly. "Freddy Jackson, captain," the sheriff said. "The worst kind of business."

# 16.

DELBERT HAD NEVER TRULY KNOWN anyone who had died. His grandmother had died, of course, and recently, but Delbert hadn't really *known* her. He certainly had no memory of her. Just a few old photos he had found hidden in the bottom of his mother's jewelry box. Delbert and his mother had left Shady Creek when he was still just a small baby and she and Delbert's grandmother had not stayed in touch. There had been a falling out in the past or so his mother liked to tell him. She always spat out that cryptic phrase -- *falling out* -- as if it contained curse words. Delbert's grandfather was an even more mysterious affair. The man had died two long decades before Delbert was even born. From liver complications. Delbert wasn't sure what that puzzling description meant either -- *liver complications* -- but his mother always alleged it in hushed tones like such a thing was catching. Like the common cold. Or worse, poison ivy.

Allison. She had been the first real person.

The first real person he had truly known to die.

It left Delbert feeling desperately cold and sick inside. Not the common cold sick or poison ivy sick, but perhaps liver complications sick. Like he could die from it sick.

It reminded Delbert of the lazy afternoon he and his mother had been on a narrow two-lane highway passing through flat and brilliantly green farmland in Nebraska. Delbert had been sticking his head out the window, eyes watering in the strong air-stream produced by the speed of their car his mother had later sold to a used car dealer in some forgotten place called Mullen when they could no longer afford gasoline or food or a motel room for the night for that matter. A monstrous lumbering semi-truck with HANSON BROS DAIRY stenciled boldly on the side had passed them at a high speed, buffeting their car, pushing it dangerously toward the shoulder, his mother screaming foul good-for-nothings as she corrected the wheel to keep from crashing into a ditch. In the same horrifying moment a beautiful Golden Labrador had appeared out of nowhere in the middle of that endless green nowhere, ducking under a barbed-wire fence and senselessly darting out into the road. Into the path of that monstrous semi-truck.

The truck driver never had a chance to react.

Never had a chance to brake.

The semi's enormous heavy-duty tires had snatched the dog like jaws and ground it up before eventually spitting the carcass out the back end. But just before the ghastly impact, Delbert was sure the dog had glanced up at the semi-truck and realized its fate. Perhaps it had been chasing a prairie dog. Tongue lolling in delight, eyes sparkling with mischief. Perhaps the dog had never been this far off the farm before in its exuberant young life. Perhaps the pooch had been running with a newfound freedom. Strong legs pumping, lungs filling with that warm summer air. Delbert had watched with horror as the Labrador had been rolled and crushed and rolled and crushed again and again by the noisy, indifferent assembly line of massive churning tires before its body was finally and rudely flung free of the thick back bumper and tossed in a bloody, indistinguishable mess back into the road.

Delbert's mother had swerved to avoid it.

Then it was only in the side mirror. Receding.

Delbert thought perhaps he saw the mangled mess lying in the road twitch before the quickly expanding distance and a slight rise robbed him of the view. Then again, or so Delbert had desperately told himself later, perhaps it had just been the vibration of the side mirror as his mother had corrected their course back into the middle of the lane, tires bouncing and skidding away from what she liked to call the dummy dots dividing the north and south lanes.

He hadn't thrown up right then.

He had only done so later. That night.

Waking with a scream from a sweaty sleep.

Delbert felt like he might finally be sick now sitting in the small living room in Shady Creek thinking about Allison. It had been positively unbearable to think about that mess of a dog lying on the highway in the middle of that nowhere back then. But no matter how hard he had tried Delbert had been unable to erase the terrible image from his mind. Or even worse, the movie of its demise playing in his head. The more he had tried, the louder and more colorful those awful moving pictures had plagued him. Over and over again. Roll. Crush. Roll. Crush. Twitch. Twitch. But to be fair, even if he could have done so, he wasn't sure he would have chosen to forget Allison even as the thought of her lying inside that stifling hot rubberized body bag pushed hot bile heavily into his throat. Even as, despite knowing better, Delbert couldn't help but imagine her to also somehow be reduced to an awful mangled mess inside that black rubberized coffin. Not unlike the once beautiful Golden Labrador twitching back there on that sticky hot Nebraska blacktop. Suffering in its final moments.

Alone.

Allison had been so kind. So sweet.

So lovely. So alive. And yet so sad.

He wondered if she was still sad wherever she was now.

Then he thought of the baby.

"Hey," his mother said. The sound of her caustic voice broke his reverie. She was drinking. Tipping a vodka bottle over a waiting tumbler. Pour. Drink. Repeat.

She nodded at the checkers board.

"You took your finger off. That's cheating," she said.

Delbert was sitting with his legs pushed beneath the coffee table, pretending to play a game of checkers. Against himself. He had apparently moved a red marker forward and taken his finger off before seeming to reconsider the move and pulling it back. He only had a scant memory of this. He had been focused on the TV.

The Bedford affiliate was showing video footage from earlier in the day. The sensational camera shot through the front window. Allison's mother brandishing the sheriff's revolver.

Swinging it. Completely unhinged.

"I wish she'd'a shot him," Delbert said.

Delbert's mother flinched. Burped. "What an evil thing to say," she said. "She didn't want to shoot nobody, Delbert. The woman was out of her mind. Plumb loco. You ever done what that girl done to herself I'd be strapped to a gurney at the funny farm," his mother said, pointing the tumbler at him. "Suppose that's where they gone and taken her now."

More earlier news footage played on the TV screen. State police troopers dragging Allison's mother from the house to a gray van. She was distraught. Arms and legs flailing. Troopers at each elbow, her legs dangling, shoes dragging on the sidewalk. Head bent backward, twitching side to side, eyes rolling crazily, apoplectic. The shot then cut to Harlan. A hard cut. Standing in the background. Trembling. Unresponsive to law enforcement around him. Like he was trapped inside a terrible nightmare and taking misguided solace in the fact he would soon be awake. That this would all end. That it could not possibly be his new reality.

Delbert frowned. "He was sweet on her," he said.

"She was his daughter," his mother said.

"Not what I meant."

Delbert's mother digested the unsettling inference.

Grimaced. Disgusted by it.

"I'm not having this conversation, you little sicko," she said.

The footage on the TV returned to a live shot.

The Barbie Doll reporter outside Allison's house.

His mother muted the TV. "Hate that blown-dry bitch."

"I was sweet on her, too," Delbert said in a small voice.

Meaning Allison, of course.

He pushed the red marker forward. In a daze.

His mother nodded.

Pushed the tumbler toward him.

"Go ahead," she said. "Strong medicine."

Delbert hesitated. Stared at the tumbler sitting on the coffee table beside the checkers board in front of him. At eye level. The liquid inside was colorless and looked so innocuous despite the fact he knew it was anything but. He sniffed the glass. He could smell nothing. He watched his hand lift the glass like the hand now belonged to someone else. The hand brought the thick-rimmed tumbler to his lips. He took a healthy gulp and instantly began coughing as the innocuous nothing in the tumbler burned like holy hell fire down his startled throat. As his offended throat narrowed and blistered, Delbert couldn't help but think of those carnival freakshows on late night TV and their traveling band of gypsies who would gobble down those long flaming fire-sticks to cheering onlookers. He thought his throat would close forever. Thought he would suffocate. Instead, he burped. His stomach lurched and he burped again with tears streaming down his face.

His mother burst out into loutish laughter at the sight of him on the day his friend Allison had died next door. Just sat there and laughed at him holding that heavy, thick-rimmed tumbler. Like it was the funniest damn thing she had ever seen.

Until heavy knocks startled them.

Delbert's mother rose from the couch. Unsteadily. Her legs wobbly beneath her like cooked pasta noodles. Her hand pushed along the wall for balance. Neither she nor Delbert noticed the live shot on the TV switch from next door to their own house, following the transition of the crime scene personnel, troopers, and deputies. Delbert's mother opened the front door and took a step back. Squinting. Sheriff Snodgrass and Captain Dwyer stood on the front stoop. She took another wobbly step back before gathering herself and managing a precarious drunken step forward.

"What do you want, Chuck?" she said.

"Heavens, aren't you the picture of health," the sheriff said.

"I see you got your gun back, Barney Fife," she said.

The captain beside the sheriff forced back a smile.

"This is Captain William Dwyer, state police, honey," the sheriff said.

Captain Dwyer tipped his hat. "Ma'am."

Delbert squeezed between his mother's pointy hip and the door jam. Noticed the large congregation of law enforcement gathering beyond the porch in the darkness.

"Boys just want to have a look around," the sheriff said.

Delbert realized with horror he was still holding the tumbler.

And quickly hid it behind his back.

"We have a search warrant," Captain Dwyer acknowledged, holding paperwork.

"On what grounds?" Delbert's mother said. Disobliging.

"On account Freddy still missing," the sheriff said.

Shortly thereafter, Delbert and his mother found themselves standing on the muddy driveway with the sheriff, bathed in the harsh white media light coming from just beyond a hastily constructed addition to the law enforcement barricade. That barricade now seemed to stretch half the neighborhood block. Despite the late hour, neighbors and curious townsfolk continued to stand behind it, too, sharing space with the makers of the harsh white light, softly murmuring at the investigation's shifting focus. Including Ollie who stood straddling his bike, staring wide-eyed at the circus unfolding before him in their small town. At one-point Ollie thought he caught Delbert's eye and waved. Ollie wasn't sure if Delbert saw him because Delbert did not return the gesture. Delbert remained focused on the white clapboard house. Beyond its thin shivering windows damp with growing condensation compliments of the autumn night's deepening cold, state police crime scene technicians were turning the house inside out.

The noise itself was unbearable. Invasive.

"Thought she kilt herself," Delbert's mother said hoarsely to the sheriff. She shivered in the cold without a jacket. Smoking nonstop. Nicotine-stained fingers trembling.

"Girl had defensive wounds," the sheriff said.

"Defensive wounds?" she said.

The sheriff noticed Delbert listening. "Close your ears, boy," he instructed, then lowered his voice, colorless lips pushing close to Delbert's mother's ear. She flinched. "Strangled with her own bra," the sheriff hushed. "Never did find her panties."

Delbert overheard every word, anyway.

The wind blowing them in his direction.

He stiffened with alarm.

And instinctively moved toward the house.

"Hey, where you going?" the sheriff barked.

Delbert froze. Scolded his feet to keep moving.

"Said where you going?" the sheriff repeated.

Delbert found his feet uncooperative. Cowardly.

"You. Sit your ass down 'til they're done," the sheriff said. "Do it." Reluctantly, Delbert sat down on the bottom porch step. Worried sick. And for good reason. It wasn't long before Captain Dwyer exited the white clapboard house holding a pair of clear plastic evidence bags. One contained the denim jacket. The other, the panties. Little Bo Peep and her lambs.

"Christ Almighty," the sheriff said. "Bingo."

Delbert's mother shuddered. Confused. Angst-ridden.

Delbert dropped his head into his lap. Crestfallen.

# 17.

**THE COUNTY COURTHOUSE STOOD AT** the center of town. It was the fourth building raised in Shady Creek after the mill, the Methodist church, and the elementary school. It had originally been a simple one room affair made of wood before a fire escaping the coal room at the turn of the century burned it to the ground, consuming the county jail in the basement. From the ashes a large red brick wonder was constructed. Inspired by Greek Revival architecture, the new and grander iteration had a portico of four massive white columns set on brick piers and a pair of narrow white staircases flanking a wide porch with tall bright white oak doors at the main entrance -- often left flung open during the warm, humid months to aid circulation.

The first floor of the courthouse contained county and political offices, including the clerk of the court, registrar of deeds, tax collector, board of elections, public works, the county commissioners, parks and recreation, and so forth. The second floor housed the courtroom. At the forefront of the cavernous room sat a rich walnut paneled judge bench beneath a plastered alcove and surrounded by decorative Corinthian colonnettes. Ornate cast iron railings of foliate design bordered the jury box and partitioned the prosecution, defense, and court officials from the public seating area composed of simple wooden benches and cast iron arm rests. A huge chandelier shipped all the way from merry old England hung from the ceiling below a plaster medallion with molded ribs extending to plaster corbels along the courthouse walls. Yet despite the courtroom's intended grandeur, the chandelier still managed to look garish and out of place and a touch too gothic, though opinion might have been assuaged if it had been commonly known the light fixture was not actually crystal, but cheap prisms of molded glass. Regardless, the courthouse was the pride of the town. Even if it, too, was a bit garish and out of place. Even if it was only in session a few days a week. If that. Presided over by a roster of departmental judges. As needed. Otherwise the lavish courtroom sat empty. An echo chamber of ghosts and polished wood.

The county sheriff department occupied a detached building behind the courthouse. A squat canary yellow brick building with tinted doors and windows. The administrative offices resided at the front of the building and on the entire second floor. The county jail was on the first level in the southwest corner. The jail consisted of only ten cells and had its own entrance, a nondescript black door beside a loading dock. The jail worked on the honor system. Inmates either served at night or during the day depending on their mill shift or similar considerations. They could order food from the diner or have home-cooked meals delivered. It wasn't unusual to find the men in yellow jumpsuits sitting out in the sun smoking with the deputies like kids at recess. The more serious infractors were sent elsewhere. To less hospitable arrangements.

There was no one outside smoking this morning.

It was overcast. Cold and blustery.

Delbert sat at a short metal table in a makeshift interrogation room which also served as the sheriff department's office supply closet. A wall of narrow shelves contained humdrum office knickknacks. Pens and pencils, copy paper and envelopes, tubs of rubber bands, and other such pedestrian items.

A small square window overlooked a grassy knoll.

Delbert watched the wind bluster outside the small window. Rise and fall. Like respiration. Pushing about dead leaves. Swirling the dead leaves in mini-cyclones before scattering them beyond the window frame and out of sight.

"Freddy gave me the jacket," he said.

Sheriff Snodgrass grunted. The sheriff was seated across the table, leaning back heavily in a creaking metal chair which appeared insufficient to his weight, threatening to crumple beneath him at any moment like a can of pop. The sheriff's thick arms were crossed over his ample stomach. His large, stocky legs pushed out before him -- a boot heel tapping the tile floor.

"Doesn't explain those panties, chief," he said.

The panties sat in the plastic evidence bag on the table.

Captain Dwyer stood in the corner of the room.

Unmoving. Like a filing cabinet.

"Told you," Delbert said. "It was just a dare."

Sheriff Snodgrass grunted again. Louder this time. "Shit, Delbert, I know the no good bastard is your old man," he lamented pitifully, chewing down on an already badly chewed cigar, "but for heaven sakes, boy, you really want to be an accomplice to murder?"

"Always an accomplice," Delbert said.

The comment piqued the captain's interest.

The captain straightened. Surprising Delbert.

Delbert had thought the man perhaps asleep.

"Say that again," the captain said.

"Always an accomplice. That's what Freddy said."

"Did he? And what do you think he meant by it?"

Sheriff Snodgrass rolled his eyes with impatience.

"Not sure," Delbert admitted.

Captain Dwyer moved around the sheriff and sat on the edge of the interrogation table, hiding the window and the soundless parade of scattering leaves from view.

"Try for me," he said.

"Maybe it means you and him," Delbert said reluctantly, nodding in the sheriff's direction, "are settin' Freddy up for somethin' he ain't done."

The sheriff groaned loudly. A belly groan.

"Uh huh," he bellowed, eyes rolling again. Like casino slots. "And you got the horny teenage girls of this town dropping their underwear for you. Sure you do."

Captain Dwyer frowned.

Delbert noticed the frown. Made a decision.

"Got herself knocked up. You know 'bout that yet?" he said.

He could see the simple statement stunned the law officers.

"Knocked up? You mean Allison?" the captain said.

Delbert nodded. Emboldened.

"She tell you that?" the captain said.

Another nod.

The sheriff was almost gleeful.

"A double homicide, then," he said.

Captain Dwyer ignored the sheriff.

Remained focused on Delbert. Leaning forward.

Voice dropping almost reverentially low.

"She know who the father was, did she?" he said.

"Her daddy, I think," Delbert said.

The words hit the sheriff like an electric shock. The chewed cigar dropped from his mouth, tumbled a couple times like an Olympic diver, and disappeared beneath the table. His plump, ruddy, gray-grizzled, pock-marked face pinched inward as if he were sucking an especially sour lemon before rippling with unrestrained consternation. "Sweet angel fuck in heaven, Delbert," the sheriff finally spat out, rising to his boots, knocking that metal chair backward. The chair made a horrible clattering noise as it hit the floor and promptly folded up. "You-- You got yourself a real head for fiction, boy," he accused. "God as my witness."

Meanwhile--

Down the hall from the interrogation room--

Lillian was sitting in a secondary lobby. Chain-smoking despite the NO SMOKING poster scolding her silently from an otherwise dreary cement wall. Even with the distance she heard the collapse of the metal chair and the reverberating boom of the sheriff's voice. She cringed. Jaw clenching.

A man in overalls and a stained white T-shirt met her gaze. The man sat in a nearby plastic chair at the end of a short line of plastic chairs in the secondary lobby. The man wore a frustrated scowl. Angry. And rose moments later, angrier still, when his son, Bobby Joe, commonly known in town as Trigger, departed from a back room with a state police escort.

The escorting trooper said, "Your boy is free to go. For now."

The man in overalls and the stained white T-shirt came to stand between his boy and the trooper.

"You want to talk to my boy again," he huffed, "tell the sheriff he comes by my house. Sits on my couch like regular folk. Otherwise, you charge him with somethin'."

"Thank you for your cooperation," the trooper said.

Trigger didn't look like he knew where he was.

Or maybe even who he was at the moment.

His father glowered. Dragged his son out the door.

Leaving Lillian alone with the trooper.

Lillian rose to her feet, pointing her burning cigarette like a sword. "I want to see *my* son," she said, trying to sound stern, but immediately discomfited by the quaver she heard in her own voice. She could see the tremble in her hands, too.

God she needed a drink. A fucking drink.

The trooper saw the shiver spread from those hands.

Mini-earthquakes seemed to suddenly possess her.

"You'll have to wait for the captain, ma'am," he said.

"I'm not waiting another goddamn minute," she said. And she pressed toward the trooper. Intending to walk right through him, if necessary. Or right the fuck over him. Her own goddamn mini-earthquake. The trooper stepped aside, his hands raised, unwilling to engage her. Fortunately, a door opened down the hall and Sheriff Snodgrass and Captain Dwyer exited. Lillian marched toward them, meeting them in the hall.

"Where's my son?" she said.

"Thought we might chat first," Captain Dwyer said.

The sheriff pushed in front of the captain. Still simmering. Gruff and authoritative. "Your boy's got a mouthful of lies n'him, Lillian," he said. "Powerful nonsense."

"Go to hell, Chuck," she said.

A hand fell on the sheriff's shoulder.

"Take five, sheriff," the captain said.

Sheriff Snodgrass's lips pulled back from his gums.

Sneering at the captain's hand on his shoulder.

"This is my office, friend," he said. "You don't dismiss me."

"I just did," the captain said.

This earned a small smile of satisfaction from Lillian.

Sheriff Snodgrass stood there for a moment in that narrow hall. Not sure what to do. The captain stood his ground. When the sheriff finally turned to leave, face red with fury, his girth pushed the captain and Lillian against the wall. Afterward, while the captain led Lillian to the coffee machine and a small alcove to talk, Sheriff Snodgrass pretended to duck into a private office in the opposite direction only to double back to the interrogation room.

He heaved the door open with his shoulder.

Found Delbert still sitting at the metal table.

Delbert flinched as the sheriff loomed over the metal table. Large hands splayed on its shiny surface shimmering beneath his substantial weight and the weight of his carefully chosen words. The sheriff spoke in that deceptively soft and mesmerizing voice. That down comforter over a bed of rusty nails.

"Thing is, Delbert," he hissed, "that day we first met, that day I gave you a ride when your foot was 'bout ready to come off like an old tire, I offered you my hand. And you shook it. Like a man, or so I thought. So listen here, you obnoxious little brat. Maybe you don't want to believe Freddy is no good. Shoot, my momma used to curse my daddy's name morning 'til night and I'd curse her right back. But you know what, chief? One day I heard he was up in Summerton with a new family. Didn't want to believe it, of course. Better to believe he was dead somewhere in the ground than to believe he'd left us, but I'll tell you what I done. I took the Greyhound up there to Summerton to see for myself. Sure did. And I grew up a little that day. Had to. Well, you puny little fucker. Time for you to grow up, too. Sure it is."

Delbert just sat there.

"Say, yes sir, boy, goddammit."

Delbert just stared. Insolent.

"I said, say, yes sir, boy. Do it."

Delbert pursed his lips.

This lit a fresh fuse in the sheriff. Incensed him. His cold eyes became enraged as he unknowingly stepped on the fallen cigar on the tile floor with the heel of his book, crushing it into a broomstick. "Then you listen here, brat," he said, table trembling beneath him, making a terrible shivering noise. "Maybe you're too stupid to know what you don't know. Or maybe stupid ain't the right word. Ignorant. That's what I'm looking for. Ain't your fault, but this little game you're playing here in my town-- It ain't gonna fly. We got a place for your daddy up on the hill. Sure we do, son. But we also got ourselves a place in this county for wayward young boys. A place with walls and rules and no mommas and quite a bit a ways from here, in fact. A place where a willful brat can sit a long spell and think about the things he gone and done and what he ain't gone and done right yet. What you think about that, Delbert? Cuz I suggest you think on it real hard, chief. And think on this, too," the sheriff warned. "A boy goes in a boy, but comes out something else altogether. Assuming, of course, he comes out at all."

The sheriff stood. Satisfied.

Satisfied with the fear he saw in Delbert.

A raw and transparent fear.

A fear of losing his mother. And father.

A fear of walls and rules and locked doors.

A fear of such a terrible unknown.

Neither he nor Delbert saw Captain Dwyer standing in the doorway until just that moment. Hands planted firmly on his hips. It was unclear how much Captain Dwyer had overheard, but it was clear the good captain had overheard enough.

# 18.

CAPTAIN DWYER DROVE DELBERT AND his mother home from the sheriff department in an unmarked black state police sedan. He invited Delbert to sit up front, hinting he might allow him to toy with the blinking lights and maybe even ring the siren. The bank of blinking lights flashing on the dashboard and on the underside of the ceiling had always reminded the captain of a Flash Gordon comic strip. Even after all these years. A sleek interstellar vehicle traveling at light speed in a distant part of the galaxy. Exploring a wilderness of strange planets, black holes, and nebulas. Delbert's mother declined on her son's behalf, though, content for the boy to sit in the back with her behind the protective grill as evening dusk settled heavily around them and where she otherwise remained completely silent for the entire ride back to the white clapboard house. Captain Dwyer turned down the muddy driveway. The media stirred from their trucks across the road. The captain parked in front of the dark home.

"I don't want you talking to the press," he said.

This earned a frown from Lillian.

"Bother my boy again, captain," Delbert's mother chided him without looking in his direction, "and I'll hold a press conference on my own goddamn front porch. Believe that, sir."

Delbert and his mother slid out of the unmarked car into the night. Questions were shouted from behind a barricade monitored by a single bored state trooper across the road. The questions scattered in a blustery wind like so many of the dead leaves.

Delbert and his mother entered the white clapboard house and flipped on the lights to find a terrible mess waiting for them. The aftermath of the hastily administered search warrant. Moving boxes dumped. Their contents spilled after weeks of neglect and darkness. Cabinets rummaged. Furniture shoved and overturned. Closets emptied. A storage alcove beneath the staircase ransacked as if by raccoons. The floor wet and trodden with boot prints.

Mud and dead leaves.

The mildew stink of the outdoors.

"You sure know how to make a mess of things, Delbert," his mother said, her voice suddenly faraway and lost. She sighed. A long tremulous sigh that shook her entire body and never quite left her hands, not even after she had poured herself a drink and sat on the cold floor in the dark kitchen, her narrow back pushed against the side of the fridge, the bottle cradled between her legs, staring for the next few hours at peeling yellow wallpaper.

Delbert climbed the stairs. His bedroom had also been violated. His private things touched and disturbed. The debris on the floor included clothes and toys. Model airplanes he had so painstakingly put together. Including the Messerschmitt. A wing broken. But it was another object which held his attention. Half-hidden beneath the old WWII plane. The corroded old railroad spike. The spike Freddy had found in the weeds outside town the morning they had gone fishing before the world had gone completely mad. Made of soft steel. Allowing it to bend without breaking. Bent in a severe L-shape. A dull spike at one end where it had once been pushed down into the rocky earth and a large rounded head folded like a mushroom on the other. Silky smooth to the touch after so many years exposed to the weather. It had once held the rail ties together and supported the moving weight of a twenty ton train.

Delbert scooped up the spike.

Stared at it sitting in his palm.

Then squeezed it with all his strength.

Closed his eyes and just squeezed.

# 19.

**IT WAS DECIDED ROSEMARY SHOULD BE** taken to the hospital down in Bedford. Unlike the rudimentary med clinic on Elm Street in downtown Shady Creek, the hospital in Bedford had a psychiatric unit. It was also considered the best medical facility in western North Carolina with a first-rate triage unit and surgery center. In other words, unlike its backwoods cousin nestled back up in the foothills like a tick on a hound dog, the hospital in Bedford was of the modern world.

The state police handled the paperwork.

And the official transport.

Sheriff Snodgrass arrived in his sheriff cruiser the following night. The journey off the mountain and out of the woods took only about an hour, but Bedford with all its stoplights and traffic might as well have been Manhattan compared to his sleepy hometown. There were tall buildings made of steel and glass with garish advertising. Skyscrapers when compared to their counterparts on Main Street in downtown Shady Creek where nothing grew over two stories. There were young, smoking, jiving hooligans hanging out on corners with nothing better to do than wait for trouble to find them or seek it out if the night became too long in the tooth. And the entire spectacle was sct to a noisy, dissonant soundtrack. The dull roar of congested traffic bouncing off those enormous structures leaning over the street. The clamor of passersby on the crowded sidewalks. The whine of sirens beyond the blinding halo of neon lights.

Sheriff Snodgrass winced.

Felt a headache coming on.

The headache began behind his bloodshot eyes and radiated out across his skull, pounding mercilessly with the beat of his heart. Like an unwelcome solicitor whenever he ventured down into this cesspool of human depravity. And it would not only be the headache. His lungs would soon rattle, too, from all the garbage in the air. Sheriff Snodgrass scowled and drove into the hospital parking lot, parking next to a curb facing the emergency room entrance. He killed the engine. Climbed out and adjusted his utility belt. Coughed hard. Then took a moment to look upward.

At a boarded window on the third floor.

Freddy had punched out that window with a local cop asleep on a chair in the hall outside his room. Freddy had tip-toed along a decorative molding running the circumference of the hospital building before taking the leap onto the emergency entrance awning. The awning was made to look like cloth from a distance, but it was only an unfortunate illusion and poor Freddy must have felt like he had slammed into the cement sidewalk itself.

It was a miracle Freddy had walked away.

Albeit leaving behind a trail of blood.

Sheriff Snodgrass cleared his throat. Spat a hunk of city phlegm behind his rear tire. Hitched his utility belt again over his sinking belly. Then with a final irritated grumble began a short walk to a pair of double electric doors offset from the main emergency room entrance. The doors would take him to a long antiseptic hall and an elevator bank. He was thinking about taking a detour to the cafeteria for a Danish before slipping into the elevators when a redheaded rent-a-cop in a silly golf cart with HOSPITAL SECURITY glazed ostentatiously in large black letters above a plastic bug shield suddenly came whining down a steep ramp, the golf cart for all the world resembling a wind-up toy. The golf cart stopped abruptly beside the sheriff. Its brakes shrieking. Blocking the sheriff from the double electric doors. “Evening,” the redhead said.

“Yeah,” the sheriff said.

The redheaded rent-a-cop in a baby blue uniform two sizes too large for his boyish frame nodded back at Sheriff Snodgrass’ cruiser parked against the curb. “Can’t park here, sir,” he said.

"I'm conducting an investigation," the sheriff said.

"Still," the redhead said.

"You Keystone cops lost my prisoner the other night," the sheriff told the freckled little jerk, his eyes narrowing and his lip curling into an impatient snarl. "Now a girl is dead."

This did nothing to impress the redhead.

"See that sign?" the redhead said. He directed the sheriff's attention to a NO PARKING ANYTIME sign.

"Said this is official business, son," the sheriff said.

"Still," the redhead said.

"Still," the sheriff mocked, unyielding.

The redhead in his baby blue uniform two sizes too large set the emergency brake on the golf cart. "Look," he said slowly like the sheriff just might be a bit soft in the head. "You might be the law up on the hill, you hillbilly sheriff, but down here in the real world, friend, you got to move that cruiser from that curb pronto. As in ASAP. Otherwise, I'll have it towed back up to the boondocks at your expense. Pronto. As in ASAP. Have a nice night." That said the redhead released the golf cart brake. The golf cart jolted forward. Whining noisily down the parking lot.

Sounding more like a wind-up toy than ever.

After finding an official use parking lot, cursing under his breath the entire time, his headache stretching down his neck and into his upper back, stiffening the muscles, the sheriff took the elevator from the long antiseptic hall without detouring for that Danish after all (his stomach was suddenly too upset to eat) to the psychiatric wing on the fourth floor only to find himself parked waiting interminably in a plastic chair in a secondary lobby, his head resting against a concrete wall behind him. But for a heavy steel door painted a dull white leading back into the inner-sanctum, the lobby was ordinary enough with framed landscapes on the walls. Verdant green fields. Maybe Ireland. Maybe somewhere in the Midwest. All very safe. The sheriff closed his eyes. Elevator music played over an invisible sound system. It quickly began to sound like carousel calliope music. Too loud and looping inside the sheriff's pounding head. Like there was hidden inside it a subversive and subliminal torment to tease out the crazy.

"You have to check that, sir," a voice said.

The sheriff slowly opened his eyes.

Heavily. Reluctantly. Mean little slits.

A nurse at the reception window pointed at his gun.

"It ain't loaded," the sheriff said. And closed his eyes.

"You still have to check it," she said.

His eyes pushed open again. Foggy and tired. Still, he smiled. His slippery smile as he made an exaggerated show of removing the revolver from its holster and loading it. Doing so in front of the other visitors in the waiting room. Plunk, plunk, plunk.

"That isn't necessary, sir," the nurse said.

He snapped the barrel into the locked position. Stood.

Dumped the revolver and belt onto the reception counter.

"I don't like formalities," he said.

Shortly thereafter, the sheriff was escorted by an orderly from the lobby through the heavy steel door painted a dull white. The narrow hall beyond the door was painted a similar dull white, but there were no verdant landscapes here. Just cold, pock-marked concrete and a smoke detector protected by a heavy-duty wire box in a high ceiling corner. An electronic door opened with the slide of a security card to a small dayroom area with thick acrylic windows protected by wire cages. Couches and chairs. A silly game show droning noisily from a small TV bolted to the wall below the ceiling. And at the forefront of the room another nurse station behind another wire cage with a narrow pass-thru slot.

Patients or inmates, the sheriff wasn't sure how to refer to them even in his own mind, were sitting around looking bored, lonely, and anesthetized in white cotton pajamas and robes. They were not drooling or ranting or having conversations with empty air or slapping at invisible bugs like he had seen in the movies. Rather, these wackos looked disquietingly normal. At least at first glance. Until the sheriff looked closer as he passed through the room. There was a young woman sitting beneath the TV. So far beneath the TV she couldn't possibly see the screen. She was covered in small crescent-shaped scars -- the size of destructive fingernails. Bloody little outlines forming small constellations all over her face and body. Her nasty little nefarious fingers were heavily bandaged; still, to the sheriff's horror, those nasty little gremlins, ever devious, continued to mischievously pick and stab and dig through the heavy gauze and tape at her face and her arms as if they had a will of their own completely independent of the unfortunate young woman's control. Very unsettling.

The dayroom led into another narrow hall.

A bank of payphones. A group room. A quiet room.

The quiet room had no furniture. No windows. Just padded walls. Something told the sheriff the quiet room was only quiet when it was unoccupied. The padded door, unnaturally short at only five feet, was swung open to the inside. The room was empty, but for an orderly with big round sweat stains under her armpits and a bucket of soapy water and a bristle brush cleaning an ugly stain from a wall composed of dozens of cork-crumb-filled canvas pouches. The orderly watched the sheriff pass with baleful eyes. Kept scrubbing.

The escorting orderly led the sheriff past several private rooms with open doors to a conspicuously closed door. The orderly used a key to open it and Sheriff Snodgrass stepped inside to find Rosemary reclined on a narrow dormitory-style bed with a thick wooden base. Her wrists and ankles were bound by thick leather straps, though the straps hardly seemed necessary. She wasn't moving. In fact, it was debatable she even was breathing. Harlan sat in a wooden chair in the far corner beneath a wired acrylic window and beside another dreary verdant landscape. This landscape, unlike the ones in the lobby, was caulked directly into the wall. There was also a small bathroom without a door.

Harlan looked like a zombie.

A scarecrow stuffed with newspaper.

The sheriff paused over Rosemary for a moment.

Lifted her hand the few inches the leather strap would allow.

Then dropped it. Indelicately. Plop.

"She dead?" the sheriff said.

"Sedatives," Harlan managed.

The sheriff grunted. Then to the orderly said:

"Waiting for a drink order, chief?"

The orderly exited without expression, pulling closed the door behind him. The heavy door shut with a sleepy muffled sound before the sudden and automatic click of the bolt. Like a rifle being loaded. Echoing in the small room. "Suppose that's for our benefit," the sheriff grunted, meaning the door lock. "Apparently they don't abide by us wandering around. Getting into mischief."

The sheriff studied Harlan.

"You look like shit, Harlan," he said.

Harlan also looked wary, refusing to meet the sheriff's gaze. Or unable to. The sheriff sighed. Searched futilely for a place to sit and sighed again. "Think that jerk would be offended if I rang the buzzer and asked for a chair?" There was a nurse button above the bed. Not that Rosemary had any hope of reaching it.

"Here," Harlan said gruffly and stood, offering his chair.

The sheriff took it.

Harlan sat on the edge of his wife's bed.

Twitching like the fingernail girl out there beneath the TV.

"Got a partial autopsy report an hour ago," the sheriff said. "It's all very preliminary, mind you, but those state boys, they do work fast. You daughter was pregnant."

He let the revelation hang in the air a beat.

There was no discernible reaction from Harlan.

"You don't look surprised," the sheriff offered.

"That boyfriend," Harlan said after a spell, intently staring at the white institutional concrete wall over his wife's bed. It seemed to strangely calm him. That wall. "That football prick from over at the high school. He always had his hands all over her."

"He's been talked to," the sheriff said, glancing at the wall, too, wondering what Harlan might see projected there from his brittle little mind. "That little jack-off swears he never played hide the salami with your little girl, not without wrapping it first."

"Mistakes happen."

"Suppose they do."

Harlan continued to stare at the wall.

The sheriff pulled out a cigar.

This seemed to break Harlan's enchantment.

"Can't smoke in here," he said, nodding at ceiling sprinklers.

"Those just for show," the sheriff said.

He lit the cigar. Puffed.

The smoke drifted about the room.

Just drifted with nowhere to go.

Unable to escape the thick and dreary walls.

"They want some blood," the sheriff said.

"Some blood," Harlan said.

He looked at the sheriff for the first time.

"For a paternity test," the sheriff said.

"Thought Freddy was the suspect here," Harlan argued, voice rising an octave. "That stupid football prick from over at the high school--" he said, head shaking with irritation and exhausted bewilderment. "He's got nothing to do with what happened."

"Your blood, old boy," the sheriff said.

Harlan flinched. The blood left his face.

He stared again at that wall.

The sheriff sighed. A heavy, troubled sigh.

Stamped out the cigar in a bed pan.

The gray smoke had formed a cloud.

An ominous weather pattern.

Floating above them.

The sheriff made a face, grimacing. Unable to watch Harlan lose his shitty mind like his wretched wife lying there on the bed motionless. He then stood for effect, his shadow filling the concrete wall in front of Harlan like a monstrous thing.

"Listen here, you sick little puppy," he said finally.

His voice subsequently fell to an aggravated whisper.

"What Freddy done before ain't to be forgotten in my mind," he hushed. "Now he's done what he's gone and done again and gone up disappeared along with it, you see? As for your little girl-- Well, I suppose nobody can prove you knew she was pregnant. Nobody can prove that. Not 'less they can crawl up inside your measly little skull," he pronounced. "Your only crime far as I can tell," he said with distaste, "is loving your little girl too much."

Harlan shuddered. Put his head in his hands.

"It ain't no motive for murder," the sheriff tried.

Harlan began to sob.

"Don't have to be, anyways."

The sheriff sighed a final time in that small claustrophobic room with the concrete walls and the bathroom without a door and the acrylic window guarded by the thick wire grate and the sleepy verdant green landscape caulked directly into the wall. He collected his hat and held it to his chest as Harlan sobbed more loudly than ever into his hands and stood over Rosemary lying inert on that narrow hospital bed with the thick wooden base, her thin wrists and bony ankles bound by those thick binding leather straps stealing the blood from her hands and feet.

And said without pretense or sarcasm:

"I was you, honey, I'd never want to wake up, neither."

# 20.

DELBERT KNELT ON HIS BED IN THE dark, his chin resting morosely on the windowsill. His belly was empty and it gnawed at him, but he couldn't eat and couldn't fathom a time when he might be able to eat again. Instead, he stared at Allison's drawn curtains across the gauze of darkness between the white clapboard house and her small bedroom window. He thought with sweet bitterness of the long beautiful day he'd spent with her when the outside world had disappeared for a few short hours. Long enough for them to share in a wonderful companionship of tears and laughter and games and quiet whispers. He could still smell her. A buttery popcorn perfume accented with a sweet fragrance of lilac. But already her face was beginning to fade. Already. Delbert was not certain why this should be, knowing desperately he didn't want it to be so. He'd made himself a promise he would never forget her after all, but still it was happening all the same. Maybe, he thought miserably, it was to protect his heart from simply rupturing and bleeding out his aching chest.

His pained thoughts only twisted further--

--into a tight, burning knot--

--when Delbert found himself thinking of Freddy hiding somewhere out there in the darkness. Stumbling dizzily, perhaps, through dark alleys leading like a maze away from the hospital in Bedford, shivering in the sinking cold. Collapsing behind an overflowing dumpster. Burying himself beneath a blanket of wet newspapers. Or maybe curled-up in the back seat of a Greyhound bus heading nowhere. Bleeding and feverish in a flimsy hospital nightgown. Teeth chattering. Ignored by the other passengers who had warm homes and warm loving families to return to and no time or inclination for a broken man slowly dying in the shadows behind them. Then again, Delbert could also see Freddy faltering in the woods outside Shady Creek, trying urgently to get back to him, but lost amongst the dark and silent trees in an avalanche of freezing fog. Every direction leading him in the same direction. Thin arms wrapped tightly around his gaunt quivering torso. Face swollen with the awful cold and his terrible beating. Wandering off into an oblivion. Never to be found. Lost again to this world.

Delbert hiccupped a sob.

Thought he heard the hoot of the owl.

*Hoo hoo-oo* he thought it said.

Somewhere out there in the darkness, too.

Delbert wiped his tears with the sleeve of his shirt and stared again past the window glass. The giant Maple had during the last twenty four hours shed the remainder of its leaves. The leaves had fallen and piled like weightless snow at its thick base, secreting the highway of roots bubbling and rippling from the black earth. Hiding the ugly toadstools and the green lawn which would turn a rusty brown in the coming weeks. And covering Delbert's own muddy footsteps from that morning and afternoon he'd last spent with Allison. Delbert absently wondered if his footprints would freeze beneath the blanketing layers of decaying mulch only to reveal themselves again in the spring beneath that magnificent umbrella of a giant tree that now stretched up toward the dark black sky above him like decapitated deer antlers.

It would snow soon. The world would change.

It would no longer resemble itself.

And in his mind's eye Delbert now saw Freddy stumble and fall in the woods of his nightmarish vision. Unable to stand. Exhausted and defeated. Staring up at a parade of falling leaves seesawing in the darkness above him, circling down upon him. Tumbling leaves turned dull shades of orange, tan, and brown. Dry and crumbling with sharp, bitter edges. Eventually covering him like the Maple leaves covering the tangle of bubbling and rippling roots. He saw in his mind's eye Freddy closing his own eyes. Dying beneath the forest mulch. Rotting, then freezing beneath the settling snow. His corpse left undiscovered until spring.

Like Delbert's footprints.

Assuming it was ever found.

Delbert turned on the clock radio if only to drown out his dreadful thoughts and the classical music filled the darkness like helium pushing heavily into a balloon. Somehow making the darkness larger and more dense on this night. Unable to soothe him. Rather, the music had the opposite effect. It slithered twitchily in his ears and wriggled beneath his thin skin. Altogether provoking and alien. Tormenting his already frayed nerves.

He never noticed the shadow in his closet.

Separating from the darkness. Pushing forward.

Its growing shape filling the narrow space.

Then retreating as another shadow filled his doorway.

His mother. A cigarette glowing. "Told you, what Freddy done ain't got nothin' to do with us," she said.

Delbert continued to stare out the window at the bare Maple, but he could see his mother well enough in the window reflection. She could barely stand. This despite the fact she was leaning heavily against the door frame for balance. And she could barely speak. Her tongue once again two sizes too large for her mouth.

"You're drunk," Delbert said.

"Just clearing my head."

Delbert glared at her in the glass.

"You're a disgrace," he said.

The room fell very quiet. Like the entire house was holding its breath. Delbert in his entire ten years on this earth had never said anything like that to his mother before. For despite her miserable faults and myriad of transgressions and motherly failings, Delbert had never dared voice his displeasure so unabashedly out of fear that his own terror of losing her would be a self-fulfilling prophecy and that she might find herself lost like his father now.

Perhaps even on purpose.

"What'd you say?" she challenged.

"You heard me," he said.

"I don't think I did you little ungrateful brat."

"Ungrateful?" Delbert said

And suddenly he was angry, too. Very angry. Like he'd never been before. An anger feeding on all that sadness and frustration and fear and disappointment of the known and the unknown bubbling and rippling to the surface like those thick tree roots writhing like a nest of snakes beneath the giant Maple and forest mulch and too soon the winter snow.

"Ungrateful?" he said again.

Louder this time.

His mother took a step back. Startled. "That's right," she said, stumbling before her groping hand serendipitously found the door frame again, stabilizing her for the moment. "Ungrateful and stupid and selfish," she said. "Cuz let me tell you something."

She pointed the glowing cigarette at him.

A glowing eye in the dark.

"I don't care what Freddy done or ain't done this time around," she said hoarsely, the glowing eye bouncing up and down and left and right with unblinking accusation. "He ain't worth it, Delbert," she reprimanded. "Not your tears. Not a lick of spit."

Delbert abandoned the window.

Stood tall on his bed. Taller than his mother.

"Let me tell you something, Lillian," he said.

The strained force of his voice saw his mother take another stumbling step backward, her grip slipping from the door frame this time. The glowing eye dipping and disappearing in the darkness. She became but a silhouette. An unreal thing. A specter to him. "Allison was my friend," he said. "And my daddy, he ain't done it this time around. And it does matter a lick of spit to me. And let me tell you something else, Lillian--" he said.

"Don't call me that," the specter said.

"I'm tired of living out of boxes," he said, his hand sweeping at all the unpacked moving boxes in the corner of his room and more of them lining the narrow hallway. "We stayin' here or not?" he demanded to know. "Or are we having this conversation?"

Even from the shadows--

Delbert could see the aggrieved look on her face.

Mother and son stared at each other. Delbert refused to break the stare. For a long moment he believed his mother would remain there for the rest of the night, dismayed but determined. That she would return his defiant stare until he collapsed from exhaustion, but in the end it was exhaustion that stole over her.

She seemed to wilt in front of him.

Like a leaf falling off the grand old Maple.

Color dulled. Twirling lifelessly to the ground.

Landing silently. Shriveling in the cold.

The cigarette dropped to the floor. She stamped it out with a shoe, nearly losing her balance again, leaving a blackish-gray ash stain on the carpet. Then without another word his mother stumbled to her bedroom at the end of the hall. The same bedroom where his grandmother had unplugged an iron and lugged it into the bathroom and slid with it against her naked breast--

--into a tub of warm waiting water.

Delbert's mother picked up the telephone.

Sat down on her bed. Dialed.

The old rotary dial made loud clicking noises.

"It's me," she said, voice flat and emotionless. "I still owe you a date." She hung up the phone, placing the receiver back into the cradle on her lap. Delbert watched her from the dark of his bedroom down the hall. No longer visible to her. "You want to unpack, Delbert," she said. "So fucking unpack."

She pushed her bedroom door closed with her foot, not looking at him, the closing door blinking out his mother's soft bedroom lamp light with it. The subsequent darkness spread quickly, rushing down the narrow hall into Delbert's bedroom like a tide of black water. Delbert found himself blinded by the sudden absence of light but for a fuzzy yellow afterimage dancing on his eyeball. Through it he slowly turned and considered the vague rectangular outline of Allison's window beyond his own. Oddly, the curtains were now open and in that corresponding portal -- *stood Allison.*

She emerged from a shimmering glow expanding inside that narrow window frame. Delbert gasped at the sight of her.

Allison was wearing a flowing white nightgown, blonde hair falling loosely about her thin shoulders. Bright eyes large and alive and devoid of pain. She was ethereal and more beautiful than he'd remembered and the classical music on the clock radio which had been so intrusive and raw only moments before now offered a soft lullaby, and suddenly the fuzzy yellow afterimage and the shimmering glow completed an impossible circuit, connecting Delbert and Allison across the intervening void and Delbert felt an extraordinary warmth rush over him even before Allison smiled and lifted a small pale hand from her round hip and waved without burden. Delbert almost decided not to wave back. Not wanting the moment to end. Wanting this moment to stretch into eternity.

But just as he lifted his hand to wave--

A whispering voice scattered the heavenly vision.

The circuit of warm light blinked out.

In an instant. Like an exploding star.

Blinding him again.

Leaving only the blackness.

A horrible hollow blackness.

From which that whispering voice--

--again tickled at his ears.

Delbert turned toward the sound of the voice. It was coming from a dark shape in the blackness of his cave-like closet. The dark shape grew larger as his eyes adjusted to the restitution of the night. Unlike the shimmering light that had only too briefly filled Allison's window, offering a glimpse into the sublime, the dark corridor of the closet promised a less favorable hallucination. A dungeon of the world. A dark passage. For if Allison had become an emissary of the Light, then it somehow stood to reason in Delbert's tender mind the dark shape rising in the closet blackness portended the opposite. And for the briefest of moments Delbert thought he could hear the scrip and scratch of sharp claws on the cedar floor and the sniffling-snuffling inquisitiveness of an elongated snout stealing his scent from the dead air. And the taut stretch of its tenebrous scales as its lizard body slunk from its dark hole. The whisper of its venomous breath tickling at his ears with its forked tongue. Baiting him. Teasing him toward the darkness. Speaking in a language Delbert could not understand. Foreign and harsh. Washing dizziness over him. Down suddenly became up. Up became down. But in this vortex the jumbled words found translation. And the monster seemed to become anything but.

"I used to play that shit when Lily was first pregnant," it said.

Delbert blinked. The voice familiar.

His pupils grew larger and the dark shape suddenly appeared to shrink before him, shaking off the heavier blackness around it, becoming smaller and smaller in his eyes. Becoming a man.

Becoming Freddy.

Delbert blinked again.

Wondering if it all was just a terrible charisma.

A clever trick of the darkness itself.

"Suppose to make your brain smart for math and such," it said.

Freddy said. Commenting on the music.

The classical music floating about the small bedroom.

Delbert blinked again. It was Freddy. Truly.

And he briefly wondered now if he had fallen asleep.

If this was all, rather, but a desperate dream.

It seemed the more plausible explanation.

More plausible than Freddy hiding in his closet.

He heard running water. His mother's shower.

Warm water rushing through the walls around him.

Making the old pipes clink and clank.

This seemed to bring the real world back.

Make it all real again somehow.

Delbert reached to kill the music on the clock radio.

"Don't," Freddy said. "It's nice."

Freddy leaned forward from the darkness.

Even in the inky gloom Delbert gasped and found it difficult to look at the broken figure hunkered in the closet or look away for that matter. His clothing was caked in dried mud, trousers torn. The left side of his face was badly bruised and his eye swollen nearly shut. Dry blood the color of chocolate caked his left ear and had splattered and congealed down his neck. He was missing several fingernails. Ripped clean from oozing, purpled flesh.

"I know," Freddy said. "I'm a sight."

Delbert hiccupped again. A lump lodging in his throat.

Choking him. But still he just managed:

'What're you doing here, Freddy?"

Delbert immediately regretted the inartful question. He didn't mean it like it sounded. He was relieved Freddy was here. Relieved Freddy was alive. But here? In his closet where the law might find him? What was Freddy doing *here*? he meant to know.

"No place else to go. Not since that sweet peach died."

"It's my fault," Delbert said.

His tears finally fell. Thick tears.

"No," Freddy hushed.

"She gave me them panties," Delbert confessed.

He could barely speak now. Overwhelmed.

"It was a dare," he got out.

Freddy shook his head. Sadly.

"Ain't your fault," he said. "Not this."

Delbert desperately wanted to believe him. Couldn't.

"This mess… It started 'fore you was even born."

Cold intrusive headlights suddenly splashed across the bedroom window, startling them. Freddy instinctively shrunk from the light like a vampire touched by the morning dawn, but not before his dreadful injuries were preserved even more gratuitously in Delbert's frail mind as the beams of light bounced about the bedroom and his beleaguered psyche grabbed onto all the horribleness as if snapping an unkind photograph.

Indeed, Freddy *was* monstrous.

Meanwhile, outside the bedroom window, Delbert heard the groan of a dying engine and the heavy crunch of a car door opening, then closing. There was no need to look out the window to know what unpleasantness made the heavy footsteps on the front porch or the heavy knocks that rattled the small house.

"Hide," Delbert hushed breathlessly.

But Freddy was already gone. Disappeared.

Delbert's mother appeared eventually in the dark hall. She stood for a moment at his door. Hurriedly dressed for a night out. Her hair wet against her face from her quick dunk in the shower. She stared silently at Delbert. Then left without a word.

Heels clicking and clacking down the stairs.

# 21.

**CAPTAIN WILLIAM DWYER STATE POLICE** Major Crimes Unit spent the evening slouched behind the steering wheel of his unmarked black state police sedan fighting off exhaustion and boredom. He had parked the car in the deep shadows at the dead end of Hilltop Street. The road overlooked the dead girl's home and the white clapboard house. The captain wasn't sure what he might be waiting for on this desolate corner of weather-cracked pavement at such a lean hour of the evening, but his instinct told him to be here and it was preferable, frankly, to stuffing his pie-hole with greasy fast food back at the motel and staring vacantly at the idiot box.

More to the point, he couldn't get the boy out of his mind.

Delbert's statement back at the sheriff station had been curious. The more the young boy had talked and the more the captain had listened, and the more the sheriff had huffed and puffed, the more curious what the young boy had said had become. And apparently the captain wasn't the only one feeling the sting of electricity in the night air. The pretty blonde reporter with large blue eyes and unnaturally white teeth from the Bedford affiliate was still camped out in her TV van across the narrow road from the murder scene with her cameraman even though all her peers had left earlier that morning. The pretty blonde had had the sense to stick around. Or the nonsense for that matter. Then again, Captain Dwyer contemplated, yawning into the back of his hand, eyes threatening to slide shut despite copious amounts of coffee from a thermos wedged in a cup-holder, the sting of electricity in the night air might be nothing more than the promise of an early winter storm. It was cold and getting colder. Captain Dwyer turned up the car heater and hugged himself, listening to the warm, musty draft blow from the vents in a series of drowsy sighs. He yawned again and was about to give in to his exhaustion and shut his eyes for a minute (or maybe two) when a pair of dull headlights appeared on the road below him, pushing aside the curtain of night.

The sheriff.

Captain Dwyer grabbed binoculars. Sat higher in his seat.

The sheriff parked his cruiser outside the dead girl's house. He was not alone. There was someone sitting in the passenger seat. Eventually, after several long beats which stirred the blonde reporter and her sleepy cameraman from the TV van, the dead girl's father, Harlan Winslow, slowly exited the cruiser and trudged reluctantly toward the dark house. Blondie shouted questions, but the dead girl's father ignored her, disappearing inside.

The house remained dark.

The sheriff cruiser then pushed down the street, making a wide and obnoxious turn, pushing the pretty blonde reporter and her cameraman back from the road before rolling down the muddy driveway and up to the white clapboard house.

The front door to the white clapboard house opened.

The boy's mother stepped out. Lillian.

The captain frowned at the sight of her under a cone of weak porch light. The woman had once been pretty, if not beautiful, he measured. Not a natural pretty like the earnest reporter across the road who had probably worn her good looks effortlessly since about the age of the dead girl, but small town pretty. Fresh and sweet and full of vigor herself before merciless life had diminished who she had once been and thought she could be. Though perhaps the vigor was still there, he decided, adjusting the magnification of the binoculars. Perhaps buried just beneath the surface like the compressed spring in a coiled snake. He had seen a glimpse of it back at the sheriff station, hadn't he? Revealed in the practiced hardness of her face and again now in the fact she wasn't wearing nearly enough for the cold, yet the cold seemed no longer able to penetrate her. As if she could refuse it the satisfaction.

Lillian negotiated heels down the crooked porch steps and across the uneven muddy ground. The cruiser passenger door popped ajar, pushed open from the inside. The captain noticed Lillian glance back at the white clapboard house before ducking inside the cruiser. The boy was in there. In a bedroom window. A round pale face in the dark before the cruiser headlights swept across the landscape and blinded the captain, momentarily obscuring the white clapboard house. The boy vanished in the interim.

The sheriff cruiser slipped into the night.

Captain Dwyer decided to follow.

# 22.

**DELBERT OBSERVED THE SHERIFF** cruiser back out of the muddy driveway. The Barbie Doll reporter and her cameraman remained on the opposite roadside shoulder, simply watching. The cruiser hesitated in the middle of the narrow street, hitched into gear, and then headed off into the darkness with his mother a ghostly visage on the other side of the passenger glass. Delbert felt a queasy feeling in his stomach.

He didn't like the idea of his mother inside that cruiser with that awful man and he couldn't imagine where they might be going at this time of the night. Her words, spoken in aggravation less than an hour earlier, "*I still owe you a date,*" droned hollowly inside his head. His mother had gone willingly, yet somehow this made it all the worse in Delbert's mind. That she would have no choice but to acquiesce. Then again, if he was to be completely honest with himself, he was also relieved to have the sheriff gone. If the sheriff had decided to enter the house and conduct an impromptu search, then all would have surely been lost.

The cruiser taillights flashed at the cross street.

Then blinked off around the corner.

"They're gone," Delbert hushed.

Freddy stepped out of the closet darkness.

"I need a cigarette," he said.

Delbert nodded. "Yeah. Okay."

Delbert hurried down the narrow hall to his mother's bedroom. She kept her reserve smokes hidden, not wanting to tempt him. Not that Delbert had any interest in smoking. His mother had cured him of this curiosity by offering him a cigarette back in Lexington. His face had turned green. He hadn't seen it turn green because he hadn't been staring at himself in a mirror, but he knew it had turned green by the way in which his stomach had instantly curled into a fist before leaping into his throat and disgorging his entire breakfast. Raisin oatmeal. He would never again be able to eat oatmeal of any kind with any peace of mind. Especially raisin.

Delbert knew all her hiding places, though.

It was a kid's job to know such things.

He had found a lot of disturbing and interesting and mystifying stuff over the years. Including cigarettes, booze, battery-operated objects, and photographs of odd persons he had never met. One of those mysterious folks had turned out later to be his grandmother. He realized now he had never found anything of his father in all those hiding places in all those years, though.

As if his mother had anticipated his snooping.

Delbert dug the cigarettes out of a bathroom drawer.

Hidden inside an old box of tampons.

He exited his mother's bedroom and shuffled back down the narrow hall, turning off lights as he went, turning the house dark. Somehow it felt safer to be in the dark with Freddy. Freddy was seated on the floor, his back against the bed frame.

Freddy accepted a smoke, nodding gratefully. Tilting sideways, the cigarette hanging loosely from the corner of his chapped lips, he pulled matches from a back trousers pocket. He snapped a match across the wooden frame of the bed.

There was an audible popping sound.

A sizzling blue flame.

A supernova in the darkness.

Freddy lit the cigarette. Shook the match out.

The brilliant fissure in the darkness collapsed in on itself and vanished like a fading TV signal. Freddy sighed as the darkness folded heavily over them again. Blew invisible smoke into that blackness. Crumbled the match between his fingers.

"You probably want to know if I killed that girl next door, don't you" he said. Freddy suddenly sounded very tired. Resigned. "Well, I didn't. Not that sweet peach."

"So why they think you done it, then, Freddy?"
Freddy stared at Delbert over the glowing cigarette.
"Sure you want to hear this?" he said.
He asked the question with reservation.
But then quickly nodded.
Convincing himself as much as anything.
"Course, you do," he said.
A terrible sigh.
"You need to hear it."

# 23.

**THE LIGHTS OF TOWN SLOWLY FADED** behind them and darkness embraced the cruiser. Lillian shrugged closer to the passenger door, suddenly wishing she hadn't taken that allergy pill this morning. The molds and fungi this late in the year tended to swell her nose shut like drying cement, but drying cement would have been preferable to the sweet-sour reek coming off the sheriff beside her. Sweat and cologne and just him. Reminding her of rotten pumpkin. Jack-o-lanterns abandoned to the side of the road long after Halloween. Decomposing. Hard shells crumbling inward. The soft insides putrefying.

The seeds turned mushy.

The odor was only made worse by his cigar.

A mishmash of ammonia and rabbit shit.

She gagged. Punched the electric window button. Nothing. Their warm expiration began to cloud the windshield, too, and she wondered how he could see past all the cigar smoke and condensation. She hit the window button again. Making a show of it.

"It's freezing and you're under-dressed," the sheriff said.

The cruiser passed over train tracks.

The tires made a loud clunking noise.

The shocks bouncing. Rattling.

They turned onto Old Stump Road.

The paved road ended at Shady Creek Bridge.

The cruiser slipped onto the bridge, rolling slowly, the wooden planks jostling and jumping beneath the heavy vehicle. Lillian felt the deep empty expanse beneath the bridge and the highway of cold air passing below them in the darkness.

She felt her tummy tumble into a slow back flip as the cruiser pushed close to the railing and she closed her eyes and imagined falling into that darkness. The sense of letting go. The weightlessness of it all as the ground rushed up to meet her from the dark. The jagged rocks waiting in the streambed.

She imagined the collision of her and the earth.

Weightlessness turning into nothingness.

The cruiser rolled off the bridge. The lullaby of the vibrating wooden planks ended. Replaced by the gravel of the dirt road beyond it. Crunching softly. Pinging.

The dirt road twisted. Meandered.

Shadowy trees like sentries hugged the edges.

The darkness grew thicker. Darker.

"Where're we going?" she said finally.

The sheriff just kept driving. Puffing on his cigar. Gaudy rings on his fat fingers glimmering in the dull instrument lights while the headlights struggled to penetrate the pockets of deepening black gloom encroaching from the silent forest. "I was talking to old Jacky-boy down at the bank," he said eventually.

"The marshmallow," Lillian murmured.

Again, she thought of rotten pumpkin.

An entire field of them. Turned.

Sweet. Sour. Mushy.

"The back taxes on your momma's place," the sheriff said. A soft whistle escaped his lips. "The bank will foreclose."

"I meet my payments."

"So far," he said grimly. A gold watch on his fat hairy wrist glittered along with the assortment of silly rings. "I know about the rooms down at the Shady Creek Motel, too," he said with a sigh. "You got the married men of this town horny as jackrabbits."

The hand with the gold watch fell on her thigh.

She glared at the hand with distaste. The gold watch.

"We didn't all marry rich widows," she said.

There was a diamond offset from the watch face.

Horseshoe-shaped. Surrounded by gemstones.

"That what they say?" he said.

"That's what they say," she said.

A photo was taped to the cruiser dashboard above all those blinking lights. The sheriff and his new wife. A pale woman standing by a young girl with glasses. Her pale hands locked on her son's broad shoulders for the taking of the photo. The young boy was a bit of a blur, however, trying to move out of the shot.

As if trying to erase himself from the photo.

"Worked for the railroad down in Bedford before the cancer, didn't he?" Lillian elaborated. "Had himself a nice life insurance policy with the company. And you swooped down in her moment of need like a bird of prey smelling cash. Like a vulture."

The sheriff smiled at the crude characterization.

His slippery smile.

"That what they say?" he said.

"That's what they say," she said.

"I can be a friend to you, too. You want that, believe me."

He squeezed the flesh of her thigh, causing it to dimple.

She pushed his hand away. Frowning.

"Where're we going?" she demanded to know again.

"Memory Lane, sweetheart," he sighed softly.

The dark trees leaned further into the narrow road.

Foliage brushed against the side of the vehicle.

Making a whish-whish sound like groping fingers.

The road grew narrower. The groping fingers louder.

"The nonsense spilling from your son's mouth, sugar," the sheriff continued, facing all that darkness. "You're forgetting what Freddy did to that little girl back when we was kids."

"We weren't kids."

"Not after that we wasn't," the sheriff agreed.

# 24.

**FREDDY FILLED A SHALLOW GRAVE** *with dirt.*
*Sweaty and muddy. Frightened.*
*Numb hands working a shovel. Cold air billowing from his mouth. Mumbling desperately to himself. "Couldn't feel no pulse," he said.*
*A final shovel of dirt. He patted down the grave.*
*Trembling badly. Narrow shoulders sagging. Unable to look back.*
*Walking away from the gruesome task into dark trees.*
*Abandoning the grave. Silent. At first.*
*But then from beneath the packed earth.*
*A faint, muffled scream.*

# 25.

**DELBERT SAT BACK, WIDE-EYED.**

"Who was she?" he said.

Freddy was now seated on top of Delbert's bed in the far corner, his long grasshopper legs spread out beneath the window, bruised face concealed by the corner darkness. Delbert sat perched on his desk chair at the edge of the bed, listening to Freddy mutter desperately in the dark about strange and awful things from the past, salty tears welling in his eyes. "I was workin' the Tasty Freeze in those days," Freddy said, his mind slipping back through the years like what had happened had happened only yesterday and not nearly a decade ago. For despite the passing of time the wound was not yet scarred over. It still felt fresh and bloody and seared with a dreadful pain. "Night janitor. She worked front of house."

He had been mopping the floor.

*A CLOSED sign hung in the window.*

*Lucy Caldwell was sitting on the front counter.*

*Thin legs swinging girlishly beneath her.*

*Freddy in his mid-twenties. Lucy sixteen.*

*"I like how you look at me," she said, smiling coyly.*

*He smiled back, leaning on his mop.*

*That night Freddy and Lucy had sex for the first time in the backseat of his car in the otherwise empty parking lot. Freddy absently noticed the large Drive-Thru sign was still lit up while they were tangled in each other. He was leaning back against the vinyl seat, pants toiled about his ankles. She was straddling him, her skirt hiked over her navel. Somehow her tits had fallen out of her Tasty Freeze blouse, her small nipples hard as bullets, striking his forehead. Freddy noticed, too, a chocolate syrup stain on the right corner pocket of her shirt and a crusty mustard stain on her sleeve. An unseasonably warm September night air blew through the open window like a hair dryer. He could feel sweat dripping down his back. It caused him to slide about on the vinyl. A car passed by on the road and for a moment he thought it would turn into the parking lot because the silly dimwit on top of him had forgotten to turn off that stupid Drive-Thru sign. It could be seen for a mile probably.*

*Lucy bounced higher and higher. Her head striking the roof softly. The thin upholstery of the interior roof of his beat-up old jalopy of a car was ripped like the worn seats below it, exposing a soft underbelly of mysterious yellow foam. She collided again and again with the sponge-like yellow fabric, leaving soft little dents in the foam. The soft little dents became larger and more pronounced the more enthusiastically she bounced.*

*She began to scream. Hoarse little panting screams.*

*Her eyes alight. But faraway, he thought.*

*Like she was fucking someone else.*

*Somewhere else maybe.*

*He grabbed her narrow hips. Pulled her down.*

*Stared into her eyes Those faraway eyes.*

*But she refused to stare back. Or was unable.*

*Not even when they climaxed.*

Freddy blinked with the recollection. The adrenaline. The feel of her soft young skin against his own. The taste of her sweet young breath on the tip of his tongue and the perfume of her intoxicating saccharine perspiration gathered at the base of her lissome neck. "I was twenty three," Freddy said. He could still feel the gentle weight of her on his lap. Bouncing up and down and sliding left and right and back and forth and around and around in the soft buzzing glow of that Drive-Thru sign intruding into the hot and musty dark car interior. The sticky mess of that chocolate syrup stain on her blouse and the splash of dried mustard on her sleeve. And the unpleasant way her eyes stared right through him like he didn't even exist. "Married," he said dimly. "A pregnant wife at home. She was only sixteen. A ripe little peach."

Freddy sighed. His own eyes distant.

The ash long and hot on his neglected cigarette.

"What was her name?" Delbert said.

"Lucy Caldwell."

It was the first time Freddy had said her name out loud for a decade. It produced a wounded smile on his dry, bloody lip. "A bad habit," Freddy said, his voice barely a whisper, "but I couldn't help myself. No way, no how. You'll understand one day."

Delbert glanced at Allison's drawn curtains.

In a way, he already understood.

"But bad habits, Delbert. They got bad consequences."

Again Freddy's mind slipped backward. Only this time it didn't slip backward as if into a warm tub of water. Rather, this time he felt his heart-rate accelerate and spiral in cold anticipation just before a set of ruthless claws snatched him by the throat and yanked him like helpless prey down into darkness. Down into its fiendish lair. Into a descending corridor of time. Amongst the odd bleached bones and disintegrated detritus of its prior victims.

And he found himself back in the--

*--backseat of that decaying old jalopy with the ripped upholstery and all that strange yellow foam. Parked on a late evening on an empty logging road. Miles from that Tasty Freeze. Surrounded by heavy darkness populated by tall dark trees. Their dull leaves drained of their autumn color. Falling. A mildewing carpet on the forest floor. The world silent but for the steady tick of the cooling engine and the drone of nearby crickets in the bitter cold.*

*Lucy leaned back against a frosted window. Pouting.*

*Her small pale hands on her abdomen. Rubbing it softly.*

*Already showing. Just a little.*

*"I want it," she said. "It's mine."*

*Freddy sat against the opposite window.*

*Drinking from a bottle. Shivering.*

*Staring intently at her belly in the pale moonlight.*

*"You sure about this?" he said.*

*"I want it," she said.*

*"Don't mean that dumbbell. You sure-- You know."*

*"Took the bus down to Bedford. Took a test."*

*Freddy shivered harder. "How far along 're you?"*

*"Almost thirteen weeks," she said.*

*"I got a pregnant wife," Freddy said.*

*"Ain't my affair," she said.*

*He grabbed her arm. A bit too roughly.*

*"Ow. Let go," she said.*

*His grip only tightened.*

*"Don't do this to me," he said.*

*"Already done, Freddy Jackson. Can't be undone."*

*"Sure it can," he said.*

*"Sure it won't," she promised.*

*A beat. Unyielding.*

*Her eyes faraway again.*

*"I'd rather die," she said.*

Lucy had spat out those final words the night before the first real snow a decade ago, daring him to tempt her resolve. Those words still rang out in Freddy's head like the bell over the Methodist church calling the faithful to service, tolling again and again. Over and over. Freddy tapped the side of his head with his fist as if he could somehow un-ring it. And felt the cold claws again on his throat. And his mind again tumble. Mercilessly backward.

*Lucy. Terrified.*

*Dress ripped. Blood on her mouth.*

*Backpedaling away from the car.*

*Sneakers slipping on the carpet of dead leaves.*

*Beneath the dark and watchful trees.*

*A shadow falling over her.*

*Lucy screaming.*

Freddy sucked in a ragged breath of air and blinked hard, pushing back his tears in the inky dimness of his son's bedroom. The ash on his neglected cigarette had grown even further, curling dangerously like slowly expanding lava. Smoldering. White hot.

"I could've stopped it," he said.

Delbert was rapt with attention. Frozen.

"But I didn't want to," Freddy said.

*Lucy Caldwell was on the ground.*

*Unmoving. Head bloodied. Eyes closed.*

*A shadow stood over her. Freddy.*

*A bloody tire iron clutched in his trembling hand.*

*He poked at her with it. She was lifeless.*

*"Christ, no," he said miserably.*

*Her head was crushed on the side above her ear.*

*Fractured. Like a dented egg.*

*Leaking blood into the moonlight.*

*The color of chocolate syrup.*

Freddy trembled badly with the telling. Exhausted. He found it difficult to look at Delbert now. Found it difficult to allow Delbert to look at him. So desperately wanting to melt away into the thin cracks in the hardwood floor of this tiny bedroom. To simply no longer exist. But that would have been too easy. "Remember when you asked me what absolution was?" he said.

Delbert managed a nod in the dark.

"I told you it meant not feeling sorry no more," Freddy said.

Delbert managed to nod again.

"Well, you're my absolution now, Delbert," he said.

His voice hitched with the admission. Painfully.

"Only you," he managed. "Got to be."

Freddy finally noticed the long curling ash on his neglected cigarette. The white hot embers cooling, turning from gray to black. Like a decomposing finger, yet still somehow managing to defy gravity for the moment. Freddy leaned forward. Peeled back the window screen. Flicked the ash. A reverse wind pulled it out into the cold darkness. A plume. Like a lost soul escaping.

Delbert continued to stare at Freddy.

Absorbing everything he had heard.

The awful horribleness of it.

"I'm not your absolution, Freddy," Delbert said finally, reluctantly, trembling himself. Swallowing hard. "You should feel sorry. You kilt that girl."

"Kilt her--?" Freddy exclaimed. "I never said that."

Delbert flinched. Uncertain he'd heard Freddy correctly.

*Freddy filled the shallow grave with dirt.*

*Sweaty and muddy. Frightened.*

*Numb hands working the shovel.*

*Mumbling desperately to himself.*

*"She's dead," he hushed. "Got to be."*

*Trying to convince himself amongst the tall silent trees.*

*A final shovel of dirt. He patted down the grave.*

*"Couldn't feel no pulse," he said.*

*Narrow shoulders sagging, he walked away.*

*Unable to look back. Abandoning the grave in the woods.*

*And there the shallow grave sat beneath the tall, silent, watchful trees.*

*Also silent. At first.*

*Until the faintest sound could be heard.*

*A muffled scream. From beneath the packed earth.*

*But Freddy was already gone.*

*And never heard it.*

*Not even when the muffled scream--*

*--became a muffled shriek.*

*Only the tall, silent, watchful trees heard it.*

*Or so it seemed.*

*Until a dark shape moved.*

*Separating from the trees.*

*Moving over the grave.*

*A man. Harlan Winslow. Ten years younger. Pale and terrified. Clasped hands bloodied. Standing over the grave and listening to the terrible sounds rising from beneath the packed earth. Tortured by them.*

*But in the end doing nothing.*

*Simply walking away himself.*

*Head tragically bowed.*

Delbert continued to stare at Freddy.

More confounded than ever.

"You see," Freddy said, "she was seeing Harlan, too. We was friends, Delbert. Lucy was like a pet between us." Freddy shook his head at the ill-mannered description before continuing: "Harlan had himself a wife at home, too. Like me, Delbert. He also had himself a little girl," he sighed. "And a real bad temper besides."

*Freddy shook Lucy in the backseat of the jalopy.*

*"Lemme alone," she cried out, kicking him.*

*"Not until you stop talking this nonsense," he said.*

*"It's my baby," she said, angry, struggling.*

*Headlights appeared on the logging road.*

*A truck. Skidding to a noisy halt.*

*Raising a cloud of black dust.*

*Harlan appeared from the dust with a tire iron.*

Freddy hung his head. "Like I said, Delbert--"

His voice hitched a final time. Barely audible now.

"--I could've stopped it."

*Freddy stood back. Dismay on his face.*

*Lucy screaming. Backpedaling from Harlan.*

*Her small pale hands raised in fright.*

*Harlan swinging the tire iron.*

*Time seemed to stand still in that moment.*

*A thwack of metal hitting flesh and bone.*

*Before time smashed forward again.*

*Finally. Jarringly.*

*Freddy blinked dizzily and came back to himself on that cold, empty stretch of logging road to find he was wrestling the tire iron away from Harlan. But only after young Lucy had stopped screaming. Only after she had fallen to the ground. The sixteen year old girl. Lying in the dirt just beyond the reach of the headlights of the idling truck. Dress ripped. Unmoving.*

*Head bloodied. Eyes closed.*

Freddy, shaking even more violently than before, eyes sad and haunted, leaned forward again and peeled back the window screen. The ash was again growing white and hot on the cigarette, again curling dangerously. "Never been so scared as that night," he admitted solemnly. And flicked a plume of ash out into the dark night. The plume hung for a moment in the darkness.

Then, like a dying scream, faded.

# 26.

**THE BARBIE DOLL REPORTER ACTUALLY** had a name. It was Stacey Wells. Well, actually her name was Stacey Wisniewski, but Wisniewski didn't flow off the tongue over live feeds and Stacey had much bigger plans for herself than freezing her cute little ass off in a satellite truck for the rest of her career. Stacey believed she was destined for an anchor desk back in Bedford. Probably something in the morning with celebrity news sprinkled in with the local headlines, traffic, weather, and puff-pieces on blue-haired old ladies turning one hundred and hound dogs who could sing the national anthem. And then, who knew? Larger opportunities beckoned beyond Bedford. Bigger cites. Brighter lights. National news. International. All of it.

But for now--

For now Stacey was stuck on another stakeout in the crummy old satellite truck with Jerry, her cameraman, and the occasional cockroach. Jerry liked to take advantage of the dish mounted on top of the truck, parking himself in front of the video monitor and chatting sports ad nauseam over a live feed with crew back at the station while snacking on bags of corn nuts with his shoes thrown off, his enormous hairy Flintstone feet resting on the small electronic console, hairy toes wiggling and stirring the already stale air. It was most disconcerting not being able to discriminate between the odors. The fucking corn nuts and his feet. Jerry had also forgotten his deodorant and they were sharing her roll-on. Its flowery bouquet was an entirely new experience on Jerry. And the radio. They were sharing that, too, unhappily. Jerry liked the Grand Ole Opry. Stacey did not. And he knew she didn't. Just like Jerry knew she didn't like the smell of those goddamn disgusting sticky corn nuts or the sight of his bunions. Just like Jerry also knew she considered the road a stepping stone and him another step.

She didn't need this shit anymore.

This drudgery. This slow torture.

Nothing could cure the boredom of a stakeout. Not paperback novels. Coffee. Or the pizzas they ordered from down the road. These hillbillies somehow always managed to fuck up their order. She assumed on purpose. Stacey hated mushrooms and anchovies and the pies consistently arrived with one or the other, giving her terrible heartburn. Then again, maybe it was Jerry messing with her. The food wasn't nearly as dreadful as the toilet situation, though. Jerry could just step outside the truck and use the long grass, often not bothering to step more than a few feet from the sliding door before Stacey could hear the sizzle of his warm urine in the cold air and the nauseating splat of it hitting the earth.

Guh-a- rowse.

Stacey had an old water jug.

It was either the water jug behind the sleeping divider in the van or hike her skirt in the weeds with the bugs and vermin or trudge a mile down the road to the gas station while Jerry remained behind in case live news broke suddenly. Stacey did make the long round trip down to the gas station for number two, however. She had no idea what Jerry was doing. And she didn't want to know.

What she wanted to know--

--was what the kid knew.

The kid knew something. That boy.

She had seen the fear on his face when the state police had shifted their investigation from the dead girl's house to the white clapboard house and she had seen the fear on his face when he had returned from police questioning. She had seen the fear on his face, too, when he had peeked out his bedroom window about a half hour ago when his mother had left with the sheriff. His mother dressed like a silly teenage girl without a father at home.

The kid knew something. That boy.

Her instincts had told her to hang around.

To watch after all the other outlets had left.

Freddy Jackson had come here after all.

He had come to that boy first.

Before he had taken that young girl's life.

If he had done that.

Her peers were home with their families at dinner tables or in front of TVs with warm meals and swirling tall glasses of wine. Stacey was eating funky leftover pizza and whizzing in an old water jug and smelling Jerry's corn nuts and feet, but there it was again.

An ash plume.

Stacey was standing outside the truck in the dark, hugging herself against the cold. A reluctant Jerry was standing beside her in a well-worn T-shirt and barefoot, picking at his ear with a sticky corn nut finger and following her gesture--

--to the boy's bedroom window.

An ash plume. Like a lopsided gray balloon.

Hanging in the cold air. Dissipating slowly.

"There… There it is again," she said.

Jerry frowned, unimpressed. "So what," he said. "The little snot got a hold of his mother's cigarettes." Jerry scratched at himself, lifting his leg to dig in just right, sighing contently. The moron was still scratching when Stacey emitted a soft squeal.

Her finger stabbing at the air now.

A man had appeared in the window.

Momentarily. Framed by the moonlight.

The boy's father. Freddy.

# 27.

**FREDDY SHRUNK AWAY FROM THE** window, disappearing back into the corner shadows, unaware he had been seen by the Barbie Doll reporter and her cameraman holding vigil across the road. Consumed by the past. The telling of it to his son. The reliving of those awful days which somehow seemed like only yesterday and which had left him to rot like a monster in a small cage in a netherworld of dim blue lights and stone walls and thick boiler-plate doors. Freddy sighed bitterly, not wanting to feel sorry for himself, not judging he deserved any pity, but feeling sorry for himself anyway. He took a long drag on the cigarette. Exhaled slowly. "Sometimes I wish she hadn't come back," he said after a long meditative beat. "I know how that sounds, Delbert, but I do. Sometimes I just wish she hadn't come back."

Delbert pushed forward in the darkness.

"*Come back*, Freddy?" he said. "What do you mean?"

"Anything but to have that little girl point the finger at me."

Freddy blinked. The past rushing forward again.

The blinding light of a screaming train in a black tunnel.

*Harlan stood over the shallow grave. Bloodied hands clasped before him. His jaw slack. Eyeballs dancing inside his skull. Ears twitching, wanting to believe it was only the wind. Angst-ridden by the faint, muffled cries rising from beneath the packed earth. But in the end doing nothing.*

*Simply walking away.*

*The muffled cries eventually faded.*
*For a moment the world became silent again.*
*Until suddenly -- they were reborn.*
*Louder and more terrible this time.*
*More desperate beneath the dark silent trees.*
*Then there was a scratching noise.*
*Dirty little fingers with bloody broken nails broke the surface.*
*Wiggling out of the loose earth like worms.*
*Digging. Scraping. Scratching. Clawing.*
*Lucy Caldwell. A ripped dress.*
*Hair matted with blood and mud and dead leaves.*
*Rising from the dead. Lurching into the night.*
*Eventually stumbling over Shady Creek Bridge.*
*Headlights appeared on the road beyond the bridge.*
*A sheriff cruiser. Patrolling behind the mill.*
*Lucy lifted a blood-soaked hand.*
*Cried out a final time.*
*Collapsed.*

*Sheriff Snodgrass was behind the wheel of that sheriff cruiser. Ten years younger. Skinnier. Wet behind the ears. No glittering rings. No fancy gold watch. Only on the job for less than a year. He hit the brakes and exited the cruiser at full tilt. Horrified. Rushing beside Lucy's fallen form. Kneeling in the pale glow of the bridge lamps. "Lord have mercy," he hushed.*

*A fractured skull. A dislocated arm.*
*Face bruised and bloody. An eye swollen shut.*
*"Who done this, Lucy?" he begged to know.*
*She mumbled unintelligibly.*
*Fell unconscious.*

Freddy stamped out the cigarette on the windowsill. It had become little more than a stub. He lit a new cigarette. A strike of a match. Blue flame sizzling. Then dying like a firework.

"She was in a coma for five days," Freddy revealed evenly from behind the harsh red glow of the new cigarette. Somehow the harsh red glow reminded Delbert of the town's lone stoplight in the dark. Blinking on and off. On and off. "Even got her last rites," Freddy said. "Lost the baby. I was charged with its murder. Second degree." A drag on the cigarette. A sigh. And then quietly from behind the harsh red blinking stoplight: "I hear she's still in the county," he revealed with a shrug. "Livin' in that trailer park off Hackberry Road down by the river there."

"She's alive," Delbert said.

The word swam in Delbert's mouth. *Alive.*

Like cold spring water on a sweltering summer day.

But Freddy didn't look at peace. Anything but.

"Yeah," he said. Only that.

And took another drag on the cigarette. Blew more invisible smoke. The old house creaked around them. Haunted old bones. Delbert creased his brow. His thoughts spinning wildly. Until he thought to ask: "How come Harlan ain't gone to prison like you?"

"This a factory town," Freddy said without expression.

Delbert frowned. Again confused.

Freddy stared at Delbert over the red blinking stoplight, the red flame dancing in the whites of his exhausted eyes, growing taller, leaping and guttering in his dilated black pupils. "You've seen the rug mill above town, haven't you?" he said finally.

Delbert nodded.

"Belonged to Harlan's rich daddy once upon a time. His daddy before him. Belongs to Harlan now," Freddy said miserably. "And that sheriff, the son of a bitch, had his hand in the cookie jar right from the beginning of this mess. Myself--? Didn't have a pot to piss in," he said, eyes turning moist. "I put that girl in the ground cuz I had me a shovel in the trunk and I was scared. Thought she was dead, God as my witness, and not because of nothin' I done directly, only what I didn't do. Need you to believe that, Delbert. Sure I do. And I didn't touch that ripe peach next door neither. Not a hair on her pretty little head even if her daddy did sit up there in that court ten years ago and lie about what really happened out there in those woods that night."

Delbert absorbed this. Contemplated it

Listened to the wind in the eaves.

Hoping it would tell him all he needed to know.

Then said finally: "I believe you."

Freddy studied Delbert. Slowly nodded. Face relaxing. Even the deep-etched lines on his forehead and against his eyes and along his pale cheekbones seemed to fade a bit into his complexion. The assortment of tics seemed to quiet, too. Perhaps it was just the dark of the bedroom corner, but Delbert felt perhaps his simple believing of the man had fundamentally altered him already. That perhaps Freddy *had* only come back for this moment.

Delbert touched Freddy's hand.

It was the first time he had touched Freddy since he had run into him that night on the sidewalk. Freddy's hand felt cold. Like Delbert imagined a corpse might feel. He could feel the bones in the hand. The tendons. The unnatural thickness of the skin. The field of colorless hair on the back. The swollen arthritic knuckles. The tiny fissures and dry cracks following the natural wrinkles of his long fingers where gashes of enflamed red tissue peeked out like deep gouges in the fragile earth's crust after an earthquake. The hand turned. Took Delbert's own hand. Squeezed. And suddenly Delbert felt the warmth. Blood still coursing through its veins. The idea of a corpse suddenly foreign and silly.

The tender moment was short-lived, however. Interrupted by a sudden knocking downstairs. The front door. The sudden knocking shook the thin walls of the old white clapboard house.

Freddy's hand slipped away.

Back into the corner shadows.

The knocking grew louder. More insistent

Delbert left Freddy in the bedroom shadows.

Tip-toed down the narrow staircase.

The Barbie Doll reporter was on the stoop.

The cameraman on the sidewalk.

Delbert peeked open the front door. Reluctantly.

"Hi, Delbert," she said.

A sugary voice. Fake smile.

"Go 'way," Delbert said.

He tried to shut the door, but she stuck the hard-pointed toe of her designer shoe between it and the door jam, wedging it there.

Delbert pushed harder.

Thought he saw her wince behind the plastic façade.

"Saw your pa in the window, kid," she said. "Game's up."

The sugar was gone from her voice.

Her smile had turned predatory.

"I just want his side of the story," she said and slipped her business card through the crack in the door. Delbert continued to lean on the door, allowing the business card to flutter to the floorboards beside his sneaker. The fluttering card strangely reminded him of the pregnancy test kit slipping out of Allison's towel that night in her bedroom and for the first time Delbert absently wondered if her father had seen it hit the floor before her bare foot had swept the test kit beneath the dresser. And he wondered with a rush of cold and paralyzing guilt if somehow that pregnancy test kit had been the reason Allison was no longer of this earth.

If he was responsible. Even just a little.

It brought hot tears to his eyes.

Barbie Doll seemed energized by those tears, an electricity bouncing off her arms and legs and from her determined eyes. Like those electric eels Delbert had seen on the late local news. The eels had killed a bunch of cattle somewhere out west. A writhing nest of them had been found in a watering hole made small by drought. "You have him out here for the camera lights in five minutes," she demanded. "I go live with or without him. Understand?"

Barbie Doll removed her hard-pointed toe.

Delbert pushed the door closed.

He trudged slowly back upstairs. He half-expected not to find Freddy in his bedroom. Half-expected the man to have slipped out the window and to have been swallowed by the night. But Freddy was still there, sitting on the edge of the bed, twitchy and afraid. Like a small animal cornered by a larger animal, muddy boots caked with dead leaves and grass and muck. Freddy shook his head forlornly. Took a moment to finish the last of his cigarette. Relishing it. Like it might just be his last. And said: "No press."

"You got to, Freddy," Delbert said, standing in the same doorway his mother so often stood, a silhouette in the darkness. "Got to tell the truth," he insisted. He could see in his bedroom mirror the Barbie Doll reporter going live beyond the front porch, presumably promoting an imminent exclusive. Motioning at the bedroom window with dramatic flair.

"Murder in the first degree," Freddy mused softly, taking a final drag on the smoke. "That's a capital offense. It's quieter on D block, I hear. Get my own cell and TV this time 'round. Better food, too," he allowed almost wistfully. "And time can be real short on D block if you want it to be. I need short time."

"No," Delbert said.

Freddy sighed. Pinched out his smoke between yellow nicotine-stained fingers. Stood. Placed a hand on Delbert's shoulder.

"You're my only absolution, Delbert. Got to be."

Delbert shook his head. Frowned.

He could feel his soft insides being crushed beneath the tremendous weight of what was being asked of him. He could not be Freddy's absolution Delbert decided right then and there in the dark of his small bedroom. It simply wasn't fair to expect him to carry that soul-shattering burden and to carry it alone.

It just wasn't right.

For either of them.

"Told you, boy," Freddy said, eyes glimmering sadly, "that's why I come back. The only reason. The only one that matters to me anyhow. Now show me the back door."

Freddy's hand remained on Delbert's shoulder.

Suddenly heavy. Much too heavy.

Delbert backed away from it.

Watched it fall. Twitching again.

"They say it's always darkest before the dawn," Freddy hushed, trying to console Delbert, the glimmer already draining from his eyes. Like a snuffed-out candle. "Remember that when you think of me," he said.

And then he tried to walk around Delbert.

He knew where to find the back door.

Had probably used it once upon a time.

But Delbert stepped in front of him.

Blocking his path.

Face red. Pinched with determination.

Head only as high as Freddy's sternum.

"No, Freddy," he said loudly. His voice echoed out the open bedroom window. But he didn't care who might be listening. Especially the Barbie Doll. "I don't want to hear nothin' about D block this time 'round or short time or none of that nonsense," he said. "And Lucy, maybe you were a damn fool. Married. Pregnant wife at home. And maybe she was a ripe little peach and a bad habit and you couldn't help yourself and maybe there ain't no excuse for that. And you're right. Maybe bad habits have bad consequences. And maybe you could'a stopped it and you tell yourself now you didn't cuz you want to believe you could'a done so. But maybe that's not altogether true. Maybe you just want to believe it's true, Freddy, cuz you had a shovel in the trunk and you was so damn scared because you didn't have a pot to piss in and Harlan's daddy and his daddy 'fore him owned that mill above town and you didn't harm a hair on her head but you knew nobody'd believe it when the story got told all wrong about what happened out there in those woods," Delbert lectured, small body trembling, but still holding its ground. "But I'll tell you what I think, Freddy," he said, smacking aside the cowlick dipping into his eyes. "I think you were tryin' to knock some sense into that girl out there in those woods 'fore Harlan showed and it all got confused to hell and I tried to help Allison and it all got confused, too, because you're right, Freddy, when you said there's always an accomplice. But what you really mean is there is always somebody to make sure the whole truth ain't heard. Somebody to say it wasn't what it was in order to save their own-selves. Harlan-- He almost kilt that poor girl Lucy that night out there in those woods and sure as the sun sets over them mountains kilt that baby that was growin' up inside of her and I think the sheriff knows it, too. And what you done out there that night or what you ain't done sure as hell don't have nothin' to do with what happened to my friend Allison next door, and I'm not gonna let you think it does. That just ain't right, Freddy. And it sure as shit ain't absolution. Sure as shit ain't that, Freddy."

Delbert sucked in air. Out of breath.

Still. The boy looked ready to fight.

Tiny fists opening and closing.

Freddy wanted to embrace his small son. Those courageous words were all he had ever wanted. They stole the cold and rot from his bones after all those years in that terrible cage on top of that ghastly mountain. And he might have been content to let his son beat on him with those small fists should it have helped, but Freddy decided then he wouldn't be taken there.

Not in front of his boy. Not like this.

Not after what the boy had just sermonized.

And maybe, just maybe, Freddy would have run, too, if Delbert hadn't seemed to grow a foot taller in the dark that night--

--and revealed, "Allison was pregnant."

The boy then nodded at Allison's bedroom window.

The curtains were fluttering.

Beyond them--

Harlan could be seen in snatches.

Boxer shorts. Bare-chested. Spindly legs.

Sitting on Allison's bed.

Hugging one of her pillows.

"Her daddy done it," Delbert told Freddy.

Freddy blinked with surprise.

And understanding.

And at just that moment--

Harlan's balding head lifted.

His melancholy face slowly registered its own surprise when he so unexpectedly saw Freddy in Delbert's window.

The two men stared at each other a long silent beat.

Across that dark and empty expanse.

Across a decade of terrible heartache.

# 28.

**THE NARROW LOGGING ROAD TWISTED** and turned. Tiny rocks echoed against the cruiser undercarriage. A hollow ringing noise as the cruiser pushed deeper and deeper into the woods. The distant fuzzy lights of the mill blinked through the dark trees for a spell on the left side of the car, then somehow shifted to the right, before vanishing altogether behind the thickening wall of forest, producing for Lillian a growing sense of dislocation. Disorientation. The world somersaulting.

The sheriff eventually parked the cruiser beneath a giant black willow. The willow provided entrance to a small clearing and a silent audience of swaying Black-eyed Susans. Flowers which had lost their color in recent days with the drop in temperatures. The bright yellows and deep oranges and copper bronzes and russet reds had now become a black and white movie. Like the undulating wheat fields in Kansas before the revelation of Oz.

A tree stump sat in the middle of the clearing.

Thick and dark and flat.

A dead thing. Buried in the earth.

For a moment Sheriff Snodgrass and Lillian sat in the murmuring warm breath of the idling cruiser heater, listening to the drone of crickets and the rustling slither of less obvious things in the woods outside. The bone-white moon appeared here and there, vanishing and reappearing from behind a shifting regiment of black clouds like a small child playing peek-a-boo in the night sky. The moon was only a fingernail, but for some odd reason the stars were absent as if the night sky had been scrubbed of them by a malevolent hand, leaving the world cold and dark and empty.

"Buried her up yonder," the sheriff said.

He motioned past cattails and tall reeds.

Toward a dark copse of trees.

He lit a cigar. It glowed like a hot coal. "A foot deeper," the sheriff said with a stony-eyed shrug, "and we wouldn't have found the poor girl 'til the animals dug her up." He exhaled, the cigar smoke floating and curling like a ghostly snake above his balding head which just managed to squeeze beneath the low cruiser ceiling. "Freddy was always lazy," the sheriff said.

"I'm tired, sheriff," Lillian said.

And she was tired. Drained.

She felt like that tree stump in the clearing.

A dead thing amongst the living.

"Tired of living out of boxes," Lillian heard herself mutter softly as if there was no longer any filter between her bruised thoughts and her treacherous tongue. "Tired of being afraid," she went on, sighing. "Tired of one ugly town after the next. Tired of flea-bitten apartments and smutty motels and the rest of it. Just tired. So fucking tired."

"Course you are," the sheriff said.

She was also angry. Near tears. "It ain't no life."

"Not 'less you're in the circus," he agreed.

The sheriff dug into a pocket.

Removed a handkerchief. Silk. Embroidered.

He handed the handkerchief to her.

"My son called me a disgrace," she said.

"Your boy is confused, Lily."

Lillian dabbed indelicately at a runny nose and leaky eyes. Sucked in a ragged breath which rattled in her throat. Then stared past the dirty windshield, the glass congregated with dead bugs, taking in that dark copse of trees beyond the clearing and rotting stump. Past the cattails and reeds. Past the hidden creek.

"Up yonder, you say?" she said.

Sheriff Snodgrass led Lillian through the clearing and through the brush and over the gurgling creek and up a steep knoll into the copse of trees with a small flashlight which only offered pinprick glimpses into the heavy darkness. Lillian had removed her heels back at the road and her bare feet initially found every sharp thorn, jagged rock, and nasty briar, but fell mercifully numb in the cold, more or less, by the time she and the sheriff finally ended their journey, descending a carpet of pine needles into a hollow.

"Show me," she said.

Cold air puffed from her mouth.

The sheriff had never offered his coat.

"Beneath that old dogwood," he said.

He gestured. To the burial spot.

Now just a mulch of reddish purple leaves.

Lillian stared at the spot.

The wind whispered in the trees.

She thought maybe she heard a scream.

She hugged herself. Shivering.

"Seen enough?" the sheriff said. "Colder than a witch's tit."

Lillian took a step forward. Stood over the lost grave.

Face solemn. Silent. Contemplative. Before: "I worked for a bank in Toledo for a year before I come back, Chuck, you know that?" she said. "The call center. Saw lots of bank documents. All manner of things. Mortgage slips. Revolving loans. Deeds. Promissory notes. Statements. --Overseas accounts."

"This have a point?" the sheriff said, nonplussed.

She fixed a glare on the sheriff in the dark.

"Jacky-boy is careless," she said.

*She stood in a bath towel. Only a few short days ago.*

*Wet hair hanging from her shoulders.*

*Jack the Marshmallow had reserved a corner room for privacy. An empty champagne bottle sat in a melted tub of ice on the night table beside the bed, the sheets coiled and tossed from their lovemaking. Dull neon lights from beyond thin curtains illuminated their clothing. Left in scattered heaps on the floor below the door with the fire escape placard. Lillian could still smell the nauseating stink of their sex. That smell always stayed with her for days after their encounters. Embedding in her pores. Like the reek of a skunk.*

*She hated this fucking room.*

*She hated he was singing in the shower.*

*Gritting her teeth and breathing through her mouth, she rooted through his briefcase.. The lock was easily thwarted. It was his mother's birthday. The marshmallow loved his mother almost as much as he loved doing unspeakable things to Lillian in this fucking motel room. Jacky-boy not only smelled like a fucking animal. He fucked like a fucking animal.*

*Teeth and claws. Grunting and panting. The fat fuck.*

*The briefcase didn't disappoint her. The fat fuck dragged the thing around like it contained the fucking codes for the fucking nuclear launch.*

*Lillian smiled. Pleased with herself.*

*And worked quickly.*

*Digging through the briefcase contents.*

*Bank documents. A mess of them.*

*Until she found something interesting.*

*Impossibly interesting. The fat fuck.*

*Right there in black and white. Pages of it.*

*Her eyes widening with disbelief.*

Lillian smiled at the sheriff in the hollow. Her bare feet sinking into the mulch of fallen purplish dogwood leaves and the carpet of pine needles, standing over the lost grave and below the old leaning dogwood surrounded by the dark copse of trees tickled by the cold, murmuring wind that also teased her hair and whispered mischievous sweet-nothings into her ear.

Encouraging her, she thought.

"I didn't know what I was looking for," Lillian admitted to the sheriff, shrugging her narrow shoulders in the darkness. "But Jacky-boy sometimes got drunk--"

*She had barely touched the champagne.*

*Usually she had to be stone-faced drunk.*

*But not on this night. On this night she had suffered.*

"--and he would start talking about offshore money," she said.

The sheriff frowned around his cigar.

Lillian thought maybe he even shuddered.

The cold seeping in despite his heavy coat.

The coat he had not offered her.

"Like a kid at Xmas, the fool," she said.

She could no longer see the sheriff's eyes beyond the flashlight. The pinprick of light was now directed at her. On her. Like a tiny laser beam spotlight finding her on a small stage.

"I thought he was skimming," she said. "Didn't expect to see your name."

*She pulled the bank records closer. Disbelieving.*

*Eyes widening further. Laughing out loud.*

*Before glancing worriedly at the bathroom door.*

*Fortunately, the shower water continued beyond it.*

*The fat fuck loved long showers almost as much as he loved his mother and defiling Lillian. She quietly slipped out of the motel room still in her bath towel and hurried to the rental office. A teenage clerk with a pimply face was behind the counter. So was an old but functional Xerox machine. The kid had to fish out more copy paper from a closet. He snuck a peek up her towel while he loaded the machine. She made sure the view didn't disappoint him.*

"I made copies," she said. "Men do anything for a woman in a bath towel."

She wasn't sure the sheriff was even still breathing.

*She returned to the motel room as quietly as she had left it, but immediately upon slipping inside the door, she saw the bathroom door was open and she found the repulsive marshmallow standing over the rummaged briefcase. Fat and angry and naked. Dripping wet from the shower.*

*He glared at her. Shook her.*

*Struck her.*

"The fat fuck never found the copies I made," Lillian said. She touched the faint bruise still around her eye. "I had the kid at the front desk mail the copies to my P.O. Box."

*Her eye swollen, but hidden behind dark glasses, Lillian opened her P.O. Box at the Shady Creek Post Office the next day after making sure she hadn't been followed inside. There was one item slid into the narrow slot. The inside address was the Shady Creek Motel. She slit open the envelope right there in the fluorescent lights and studied the copies of bank documents stolen from the marshmallow's briefcase. She shook her head with amazement.*

*Smiling, she tucked the records into her coat pocket.*

*Singing to herself as she exited the post office.*

"This was stuff Jacky-boy didn't keep at his office at the bank," Lillian said. "Wire transfers. A bank in the Grand Caymans. Records for a shell company. Incorporation papers. Drawn up by a fucking ambulance chaser in Bedford," she said. Her warm, excited breath crystallizing in the cold air. "You and Jack listed as the managing officers."

Lillian nodded down at the mill lights.

The hollow was set in the side of a hill and the fuzzy mill lights could just be seen blinking in the distance beyond the old dogwood and the hollow's bowl-like bottom lip.

"Mill money, sheriff. A scam. Blackmail. Dirty laundry."

Sheriff Snodgrass remained silent.

Deafeningly silent.

"I may be dumb, but I ain't stupid," she said.

He was only a large silhouette behind the pinprick flashlight.

And that smoldering cigar.

"And I was always good at math," she said.

His deafening silence continued for a beat.

Before, in an eerily calm voice, he said finally:

"You done playin' Nancy Drew?"

She toed the dirt beneath the purplish flowers.

"The shell company was formed ten years ago," she went on, not yet finished. Not nearly. In fact, for the first time in her life she was just getting started. "A few days before that little backseat slut Lucy came out of her coma. Before, sheriff. Before she could have said a goddamn word about any of what goddamn happened to her out here in these goddamn woods to goddamn anyone."

"You nosy little bitch," he said.

"I want my cut, Chuck," she said.

# 29.

**CAPTAIN WILLIAM DWYER FOLLOWED** Sheriff Snodgrass and Lillian as far as Shady Creek Bridge. He kept his headlights off to avoid any obvious detection, but decided it was too hazardous to continue tailing the cruiser over the narrow bridge into the thick backwoods. The tight logging road twisted and turned in the dark trees, offering dark blind corners and steep ravines. Instead, he parked his unmarked black sedan in a field opposite the bridge and creek -- hiding in the shadows behind an abandoned barn or shed. Its wood black and rotted. An unsteady, leaning structure of lumber loosely held together by rusted nails, corroded wire, and gumption. He could hear the feeble construction creak and moan in the slightest of wind gusts. Upon closer scrutiny, however, it appeared a lot of the building had already wandered off into the field, evidenced by gaping holes and hollow slats in its shambled walls and sunken roof. He imagined those black rotten boards of wood hiding out there in the rustling grass, rusted nails exposed, waiting for a misstep from an unsuspecting shoe or tire. He yawned. Sank back in his seat. Allowed his eyes to shut briefly. There was only one way out of those woods.

And, fortunately, this was it.

In the end Captain Dwyer wasn't sure how long his eyes were actually shut, but he thought it might have been for more than a few minutes when he woke suddenly, shaking himself.

Dull headlights were bouncing around in the shadowy woods, dancing in the trees like fireflies in tandem, following the schemes of the winding logging road back to the narrow bridge.

The sheriff cruiser.

Captain Dwyer rubbed his eyes.

Sat taller. Squinted.

The cruiser rolled slowly across the bridge, the wooden planks jostling. At first the captain thought his drowsy eyes might be deceiving him at this distance, but as the cruiser passed beneath the bridge's fuzzy lamps he realized the sheriff was alone.

Captain Dwyer snatched the binoculars from the passenger seat where they had been taking a catnap and pushed them to his forehead. The cruiser leapt toward him in the strong magnification and suddenly the sheriff's gray visage was only a few feet from his own. His eyes mean little slits. Fat lips puckered over a cigar. Cheeks pinched with distaste.

The seat beside him empty.

Captain Dwyer frowned. Leaned forward to fire the ignition, preparing to exit from behind the dilapidated barn or shed or whatever the rotting pile of lumber had once been in its former life when the sheriff cruiser surprised him by pushing into the roadside shoulder after crossing the bridge and making a quick, tight U-turn to face the woods. There it then sat. Idling.

Like a cat in front of a mouse hole.

Captain Dwyer glanced at his dashboard clock.

Decided to wait. To watch.

The minutes slowly ticked off.

Nearly twenty three minutes later a lone dark shape materialized from the wilderness like a floating apparition. A slight figure. Shuffling forward along the logging road from the tunnel of blackness. Barefoot and limping and without a coat. The slight figure hesitated at the threshold of the bridge when it spotted the idling cruiser on the other side.

The fuzzy bridge lamps revealed Lillian.

The sheriff was making a point, Captain Dwyer decided. It was indelicate and inartful, but a point nonetheless. After all it was here the sheriff had serendipitously discovered Lucy a decade ago. Stumbling from these very same woods. Stumbling onto this very same bridge. Half-dead. Bleeding. Muddy and shivering.

Skull fractured. Delirious.

Lillian didn't appear the least bit enlightened by the sheriff's lesson, however, and Captain Dwyer watched the woman with increasing admiration as she staggered across the bridge beneath the dull cones of light and shuffled *past* the sheriff cruiser. The sheriff was forced to reverse the cruiser to keep pace with her along Old Stump Road and eventually turn ninety degrees into her impertinent path on the roadside shoulder.

Only then did she stop. Glowering.

Staring over the sedan. Off into the darkness.

The sheriff pushed open the passenger door, anyway.

Still she hesitated. Defying him. Ignoring him.

The sheriff said something. Barking it.

Demanding. But also, perhaps, relenting.

Evidenced by the reluctant slump of his shoulders.

And an exasperated, mulish chomp on the cigar.

Captain Dwyer thought he even saw her smile.

Only then did Lillian climb inside.

The cruiser revved, tires spinning momentarily in the soft earth. Like an angry child. Before turning back onto Old Stump Road and proceeding toward the town lights. Captain Dwyer prepared to follow again when his radio crackled, startling him.

It was his girl. From state. Using local dispatch.

"Possible suspect sighting. Over," his girl said.

Captain Dwyer grabbed the radio mike. "Say again. Over."

"Possible suspect sighting, captain. Over."

"What you got, Jenny?" he said, starting the car.

"Your suspect on the evening news in about five minutes."

# 30.

**FREDDY STOOD BEFORE THE MIRROR** in the foyer of the white clapboard house in the small foothill town of Shady Creek and frowned at the old man staring back at him. The sag of his throat. The deep-rooted lines and hollow crags about his face. The gray flecks sprinkled in his long and scraggly hair. The exaggerated stoop of his slight back. The sink in his bony arthritic knees. The concave of his narrow chest. The bird-like atrophy of his shoulders.

Delbert stood at the window.

Peeking past the curtains.

Freddy had been a handsome boy like Delbert once upon a time. A boy with the entire world right at his sneakers. A world full of adventure and possibility. What had happened to that boy? Freddy wondered. Where had he gone? The young boy who had dreamed of flying off into space and exploring alien worlds or battling Indians on untamed frontiers or vanishing into thick South American jungles and living amongst mountain gorillas and flying around on long ropey vines in the high sun-dappled canopies like Tarzan. The young boy who had played chicken with passing trains and fished below the bridge before the water had turned to black sludge. The boy who had found treasure amongst the garbage in the town dump that had once been his home and from which all the adventures in the entire world had seemed possible.

Was that boy still inside him? Perhaps not.

But perhaps he was standing in front of him.

Peeking past the curtains at that ambitious blonde reporter from Bedford going live on the front stoop, anticipating Freddy stepping out the front door and into the bright camera light.

Freddy studied Delbert in the glow of that camera light. At the sparkle in his optimistic young eyes holding fast the conviction anything was possible if you just believed it strongly enough. The belief Freddy could just walk out the door and unburden himself and it would be enough. The truth. That the truth would set him free. Finally. It couldn't return his lost youth, of course. Not that. Nothing could or would ever be able to do that again. But, perhaps, by offering what the boy desired so badly, Freddy could preserve it for Delbert. For a little while longer, anyway.

The wonder in the world. The infinite possibility.

More than sneaking out the back door.

It was only fair to offer the boy that much. His trust.

For hadn't the boy already offered his own?

But even as Freddy entertained these stirring thoughts he couldn't help but accept Delbert also implicitly understood the cold reality of the situation. The cruel convolutions of an imperfect adult world. He could see it in the way the boy clenched his jaw and gritted his teeth in the window glass. This made Freddy sad and it made him proud. That his young son could appreciate the gravity of this moment while still grasping at hope.

Delbert turned from the window.

As if able to read Freddy's thoughts.

He took Freddy's hand into his own.

Small fingers interlacing Freddy's larger fingers.

Delbert then opened the front door.

It creaked softly as it rotated.

The camera light was bright and blinding.

Harsh and white.

Freddy thought he heard Delbert say:

"Here's your dawn, Freddy…"

Freddy had always quipped such platitudes. Had done so his entire life just like his old man had done, but those platitudes had always felt empty in their saying. Words to fill empty space by pushing more empty space. A vacuum into a vacuum. But such words spoken now by his son with such earnestness offered him additional comfort and those words were still dancing around in his head while his free hand, the hand not holding Delbert's hand, lifted slowly to shield his eyes from that blinding harsh white light swallowing them whole -- when suddenly--

--a GUNSHOT EXPLODED.

A loud and alien noise in all that whiteness.

The world slid out from under his boots.

And Freddy found himself on the ground.

Blinking. Confused.

Lost in the whiteness.

Delbert was still standing. Pointing.

Beatific in that swirling milky white galaxy.

Freddy followed his finger.

A man stood beyond the radius of the harsh white camera light. That harsh white light shifted and consumed that man into its hungry embrace. He was holding a smoking shotgun and shaking bitterly in the cold in a T-shirt soaked with perspiration, having snuck up on them in the dark from around the sagging porch corner. The cameraman took a stumbling step backward on the rickety porch like the man might shoot him next, nearly tripping over a warped porch floorboard; yet, the consummate professional, kept filming. Even adjusting the light over his camera to capture the entire porch -- perpetrator and his victims. The pretty blonde reporter, meanwhile, inconceivably took a step toward the man with the shotgun, her microphone extended like she was somehow removed from the events and immune to any of its dangers.

Harlan stood there in that sweat-soaked T-shirt.

Saying nothing. Seconds stretching into hours.

The shotgun still in his hands. Trembling.

Somewhere in all that awful eternity--

Freddy realized he'd not been hit. Neither had Delbert.

Only the old porch swing gathering cobwebs.

Swinging wildly. Rusty chains twisting and screeching.

Harlan began to sob. Heavy heaves.

Dull headlights and a roaring engine jumpstarted time again. The dull headlights and that roaring engine swiftly approached the whiteness, tires grinding dirt clods on the muddy driveway, throwing loose rocks out into the darkness somewhere.

A door popped open. The sheriff. Yelling.

Another door. Lillian. Screaming.

Shadows beyond the wall of white and sticky cotton.

Sticky for the gunshot had deafened Freddy.

The sheriff entered the whiteness first.

Still yelling. Face red. Eyes bulging.

Harlan shrugged like a puppet cut from its strings.

Dropping the shotgun. Falling to his knees.

Lillian followed. Embracing Delbert. On her knees.

Delbert remained standing. Rigid.

Still holding Freddy's hand.

Larger sound returned like a scratchy radio.

Voices and tears and shouts.

A state police captain appeared.

The fella from the local papers. Captain Dwyer.

His gun drawn. Over Harlan.

The sheriff slipped handcuffs on his friend.

Harlan offered no real resistance.

The camera captured everything.

Freddy managed to stand.

Assisted by the captain.

It was over. Or so it seemed.

Until that HORRIBLE WHISTLING NOISE.

Later Freddy would not be entirely certain if he had actually heard the horrible whistling noise or just felt it. Felt it disturb the cold night air. Push through it. Through the darkness.

Into the white orb.

Freddy collapsed. Something sticking out of his chest.

The blonde reporter went down, too.

Gripping her right shoulder.

Bleeding through her fingers.

For the rest of her life whenever the blonde reporter whom Delbert secretly thought of as the Barbie Doll reporter lifted her arm to shove a microphone into a subject's face or simply to apply deodorant in the morning she would remember this night.

An arrow had sliced through the side of her arm.

Winging her. Taking flesh.

Before slamming into Freddy's chest.

Fracturing his breastbone.

Plunging beyond.

Nobody had noticed Trigger arrive in the night amid all the confusion. He lived just a few blocks over on Grand Avenue. He had seen the Barbie Doll reporter's promo on the TV. With salty tears burning his swollen eyes and staining his sunburnt cheeks, leaving trails on his otherwise dusty face, steaming in the frosty air, Trigger, more commonly known as Bobby Joe, had snatched the compound bow from the gun rack in the back of his truck window. The bow had been a gift from his paternal grandfather on his thirteenth birthday. The bow had resided comfortably in the back of his truck since the start of hunting season. Well-oiled.

Wooden limbs laminated with fiberglass.

Cast magnesium risers.

Six wheel plastic pulleys.

Steel cables. Dacron strings.

The furious mounting tension of the expanding strings set in the slow rotation of the plastic pulleys and in the wide and yawning stretch of the wooden bow and most intimately felt beneath his curling trigger finger had been an almost religious moment for Trigger. And the releasing of the wooden arrow the answer to a prayer. An eye for an eye.

Slicing off into the night.

Picking up speed. Whistling.

Red and green feathers spinning wildly.

Trigger hadn't meant to hit the reporter.

Only Freddy.

It was a sweet amen when Freddy went down.

Crumpling to the old porch.

Trigger wasn't sure how long he stood there in the cold darkness admiring his moral vengeance before the state police captain materialized from the night and tackled him to the ground, the compound bow clattering off into the shadows. Despite what he had told the state police and the sheriff, Trigger had never slept with Allison. She had told him she was a virgin, more or less. He didn't understand what she'd meant by more or less, but was certain it could and would be overcome in time by his boyish persistence. Allison had told him she loved him. He had not said it back. Trigger decided now maybe he did love her. But Freddy had taken that all away. It was a mystery to him why Freddy had done that, though Trigger remembered an English teacher in school talking about past being prologue and thought maybe he had his answer.

The only answer he was likely to get anyway.

The cold night air whooshed from his lungs.

And for a moment he could not breathe.
The captain landing heavily on top of him.
But Trigger knew he would breathe again.
Finally. Again. Breathe.
Now that this had been done.
As for Freddy back on the porch--
Freddy stared at the arrow sticking out of his chest.
Stared at it stupidly, Freddy thought to himself.
Like it might only be a terrible hallucination.
Or he a cowboy on that untamed frontier.
And it the play thing of a child's imagination.
He tried to grab at it. The arrow.
If only to remove the weight of its pain.
It was as if a rhinoceros was sitting on his chest.
But his hand failed him. Fell to the ground.
The harsh white light again upon him.
Harsh and blinding and absolute.
His eyes fluttered.
Closed.

# 31.

**A FRACTION OF A MILLIMETER.**

A fraction of a millimeter further and the diamond-shaped steel arrow tip would have penetrated not only the sternum and left lung, but sliced into the soft tissue of the heart.

The surgeon had used a lot of fancy medical lingo describing the extent of the injury, but Freddy only needed to understand a fraction of a millimeter. If the arrow had not winged that unfortunate blonde reporter and lost velocity, the wretched thing would have ripped into his heart and he would have died right there on the porch in that harsh white light in front of his son.

Instead, Freddy survived a furious ride down to Bedford in the back of the captain's speeding unmarked black sedan and made it into surgery. The surgery lasted twelve hours. He woke in the same hospital room he had occupied only days before hooked to a tree of IV bags with more tubes sticking out of his chest, sucking crap out of his collapsed lung. The window he had punched out only days before was now boarded over. A plastic sheet was draped over the plywood, taped heavily around the borders, billowing and sucking in oscillating draft gusts penetrating the invisible cracks in the wood. Billowing and sucking like his damaged lung.

But he was alive.

There was a state trooper in the hall.

But he was alive.

His left ankle was cuffed to the bed frame.

But he was alive.

There was no escape this time, however.

Not unless he dared unhook himself from all the life-saving machines and somehow reckoned the impossible physics of squeezing himself out the window again with the four hundred pound hospital bed secured to his leg.

He went in and out of consciousness.

Waking for indeterminate, if agonizing spells.

It was the pain that woke him. Always the pain. It was the cresting wave of fuzzy painkillers that would finally put him back to sleep. A colorless concoction streaming through one of the assortment of IV tubes. Weightless and numbing. Pure sunlight. The pain found him in the deep and undulating troughs not long after the morphine timer clicked off. Angry black water.

Suffocating and roiling.

At one point Freddy woke to a man sitting in a chair. Sitting in the corner of the hospital room shadows. For a strange and confusing moment he thought it was his son. His son now a grown man. Delbert. Maybe he was dead after all, Freddy thought.

"Thought we might chat," the man said.

"Okay," Freddy said, his voice a dry, croaking noise.

The man turned on a small table lamp.

The lamp revealed him to be Captain Dwyer.

"Oh," Freddy said. And felt a dull spear of pain.

Distant, but there. Stalking him patiently.

The captain formally introduced himself.

Then said: "You sent away the public defender."

Freddy had no memory of sending away any public defender. Well, maybe a hazy, dreamlike recollection of such a thing from a moment in this room disconnected with time. A flash of a pixilated memory. A garbled conversation of which he had only seemed a sleepy witness rather than a participant. An unremarkable pale face above a cheap floating suit and a scuffed briefcase appearing above the black water crashing over his head. Again and again.

"Don't trust nobody in that town," Freddy said.

"Not sure I blame you," Captain Dwyer said.

At least Freddy thought that was what he said.

It was still hard to trust his ears.

The shotgun blast. Reverberating. Ringing.

"The sheriff pulled some strings," the captain admitted, shrugging his shoulders. "Got Harlan before a local magistrate in the middle of the night. Processed and released on an unlawful discharge of a firearm for now. Course, don't think Harlan intended to shoot you," the captain supposed. "He certainly meant to pull the trigger. But perhaps that was only the extent of it."

"Guns ain't his style," Freddy managed in response, chafed throat feeling as if coated in sawdust, "and I ain't knocked up."

"That right," the captain said.

Freddy nodded. Felt another spear of pain.

Cruel. Playful. Merciless.

The captain nodded attentively. "As for Bobby Joe--" he went on, "the youngster will remain in custody at least until your fiddily-diddily court is back in session next week and a bond hearing is completed. He's looking at attempted murder and other charges. But there is no evidence to suggest there was any coordination between Bobby Joe and Harlan. Quite the contrary, in fact. It appears both were exploiting a window of opportunity."

"Bobby Joe," Freddy mulled.

"The dead girl's fella. Yeah," the captain said.

"Allison," Freddy said, putting it together.

It was the first he'd heard of it. His shooter.

"What do you think about that?" the captain said.

"What do I think about what?"

"About that boy shooting you, Freddy."

Freddy considered it. Winced.

"Just thinks I done again what I done before," he said finally.

"Suppose you're right," the captain said.

"Not no different than anyone else in that town."

"Suppose not," the captain agreed.

"Don't blame him. But it don't make it true neither."

"Tell me," the captain said, pushing closer.

The cresting wave had lost its momentum and was now threatening to fall out from under itself. Collapsing beneath its own weight. Glorious whitecaps almost gone. Foamy water fizzling. Turning dark and foreboding. Preparing to drag Freddy down again into that angry maelstrom. Into the shadowy black depths waiting like an open mouth full of sharp and hungry teeth.

"Freddy?"

"Yeah."

The ringing in his ears had grown louder, too.
The room spinning again. Faster and faster. Roiling.
"I don't much like your sheriff, Freddy."
The captain was spinning with it. A blur.
"In your own words, tell me why I shouldn't."
His voice was also spinning. Full of static. Scattered.
Becoming incoherent in the rush of black water.
And in the residual echo of the shotgun blast.
Freddy closed his eyes. Tumbling again.
The cold darkness embracing him.
Freddy prayed the light would still be there.
Up there. Waiting to welcome him eventually.
To warm him on the next cresting wave.
Sunlight.
Pure.

# 32.

OAK RIVER MOBILE HOME PARK SAT at the southern edge of town beside a slow-moving muddy river and an oak forest choked with impenetrable hedges of poison ivy. It was hidden from plain sight down Hackberry Road like an unspoken family secret. The narrow dirt road wasn't graded and had a tendency to flood in the wetter months, leaving the passage a mucky mire with deep treacherous potholes for days afterward. The park was home to sixteen single-wide mobile trailers. None of the trailers had functional tires, so the homes had long ago sunk into the soft earth -- small rotting domiciles with flat metal roofs and cheap vinyl siding that tended to rip off in violent gusts of wind. Overrun by fields of overgrown weed and river rat, cockroaches and other critters. The interiors were no less distinguished. Ugly wood paneling, vinyl furniture, and aimless souls subsisting on government checks. The walls were protected by only an inch of crumbling insulation, insuring the small boxes became virtual ovens in the summer and ice chests in the winter with water pipes freezing, cracking, and flooding. There were unauthorized additions and inadequate plumbing and hazardous electrical panels and low-cost particle sub-floors. The mobile units were not parked on graded land with proper drainage, so rainwater and water leaks collected in puddles beneath the residences and the belly-boards were rife with mold and rot. A screen in the community well had rusted out and now sand was being pumped through the water system, turning toilet water orange and rendering anything out of the faucets basically impotable. A fetid swamp of raw sewage was collecting in the southeast corner of the property. It had become a breeding ground for mosquitoes and produced a hazy chemical cloud which turned various shades of dull rusted color as the sun circled. There was an illegal burn area for trash just beyond it, threatening a bona fide catastrophe in the future.

Delbert and Ollie hid in the long grass at the top of a steep hill overlooking the mobile home park this early morning, staring out cautiously from between tall swaying stalks and beneath a web of electrical and phone lines. The electrical and phone lines snaked down to the individual mobile home park units like strings of alien umbilical cords from splintering old utility poles with corroded, bird-splattered transformers riding the crest of the hill.

A woman stood outside a trailer at the forefront of the property. Unlike the other units, this trailer had a hardy stucco exterior and a peaked roof constructed of drywall. A small wooden sign read simply MANAGER'S OFFICE. The woman stood in profile, hanging wet laundry out on a line. The sun was up, but it was only a pale orb in an overcast sky and the morning was cool. Delbert wondered if the laundry would even dry by sundown.

The woman was in her mid-twenties. Young and pretty, if careworn. Her house dress appeared secondhand and was not particularly flattering on her. She was barefoot despite the chilly morning. She had long brown hair that looked like it hadn't been brushed properly for days, if not years. It fell in knots and tangles about a sunburnt face from a loose, ill-conceived bun. Her thin fingers worked fussily. Not because she enjoyed the chore of hanging out wet laundry, but because it occupied her. The simplicity of the task putting her mind at rest. If only for the moment. And for the moment Delbert couldn't help but think of the woman below him as an injured bird. He had always thought there was something majestic, if indeed frightening about birds. The fact they had those hollow bones and were nearly weightless, yet survived in a harsh and predatory world of rock and teeth and claw and had done so for eons, harkening back to prehistoric times. Modern dinosaurs with sharp beaks and talons of their own capable of tearing sinewy flesh from bone. Brutal and resilient little creatures capable of the most magical of inventions. Flight.

Deities of worship through millennia.

Fragile and eternal.

Delbert blinked. "You sure that's her?" he said.

"Everybody knows crazy Lucy, doofus," Ollie insisted, his broad shoulders shrugging. "She's a freak."

Dirty small children ran around the overgrown yard. Screaming. Over-excited. Also barefoot. Teasing a ragged dog on a heavy chain. A thick leather collar choked at the whining animal as it pulled excitedly against the restraint. The jangling chain was clasped to a metal stake buried in the ground, offering the poor beast a ten to fifteen foot radius to chase the children who managed to instinctively dance in and out of the invisible circle, aware but unaware of the dog, always just out of its lunging, whimpering reach. Its long tongue hung halfway out its mouth. Its dark almond-shaped eyes tracked the movement of each child. It snapped at their heels and scratched at the ground and moaned. Its hair was matted. Badly in the need of a comb or a washing. Eventually the mongrel whose breed escaped any exact description coiled itself in the twisting chain chasing the largest child of about seven years. The child stopped briefly and giggled with a bubbling delight when the clattering chain spun the beast dizzily in the mud, frustrating the dog, but also leaving it pleased with the attention.

The woman, meanwhile--

--turned toward an approaching car.

It appeared on the muddy road bending from the trees.

As the woman turned, the woman Delbert now knew to be Lucy, her profile shifted, revealing a jagged scar on the left side of her face. She frowned when the approaching car revealed itself to be a sheriff cruiser. It rolled to a stop outside her trailer.

"Oh shit," Ollie said.

The boys ducked lower in the grass.

Sheriff Snodgrass stepped out of the cruiser. Hitched his belt. His pock-marked face hidden in shadows beneath the brim of his hat. Still, Delbert's blood chilled a few degrees when the lawman seemed to instinctively glance at the grassy hill overlooking the mobile park, the cold sunlight reflecting off his mirror sunglasses.

The boys ducked lower still.

"Double fucking shit," Ollie said.

But when the boys eventually dared to peek back through the tall stalks of grass, Lucy had already gathered her children and was grudgingly following the sheriff into the mobile home unit with the hardy stucco exterior and the peaked roof constructed of drywall and past the simple wooden MANAGER'S OFFICE sign. Her cheeks red with agitation but for the jagged scar. It remained pale. Even more pronounced on her countenance.

Like a zipper.

# 33.

**SHERIFF SNODGRASS TRIED TO GET** comfortable on the threadbare couch. Loose springs hidden beneath the thin fabric poked mercilessly at his behind, however, making the effort impossible. The couch was also altogether too big and made the narrow space in the trailer seem even smaller. Or maybe it was all the dark wood paneling and the round coffee table that resembled a giant toad stool bumping at his knees. Thank the Lord the silly wobbly thing was round; otherwise, the obnoxious little screaming brats running circles around the scant room would have cracked open their lopsided melons a long time ago.

The sheriff frowned.

He could hear the toilet running constantly in the room behind the kitchen and the horrible little rat's nest smelled of stale coffee and maybe last night's dinner and bleach and cigarettes and kitty litter that needed to be turned. At least the sheriff hoped it was kitty litter. Frankly, he hadn't seen any cats slinking around this coffin yet and quivered at what the odor might actually be if there were, in fact, no four-legged varmints in residence.

The appearance of what appeared to be old pet stains on the carpet eased his mind only slightly.

His frown deepened as he soaked in the cluttered appurtenances decorating the small space. Odds and ends and knickknacks which only added to the sense of claustrophobia. Like someone had vomited a flea market or a garage sale. Stuff a person with half a brain had the sense to unfetter from their own home before such nonsense could take root. This included a series of ugly sunflower watercolors, a wall of wooden birdhouses, and a dusty collection of Raggedy Anne and Andy paraphernalia. Ceramic figures, magnets, and the spooky little dolls themselves. Raggedy hair and churlish little smiles of bright red yarn and big plastic black buttons for eyes peeking out from constellations of dull red freckles. Mischievous little spirits mocking him.

Like the obnoxious little screaming brats.

The sheriff was relieved when Lucy herded the noisy brood into a bedroom at the end of an even narrower hall.

Stuffing them like shoes in a closet.

Lucy closed the bedroom door and returned to the living room. She sat on an ottoman with stuffing choking out of various rips and gashes in the washed-out fabric. Fabric so badly faded the sheriff could no longer make out the pattern -- sunflowers or sunbursts or maybe The Starry Night by Vincent van Gogh.

Her husband, Willy, was parked on the opposite end of the couch, staring with glassy eyes at the sheriff, hands twitching. Willy was an alcoholic and was apparently allergic to a razor. He was only half-dressed and half-awake, flinching only slightly when that feral beast on the chain outside the thin walls began to bark ferociously at the wind, its snarls and howling bellows and hysterical woofs quickly germinating a nasty little headache behind the sheriff's weary eyes. It would be a doozy, promising to radiate across his skull and ruin his entire fucking afternoon. Sighing, the sheriff produced an envelope from a coat pocket. He slid it across the toad stool of a coffee table. A wad of money peeked out its flap.

He let it sit there. Conspicuously.

The headache began to thump. Like a distant war drum.

"Just know, there's more where that come from," he said.

"Every month, right?" Willy said.

The sheriff had talked to Willy on the phone. He wasn't sure what state of mind the moron had been in during that conversation, but ostensibly he had been capable of relaying enough of the details to Lucy here because Lucy had begun to frown grumpily, thin arms crossed over her thin chest, even before the sheriff had produced the envelope. She just stared at the envelope now.

Reluctant to touch it.

"Buy a lot of pampers," the sheriff said.

The moron handled the money. Greedily.

"Think of it like social security," the sheriff said.

Lucy hugged herself even tighter. Looked away.

Toward the vinyl door.

And the sound of the barking dog.

There was a crashing noise in the bedroom. Giggles.

Gremlins. Little hairy gremlins on crack.

"Listen, sugar," the sheriff said deliberately, finding it difficult to breathe all of a sudden, all that dark wood paneling pushing in on him, reminding him again of a fucking coffin. "Take the money. You don't want to know what's behind door number two." He slapped his knee for effect. A hollow retort. "You really don't."

# 34.

**JACK THE MARSHMALLOW SAT BEHIND** a big important mahogany desk in his office at the bank. The large bug-eyed man was fuming a blistering hot fury. The fury seemed to rise off his fleshy, malodorous body like shower steam after their stomach-turning encounters in the small dirty rooms at the Shady Creek Motel. The marshmallow leaned forward and squeezed the corners of his desk, the blood draining from his plump fingers. His teeth clicked like a rodent and he spoke in a hissing, conspiratorial whisper despite the fact his office door was closed and reasonably soundproof, managing to veil the hustle and bustle of the main bank beyond it. "Sheriff asked me to open an account for you in your name," he said eventually. Unenthusiastically.

Lillian sat in a client chair.

Smoking defiantly.

"In this bank?" she said.

She shook her head at the very idea and then savored the displeasure registering on the marshmallow, revealed in thick undulating waves coursing beneath his banker's suit and sending his podgy flushed cheeks aflutter. She absently wondered what she would do if he had a heart attack right then and there.

His teeth clicked again. The fat rodent.

"Deposits will be made quarterly," he said.

She continued to shake her head.

"The transactions will resemble dividend payments."

She grunted. Head still moving in opposition.

"Offshore investments," he said.

"This is mill money," she responded finally.

"Nobody can prove that," he said.

"Bullshit. Why you think we're having this conversation."

She winked at the marshmallow's briefcase on the table in the corner. The violated briefcase. It sat next to old baseball trophies. Perhaps artifacts from high school or maybe the marshmallow had kids. There were a couple framed photographs sitting on his desk, too, but the photographs were turned away from her and Lillian didn't care enough to walk that far.

"In for a penny, in for a pound," he said.

"I want cash. Like Lucy," she countered.

Lucy was receiving cash. Of course she was.

Otherwise, she'd have appeared on those bank records.

"Cash?" the marshmallow snarled, slamming back in his chair like someone had just crushed down on the brakes at a hundred miles an hour or like he was strapped in one of those G-force training centrifuges that spun astronauts around and around until they passed out, chins buried in their chests.

His podgy flushed cheeks clenched. His plump fingers clutched the corners of his desk even harder than before, turning colorless. Like uncooked chicken sausage. The wood creaking.

He rose. Absolutely beside himself. Shaking.

She exhaled smoke. Quite comfortable.

He pointed a fat, fleshy finger.

She imagined his heart the size of a ham.

Banging angrily against his chest wall.

In exasperated spasms.

"This ain't the Shady Creek Motel, you slut," he spat.

"Ten thousand. By sundown," she said.

"Ten thousand? Fuck you, Lillian."

"Not anymore," she said. And stood.

She dumped her cigarette on the carpet and stamped it out with a heel. Leaving an ugly ash stain. She then headed slowly for the office door. Swinging her skinny little tush. Swinging it all the way out to the sidewalk. Humming in the cool morning air.

# 35.

**HARLAN WINSLOW ARRIVED AT THE** hospital in Bedford just after ten in the morning to discover Captain William Dwyer waiting for him in the main lobby before the elevators. The state police captain was seated with a Styrofoam cup of coffee and a half-eaten bear claw resting neatly on an unfolded napkin on his lap. The captain was using a plastic fork and knife to eat the sticky Danish. It was a fastidious exercise and gave Harlan as much pause as finding the state police captain sitting there in the hospital lobby in Bedford in the first place.

"Hungry?" the captain said, lifting a paper bag.

Harlan could see a second bear claw inside.

"No," Harlan mumbled.

"Pity," the captain said. "Mind if I finish?"

Harlan stood there before the elevators, disconcerted. It had been cold outside. The weather was turning. But now he felt altogether too warm. He could feel hot air pushing down from a ceiling vent above him. He stepped aside to evade the unrelenting current only to feel a chill subsequently pass through him.

The captain took his time, slicing the donut into neat little bite-size pieces before popping them into his mouth and dabbing at the corners of that mouth with another napkin. Eventually, after he had finished, with Harlan standing there stupidly in the middle of the crowded lobby with the elevator doors opening and closing, the captain made a show of removing a piece of paper from his pocket. A court document. A warrant with a full Christian name. Fifteen minutes later Harlan was seated on a narrow stainless steel table in a small examination room on the second floor, sliding about on one of those crinkly sheets of thick tissue paper beneath him. His right sleeve rolled to his elbow. A young nurse who refused to look at him directly in the eye dabbed at his exposed arm with a cotton ball coated with rubbing alcohol before slipping in a long frightening needle. Harlan frowned and watched his blood flow through the needle's transparent tube to a waiting vial.

"You look pale," Captain Dwyer said.

Harlan felt pale. Dizzy.

"Some folks just don't like the sight of blood, I guess."

The captain was standing in the corner by the door. As if anticipating Harlan might abruptly decide to run. As if the mere sight of his own blood might condemn him and Harlan knew it. Harlan blinked. Could not help but watch the blood swirling inside the round tube, climbing its plastic walls, bubbling and frothing outside his body, filling the vial. He was glad to be sitting down.

"Do you have to be here?" he said to the captain.

"Afraid this is evidence. Crossing the t's. Dotting the i's."

The nurse pursed her lips. Uncomfortable.

"Speaking of which, Mr. Winslow," the captain said, frowning at a crumb on his tie. Sighing, he swiped at the crumb. It was frosting and he swiped at it carefully, not wanting to smear the water and sugar. "I'll need to speak with your wife again at some point," he continued finally, vaguely nodding toward the psychiatric wing two floors above their heads while critically inspecting his tie. "How's she doing, anyway," he wondered, "your wife?"

"Not well," Harlan managed.

The nurse removed the needle. The vial was full.

"Suppose not," the captain agreed, frowning.

The frosting had smeared after all.

"Suppose not," the captain said again.

# 36.

**SHERIFF SNODGRASS EXITED LUCY'S** trailer, having to duck his head to avoid cracking his forehead a good one on the narrow door's low aluminum frame. The frame already advertised a noticeable dent, suggesting Willy had misjudged it on more than one drunken occasion. The sheriff stood for a moment on the briefest of excuses for a porch, savoring the cool morning air after being inside the poorly-ventilated trailer before noticing tracks of both fresh and calcified rat droppings parading across the weather-stripped planks. The rats were likely as big as cats out here, he supposed grimly. He also supposed the country bumpkins moldering inside these death boxes against these swampy woods like modern day hillbillies ate squirrel like chicken, so it didn't stretch the imagination to conceive they ate river rat, too. After all, what was one disgusting rodent compared to another on the old barbecue spit. The idea made his stomach lurch and his headache twinge as if a writhing, gluttonous rat was inside gnawing at his brain. Lucy's loathsome dog yapping obnoxiously at the end of its taut chain in the yard only made his headache worse. He rubbed his eyes. Heard the screen door slapping behind him.

Footsteps. Willy.

"You sure she ain't talked to nobody?" the sheriff said.

"Naw. Not nobody," the drunk said.

The sheriff contemplated the stupid silly son of a bitch scratching at himself like a monkey infested with bug bites. The man's toenails were almost black. His legs beneath his faded boxer shorts skinny and malnourished and tragically bow-legged.

Lucy watched them from the kitchen sink.

Frowning behind window slats.

"Saved her life, you know," the sheriff said to Willy, but staring at Lucy. "If I hadn't been making a last run 'round the mill that night ten years ago--" he contemplated, sighing ruefully with the thought. "You'd do well to remind her. Sure you would, chief."

Willy patted the envelope in his pocket.

"You can count on me, sheriff," he said.

The screen door slapped open and closed in rapid succession and the circus of dirty children scrambled across the porch and back into the overgrown yard. The barking fleabag yanking frantically at the end of his chain hardly offered the little brats any attention on this occasion, however, earning the sheriff's curiosity. The sheriff plopped his hat back on his head and shoved the mirror sunglasses over his fatigued eyes and followed the hound's exasperated sightline into the pale sun toward the crest of the grassy hill. The sheriff grimaced at what he thought he saw.

He moved quickly. Stepping off the porch.

Stomping across the overgrown yard.

Yanking the stake from the ground.

Freeing the beast.

Liberated, the four-legged monster burst for the hill with a desperate whine, quickly disappearing into the tall grass beginning at its base only to have its broad arched back, its coarse hair standing on end, reappear here and there further up the steep incline, chain and iron stake dragging along the bumpy ground behind it, swishing back and forth, creating waves in the long hearty stalks like a large jungle snake moving at high speed.

On the crest of the hill there was movement.

Delbert and Ollie. Rising. Ducking again.

Hopelessly trapped in the tall grass.

The beast reached them in only seconds and stood on higher ground above their bent heads, the length of its body a trembling, coiled muscle, snarling and growling and scratching witlessly at the rocky earth while snapping its salivating jaws, black lips pulled from its black gums and gnashing teeth, shoving the sharp bristles of its snout toward their hand-covered ears, its high-pitched protestations quickly rendering the huddled boys deaf.

The sheriff hiked up the hill. Slowly.

Coming to stand over the boys.

He used the chain to pull back the choleric dog.

Then said: "Stand up, you little shit."

Ollie stood. Afraid. Eyes cast downward.

The sheriff hit him with the back of a hand.

The gaudy rings made a hollow thwacking noise.

Ollie fell hard against the steep grade.

"That's for sneaking around like a jealous woman."

Blood trickled from Ollie's mouth. Ear.

"Don't you blubber on me, doofus," the sheriff said.

Ollie fought back tears.

The dog bellowed again. Louder.

Pulled at the chain. Nearly pulling over the sheriff.

"Get in the car," the sheriff barked.

Ollie offered Delbert -- who was still on the ground, staring wide-eyed from behind the tall and silently swaying stalks -- a final distraught glance. The delay only earned Ollie another thwack. The boy moaned. Buckled. Then grudgingly sniffled down the hill.

The sheriff then regarded Delbert.

Looming over him like a black cloud.

Delbert could see himself in the mirror sunglasses.

He looked incredibly small and terrified.

The sheriff removed the sunglasses.

Revealing those cold, penetrating gray eyes.

Annoyance became scorn. Scorn became hate.

Devoid of empathy or humanity.

Delbert had once spent a long hot summer in Sunday school when his mother had dated that preacher in one of those many small dirt clod towns she and Delbert had too briefly passed through during their travels. Delbert had been taught about the ten commandments and not to take the Lord's name in vain. He had sung songs with the other children about the baby Jesus. And learned about sin and temptation and the corruption of man.

And the devil.

Delbert had never been sure he believed in the devil.

It seemed like a ridiculous cautionary tale.

Like Santa bringing coal for naughty children.

Until now.

"You're in the wrong place at the wrong time, kiddo," the sheriff said, hissing in that strangely soft and mesmerizing voice which seemed so entirely contrary to his enormity and somehow entirely more venomous because of it. "Just can't have that. If your momma won't teach you right from wrong, then somebody ought to. Sure enough, son."

The sheriff dropped the chain.

Grabbed the dog stiffly by the collar.

The dog rose to the occasion. Snarling and barking as the sheriff shoved its snapping jaws at Delbert. Inches from his nose.

The beast's breath hot and rancid.

"I think he wants to bite your face off, Delbert," the sheriff said softly, gleefully, kneeling down beside the enthusiastic animal, wanting an unobstructed view.

The beast became hysterical.

Straining. Yowling. Black gums dripping.

Nostrils flaring. Bristles sharp as sewing needles.

Black eyes wild. Bulging out of its head.

A shadow fell over the sheriff and the dog and Delbert.

"BUSTER! HEAL!" it said. A woman's voice.

The life drained instantly from the dog.

It whimpered. Crawled to her feet.

The sheriff turned.

Surprised. Annoyed.

"Lucy," he said.

"I want you off my land in two minutes, sheriff," she said.

"Or what, sweetcakes?" he growled. Eyes narrowing.

"Sure you don't want to hear that answer," she warned.

She stood tall on that hill. Lucy. Even though she was a good deal shorter than Sheriff Snodgrass she had the advantage of the slope and she didn't flinch. Her resolution seemed to both unnerve and incense the sheriff. He rose, shifting his weight this way and that to defy gravity. Then pointed threateningly at the scar zippering down her sunburnt face. "You just remember," he said.

"I remember," she said.

"Be sure you do. What was done and been done," he said.

"One minute," she warned.

Delbert thought she might even be counting.

"Careful," the sheriff warned. "Careful."

She just stared at him. Unimpressed.

The sheriff scowled. Discombobulated. His own nostrils flaring. Teeth gritting. He offered Delbert a final hateful look. "Don't make me get ugly boy," he said, then surprised Delbert by trudging down the hill without another word. Hitching his belt.

Cursing beneath his breath.

# 37.

**DELBERT SAT WITH LUCY ON THE** crest of the hill overlooking the mobile home park. The dog whose name was Buster (which already made it seem less formidable in Delbert's mind) was slouched contently between them, snoozing in the pale morning sun. Only one eye half-open while Lucy scratched behind a tattered ear. Delbert and Lucy sat in relative silence with only the birds chirping in the trees around them and the drowsy hush of the crickets buzzing in the tall grass. Below the muddy river pushed lazily toward the horizon where it grew thinner and thinner until it vanished from recognition as if falling off the edge of the world. "My momma run off when I was seven," Lucy said after a spell, staring out at that vanishing act of a muddy river. Here and there the cold sun glinted off its deep, dark waters, producing blinding sparkles of white light. Like a thousand Tinkerbells from Peter Pan. "My daddy, God bless his miserable drunken soul, wasn't much to write home about," Lucy said. "This land--" She gestured at the trailer park. "The white trash lottery."

Her voice was low. Ashamed.

The dog sighed. Closed the one eye.

Delbert found himself staring at all those knots and tangles in her hair falling over her sunburnt face from the ill-conceived bun secured loosely by a butterfly clip. Something a child might wear. Beyond the knots and tangles were pale bald spots. Patches of scalp where hair no longer grew. As if the hair had been plucked clean by naughty little fingers. Delbert thought he could even see little bloody striations where those naughty little fingernails might have dug into the flesh. He imagined all her hair might eventually fall out in knotted and tangled heaps from her head and scatter to the wind. Delbert had never seen a woman without hair and he wondered what would become of her. Lucy the freak.

He imagined she might drown herself.

In that deep, dark river maybe.

Never to be found.

"My daddy," she said. "Worked at the rug mill in town like everybody 'round here. Worked for Harlan's rich daddy, too. Got himself a promotion at the mill and the deed to this land after what happened to me. I didn't have no choice but to lie in those courts."

She shook her head with the thought.

The head with all those bald spots.

"My daddy-- He died not long ago. Drunk himself to death," she revealed without a trace of grief. "And that was that and this is this. Don't suspect I'll have the land much longer anyhow. Taxes haven't been paid in years and there's a mountain of code violations from county. Most folks here don't even have leases no more and haven't paid rent in god knows when."

She noticed Delbert's eyes settle on her scar.

The pale zipper zigzagging down her cheek.

She gently reached for his hand.

It startled him. Her hand on his own.

Her skin felt calloused and rough.

She lifted his hand in a non-threatening manner and placed his fingers on that zigzag of a scar. It felt strange. Foreign. Leathery, yet plastic. That jagged scar. Reminding him of a glob of model airplane glue that had accidentally spilled from the dimpled tube and dried in a puddle on his desk. He supposed her disfigurement in its own way was holding her face together.

She returned his hand to his lap.

"Still get the nightmares, you know," she said. "I'm beneath ground. I can't breathe. Can't make a sound. And I can hear them up there somewhere in the moonlight. Drunk and cursing and groaning and shovels of dirt slapping down on me like wet sand."

She fell quiet for a moment. Shivered.

Like she was below ground again.

"Course, sometimes I'm above ground," she said. "Those are worse to be honest. I can hear my baby crying down beneath the earth. Suffocating. I dig until my fingers bleed."

She shivered again. Harder.

Tucked her hands beneath her armpits.

Turned to Delbert.

Eyes solemn. Full of regret.

"Harlan kilt his own girl. That what you think?"

Delbert nodded.

"Then it's my fault," she said.

He followed those solemn eyes down to her mobile unit far below. Her husband was sitting on the front porch in his boxers in a lawn chair. Scratching himself. Sipping from a large bottle of malt liquor beneath the wooden MANAGER'S OFFICE sign.

His muddy eyes focused on Delbert.

Knowing the boy meant him trouble and a half.

"Don't worry 'bout him," Lucy said.

Delbert wasn't so sure.

"Lush don't even know what day it is half the time."

Delbert turned back to Lucy. The cold sun had found her hair, exposing blonde highlights hidden in the dark and tangled knots. For a moment in that slant of pale sunlight he could imagine her as a young girl. As she had been. Her life in front of her.

Before she had met his father.

"Freddy bad, too, isn't he?" Delbert said.

Delbert studied Lucy intently, desperately, no longer able to draw breath. Fretfully awaiting her response as that slant of pale sunlight shifted and left them in the shadows again. Appreciating only now in this moment it was the very reason he had come out here in the first place. To ask her that question. The gravity of the world seemed to hang on her answer.

"Suppose only you can answer that question, Delbert," she said finally. And that was all she said about that business.

Staring again at that vanishing act of a muddy river.

# 38.

**DELBERT SHUFFLED HOME.** Gritting his teeth. Thinking about what Lucy had said. And hadn't said. Thinking about what his ankle was saying now.

The ankle had just about healed before this morning. The discoloration and swelling just about gone. There had still been the occasional dull splinter of pain and some residual tenderness, but otherwise the offended ligament had snapped back into place.

Like the rubber band he knew it to be.

At least until Buster had made his charge.

Delbert had panicked and without thinking had stabbed the bad foot into the slanted ground, intending to leap up and run. Unfortunately, the foot had twisted funny on the uneven slope and fresh bolts of fiery hot pain had immediately shot up his leg. If he didn't know any better, hobbling home slowly now, Delbert would have believed he was wearing the foot on backward.

The misery was mollified somewhat by Ollie.

The boy had not left his side on that hill.

Of course, it might have had something to do with the fact Delbert had latched onto his wrist with the strength of Thor and dragged Ollie back down into the dirt. Still, Delbert had no doubt the big country boy (who had probably skipped a few grades) could have fought free and escaped into the woods above the hill if he had truly desired to do so, thereby abandoning Delbert like a raw steak for Buster's complete and undivided attention.

Yes, Ollie was becoming a true friend.

It made Delbert's ankle feel a tad lighter.

Just the thought of it.

But the weight of agony tumbled right back down again into that ankle when he turned from the road and limped down the muddy driveway before the white clapboard house to find a familiar brown sedan parked in front of the porch. SHADY CREEK SAVINGS AND LOAN stenciled on the side. A familiar piggish man with a pale balding dome and banker's suit was slouched behind the wheel, observing him with familiar small fleshy eyes.

The marshmallow.

The driver side window down.

Delbert had half a mind to pick up a nasty rock.

Maybe even throw it, too. He had a live arm.

Ollie could attest to that. Or at least Ollie's sister.

"Give this to your momma, brat," the marshmallow said.

Extending a large envelope from the window.

His fat cheeks crimson.

"And no peekin'," he told the boy.

Delbert hesitated, staring at the envelope.

"C'mon, stupid," the marshmallow said.

Shaking the envelope.

Delbert took a cautious step forward. He saw a rock embedded in the mud. A sharp-looking blade. Serrated. Like half an arrowhead. He could snatch it up in the blink of an eye, but suddenly he thought of Lucy's face. Her scar. The zipper. And Delbert decided to leave the stone half-buried in the cold sucking mud, grasping at the large envelope instead.

It was heavier than it looked.

The envelope.

Delbert almost dropped it.

The marshmallow, meanwhile, slammed the car into reverse and pounded his fat marshmallow foot on the gas pedal. The car jolted backward abruptly, bouncing in reverse along the pitted driveway, throwing mud and muck and rock before peeling onto the paved road with more mud flying. The marshmallow then slammed the car into Drive and without looking back screeched off down the road, leaving burnt rubber on the asphalt.

Delbert climbed the porch.

Sat on the top step.

He glanced warily behind him to make sure his mother hadn't come to the door or window, then peeked open the envelope.

It was stuffed with money. Big bills.

"Holy shit," he said.

# 39.

**CAPTAIN WILLIAM DWYER AND SEVERAL** of his uniformed troopers sat crowded, shoulder to shoulder like packed sardines, on the threadbare couch across from Lucy and her husband. Willy had dressed for the occasion, resplendently decked out in oil-stained coveralls without a T-shirt or shoes. The idiot was drinking beer with a scrum of crushed empties on the small round coffee table before him. Lucy had managed coffee. And a tin of stale cookies.

"Where's the sheriff?" she said.

The state police exchanged furtive glances.

The glances unnerved Lucy.

"Is he coming?" she said.

Captain Dwyer cleared his throat. He could hear what sounded like a herd of ferrets bouncing off the walls behind a closed bedroom door at the back of the trailer along with the drone of a television at full volume. "The sheriff has been excused from the investigation, ma'am," the captain said and sipped his coffee.

It was bitter. Tasted hours old.

Lucy blinked with surprise. "Excused?"

"A procedural matter," Captain Dwyer said.

"Is he under suspicion?" Lucy said.

Willy gave his wife a look.

The captain put down his coffee. Pushed forward, the springs beneath the couch releasing with an unsettling popping and grinding noise. He offered his most welcoming expression. "Why don't you tell us what you mean by that, Lucy?" he said.

Willy gave his wife another look. Reprimanding.

Lucy ignored it. Stood. "Wait here," she said.

Lucy disappeared to the back of the trailer, passing through the closed door where her small children were crawling all over a narrow bed in front of a TV. Willy quickly followed her inside the bedroom, closing the door behind him.

"What the fuck you doing?" he said.

"Stay 'way from me," she said.

She dug the envelope with the money from a bureau.

Tried to walk past her husband.

Willy grabbed her wrist. Hard. Spun her.

"Said what the fuck," he said.

"Said stay 'way from me," she said.

The children had stopped horsing around.

Watching their parents now with nervous anticipation.

"Don't make me break it," he hissed.

"I dare you," she spat.

He twisted her wrist harder. Higher.

They stared at each other in the small dusty bedroom.

Her face reddened with determination and anger. Except for the scar. It adopted its restive white pallor. The shades were drawn over the window above the bed, casting the bedroom in a dim light and the scar seemed to preternaturally smolder.

She felt Willy let loose her wrist.

And she was out the bedroom door.

Marching back into the living room.

She dumped the envelope full of that dirty money on the round coffee table beside all the empty cans of beer and the bitter coffee and the tin of stale cookies. The money spilled out in front of the state police, fanning, exposing itself. Crisp hundreds. Uncirculated tender. Straight from the bank vault. Sharp dangerous edges that cut covetous fingers. But still dirty. Dirty as it got.

"You'll find the sheriff's filthy fingerprints all over that envelope," she said. "Suppose all over that money, too, maybe. As for where it come from," she said, frowning, staring down at the awful pile of it. "I can tell you that, too, if you like."

# 40.

**I**T **HAD BEGUN TO RAIN. A COLD RAIN** that would turn to sleet by nightfall. The Barbie Doll reporter -- known to her viewers as Stacey Wells, and formerly known as Stacey Wisniewski by those who knew her back when -- fought the sticky muck grabbing at her galoshes while trying to ignore the sanctimonious grin on her cameraman's face. Jerry had insisted they ditch the satellite truck back on County Route 3 beside that cow pasture. He'd taken a single glance at the mud pit that was Hackberry Road and shaken his head. That road was now turning into a soupy quagmire and it was almost certain the satellite truck would have been buried to its fenders if he had listened to her reservations about walking. Abandoning the truck on the paved county road had required a half mile hike through this deepening bog to the trailer park hidden beyond the curtain of trees. Not an easy exercise with an arm in a sling against her heaving chest. Jerry made it look easy even with the camera on his shoulder, but Stacey kept slipping and sliding and getting stuck in her galoshes, her lanky legs finally buckling beneath her slicker, sending her knobby knees into the stinky mess to Jerry's amusement as the rain fell harder.

"Shit," she said, refusing his help.

She struggled to her feet.

Then promptly fell again.

Splattering mud.

Stacey had refused to return to Bedford for her injury. Instead, she had opted for the small med clinic here in this hillbilly town, wanting to project an air of valor and invincibility. However, the truth was more self-serving. She had not wanted to be replaced in the field. God forbid she ended up back in Bedford covering some stupid cupcake drive down at the local elementary school while someone younger with bigger tits dragged her pretty little butt up the hill and fed off this delicious carcass of a story. This was her story. And she was now a part of it.

The other affiliates were back in town since the well-publicized crossbow incident and her competitors were putting her in front of their cameras. Her grandmother in Wilmington along the coast had actually seen her interviewed. Stacey knew it was only a matter of a time before the Bedford news director offered her that coveted desk job. Stacey intended to milk the sling and what amounted to a field dressing beneath it until that happened. In the meantime, Stacey wondered if there was a newsroom equivalent of the Purple Heart. She felt like a war correspondent.

Bombs and bullets flying around her.

Of course, Stacey wasn't sleeping much. Her arm felt like it weighed as much as that fucking camera on Jerry's shoulder and she was popping painkillers like Pez candy. Combined with copious amounts of caffeine, she was having a hard time putting one foot in front of the other and remembering what day it was or why she was humping doggedly out here in the rain toward the ugly, dilapidated trailer park appearing past the trees like a bombed-out battlefront until she turned a long rounded corner in what could only politely be called a road and finally saw the state police vehicles parked outside the stucco trailer with the peaked roof.

The boy was waiting on the hill.

Standing in the rain. Like a drowned puppy.

He limped down the hill on a bad foot.

Holding her business card.

"Thanks for calling kid," she said. "What's this about?"

"Absolution," Delbert said.

It turned out the woman living in the stucco trailer with her husband and kids and the snarling dog chained to a stake in the front yard was a Lucy Dykes. This, of course, in and of itself, was not a particularly interesting fact to anyone. The interesting part of the matter and a matter overlooked by Stacey and the other media vultures who had descended upon this town in the aftermath of Allison Winslow's death (and again after the crossbow incident) involved the woman's maiden name. Caldwell. And now, apart from the state police, Stacey Wisniewski, now known as Stacey Wells, was the first to have it. The first to know Lucy Caldwell was here. Still in town. After all these years. Hidden in plain sight thanks to a suspicious misfiling at the county clerk office of her marriage license. And what a story the woman had yet to tell.

Lucy Dykes. Formerly Lucy Caldwell.

The girl who'd dug herself out of a grave a decade ago.

# 41.

**THE COLD RAIN, INDEED, TURNED TO** sleet by nightfall. Captain William Dwyer and a couple of his boys from state braved the storm and headed down the winding mountain highway to Bedford that very night. The captain and his state boys found Harlan sleeping fitfully in a plastic chair beside his wife's bed on the psychiatric wing. They roused him from his troubled slumber and placed him in handcuffs. Harlan blinked and blinked. Disoriented. Still half-convinced this was all only a nightmare from which he could still wake himself.

The paternity blood had come back and the statutory rape of his late daughter was only the starting point. Lucy was now cooperating with authorities and additional charges would soon be filed. Charges related to crimes from a decade ago. Another lifetime. Charges immune from any statute of limitations.

Harlan seemed to finally accept the gravity of what was happening to him as the handcuffs were tightened on his wrists.

He began to sob like a child.

A broken soul.

He was escorted from the hospital room for a quick ride down the elevator and a long drive back up the mountain into the heart of the storm, his bald head bent low into his sunken chest. His wife, Rosemary, Allison's mother, was now awake, too. She had been awake for the last thirteen hours, more or less, slowly being weaned off the fluffy cloud of sedatives, leaving her raw and emotional. She struggled against the leather straps so that she might sit upright in the hospital bed facing the bathroom without a door and the dreary verdant landscape caulked directly into the wall. She watched with quiet satisfaction as her husband was led past her and out of the room. Her unforgiving gaze followed him until he was out of sight.

There was another witness to the arrest.

Freddy Jackson.

Freddy stood before a dark window in a dark dayroom at the end of the third floor, watching from behind the dark glass as the state police escorted Harlan into the wind and freezing rain to a waiting state police sedan idling in the parking lot below, its light bar spinning steadily and silently, throwing red and yellow into the stormy night.

Freddy felt nothing.

Only a vast emptiness.

# 42.

**THE SLEET AND FREEZING RAIN** transformed the small foothill town of Shady Creek into a cold, silent, magical world of glistening frozen water. The ice made the roads impassable and sidewalks treacherous for the earliest hours of the next morning and the town patiently settled inside the warmth of their homes in front of cozy wood stoves, content to simply stare at nature's majesty. The splendor of such a creation was only short-lived, however. The sun gradually rose in the morning sky and the ice began to inexorably melt for now. Stunted icicles hung from trees and gutters, dripping and refreezing in the lingering shadows, elongating in stubborn defiance, before relenting to the warming temperatures, sliding and crumbling to the frosty earth.

It was through this gathering slush a small parade of four state police cars led by Captain Dwyer's unmarked black sedan snaked slowly from downtown Shady Creek up to Hilltop Street before turning down a private road still known by many in the town as Winslow Place, but officially recognized by the planning commission for the past decade as Promontory View.

A single house sat at the end of the road.

Overlooking the town and the rug mill.

The large beautiful home at the end of the private road set against the national forest had once belonged to Harlan Winslow and his daddy before him and his daddy's daddy.

It was a three story mansion constructed in an enthusiastic amalgam of Victorian architectural styles from Italianate to Queen Anne to Eastlake with a dash of gothic influence. Steep rooflines and tall windows with ornate pediments. A wraparound porch with gingerbread adornments. Large bay windows on the east and west walls to capture the sunrise and sunset, respectively, along with an assortment of gables, turrets, and decorative pillars, including a romantic cupola on the south end with a mansard roof and dark arched windows. Huge mahogany front doors greeted visitors with hand-carved panels and ornamental bronze handles. The interior featured sixteen foot ceilings and marble fireplaces and crown molding and plaster medallions and thick tiger-oak doors. There were five bedrooms and four and a half bathrooms. A spiral staircase curled to the upper levels of the majestic domicile. A cut-crystal gasolier from the previous century hung in the grand parlor downstairs and had never been converted to electricity.

The home had once been known as Winslow Manor. It now belonged to the large man with the ruddy, gray-grizzled, pock-marked face and brooding eyes standing before the woodpile in the front yard. The tarp had not been properly secured by his stepson and had blown off during the storm. The firewood had been exposed to the sleet and freezing rain and become warped in a tomb of hardening ice and waterlogged as the ice melted. It would now be difficult to split properly and troublesome to burn.

And the axe.

The axe had been on the stump.

Left in the weather, too. Neglected.

The hickory handle swelling. Splitting.

The boy had done this. The boy who was sweeping leaves off the porch with short surly strokes of the broom. There were still fresh bruises on the boy's face from the other morning at the trailer park. Not that those bruises had learned the boy any damn sense. The man with the ruddy, gray-grizzled, pock-marked face felt the cold ripple through him, fueling his ire as his teeth bit down on the cigar in his mouth and his forehead furrowed and his boots kicked through the slush as he marched toward the truculent boy sweeping the porch. The ungrateful, snot-nosed little brat would soon learn a thing or two whether he wanted to or not.

But Sheriff Snodgrass only got a few short steps.

Before noticing the line of four state police cars.

Appearing from the shadows in the trees.

The boy on the porch noticed them, too.

And leaned on the broom to watch.

Captain Dwyer and his state boys parked their vehicles side by side in a turnaround beside what had once been a horse stable, their tires leaving muddy tracks in the melting frost. Sheriff Snodgrass discovered the axe in his hands with the split hickory handle. Melting frost dripping off its weather-dull blade as he turned from the house and approached the state police contingent disembarking from their official cars. Adjusting hats. Looking all-business.

"--hell is this, captain?" he said. "The Seventh Calvary?"

"Harlan just confessed," Captain Dwyer said evenly.

The sheriff stopped cold.

Boots half-buried in the slush.

There was a subtle twitch of his chin.

Dread, perhaps.

"To what exactly?" he said slowly.

"Put down the axe, sheriff," the captain said.

The boy on the porch, Ollie, watched with fascination as the next several moments unfolded. The sheriff remained where he stood for an unsettling amount of time, his boots rooted in the ground beneath the slush, as if he could simply outwait the half-circle of men in front of him, only coming unglued when those men forcibly removed the axe from his possession.

He cursed and spit. The sheriff.

But never swung the blade.

The axe fell in the slush. Lay there.

The sheriff was knocked down. Pinned.

"You boys--" he griped. "This is my town."

His voice was full of false venom. Cracking.

He was placed in handcuffs.

Face pushed in the mud.

"This was your town," Captain Dwyer said.

A small woman in a simple house dress and apron exited the house. She stood behind Ollie, her son, on the wraparound porch. Watching. Unblinking. Pale and frightened. The fear, however, gradually appeared to leave her eyes, replaced by a weary hopefulness, as she digested the unfolding scene in front of her.

The sheriff called out to her.

A suppurating, bleating noise.

She offered him no discernible reaction.

Other than to dry her hands on the apron.

The captain contemplated the woman on the porch.

"The alleged rich widow," he said.

He let the words hang in the cold morning air a beat.

Before adding: "Alleged being the operative word."

The captain offered the woman a nod.

"Ma'am," he said.

The sheriff was lifted roughly to his feet.

Mud and frost sticking to cold sweat on his brow.

The captain removed the crushed cigar from the sheriff's trembling mouth, chucking it into the weeds along the hill facing the town and the mill. "We did some checking down in Bedford," he said to the sheriff. "Turns out your wife's first husband's insurance policy barely covered the medical and funeral bills," he revealed drolly. "Cancer and all that. She, your wife, didn't have two nickels to rub together when she married you. Imagine."

The captain considered the mansion.

The monstrous monstrosity looming above them.

"Nice house, sheriff," the captain said without a trace of sincerity. "And a funny business, too. And I'm afraid it's only the beginning from what I've already gathered," he went on. "This funny business. This funny business in your town, sheriff."

A young girl with glasses appeared on the porch.

Ollie's younger sister.

No tears. Not today.

Not as the sheriff was led to the state police vehicles.

Ollie continued to lean on the broom.

Smiling unabashedly now.

"Wipe that look off your face, doofus," the sheriff growled at his stepson, the ugly, sniveling, snot-nosed little turd. "I'll smack your ass into next week," he said, struggling against the state boys on either arm, his boots dragging in the mud beneath him.

"Don't call me doofus, doofus," Ollie said.

And his smile grew wider. And wider yet.

As the sheriff was dumped into a state police car.

And subsequently locked behind the tinted glass.

The first of many cages to come.

# 43.

**CAPTAIN WILLIAM DWYER AND HIS BOYS** from state entered the Shady Creek Savings and Loan just after it opened for business at nine in the morning. They pushed past a startled receptionist, politely, but steadfastly, and burst through the closed office door of the bank president without knocking first to find Jack the Marshmallow standing above a pile of shredded documents strewn like party confetti over an open briefcase. He was moist with perspiration. The marshmallow.

Looking wild-eyed, if slightly sanctimonious.

"You needn't have bothered, Mr. Seymour," the captain revealed, head shaking with amusement. "Apparently someone at this institution has a conscience." The captain held up a court warrant in one hand and a plastic evidence bag in the other. Copies of bank records. Wire transfers. Overseas accounts. "We received all this anonymously a few days ago in the mail," he explained.

Jack the Marshmallow sunk into a chair.

"That bitch," he said.

Lillian. But no one would ever be able to prove it.

# 44.

**BOBBY JOE AKA TRIGGER NEVER FACED** charges. The boy was cooperative with state investigators and the county prosecutor's office. He admitted with full honesty he had meant to kill Freddy Jackson and apologized for winging Stacey Wells with the wayward arrow. Even apologizing on camera in a primetime exclusive interview with the Barbie Doll reporter. And from a practical point of view, despite the boy's homicidal intentions and the gross negligence and injury involved on the night in question, the county prosecutor, facing a tough election battle, concluded a jury would be unlikely to convict the heartbroken young man given the circumstances of the case.

Bobby Joe aka Trigger returned to school.

A footnote to a scandal.

Meanwhile…

Allison Winslow never received a funeral service. She was cremated and her remains taken by her mother, Rosemary, to Tennessee where Rosemary had family somewhere outside Crockett's Cove. There was talk Rosemary would not return to the town of Shady Creek. This talk appeared confirmed when a FOR SALE sign appeared one morning in front of the grand old Maple. The house beside it remained dark and quiet and empty.

There was also talk, of course, and a very great deal of it, in fact, about the rug mill and malfeasance, financial and otherwise.

The town only existed because of the mill. The thought of the mill standing dark and quiet and empty sent a tremor through the town until federal, state, and local authorities in conjunction with the courts made preliminary legal assurances neither the mill nor the town would be allowed to suffer the same ignominious fate as the young girl who had lived beside that grand old Maple.

As for the rest of the sordid business, a change of venue was ordered and the entirety of what was to come transferred off the mountain (and from its garish red brick courthouse at the center of town) down to Bedford in the valley, leaving behind only the anamnesis of a terrible nightmare.

# 45.

**LILLIAN HAD NEVER KNOWN HER** own father.

Only his first name. Jasper.

Otherwise, her father had been like Santa Claus or the Easter Bunny or the fucking Tooth Fairy. Something she had believed in with all her heart as a small impressionable child until she grew up and realized it was all a grotesque lie. The idea he might care about her and might someday return to invite her into his life. As a child, she had romanticized him a valiant king, far-flung out into the large world on a grand adventure seeking fortune and the return of his rightful crown, battling monsters and barbarians and all the while searching for his long-lost princess. The absurd nonsense found in picture books about girls with golden hair.

But her father had never come back.

Of course he hadn't.

He had not been a valiant king.

Not her father. Not Jasper.

Nor she a princess.

Jasper had been a gambler, Lillian had learned later. A debtor hobo moving about the country, always one step ahead of degenerates he owed money. He had died squatting in an abandoned foreclosed home outside Biloxi from septic shock compliments of a fatty liver. A condition spawned by neglected diabetes and a lifetime of alcohol abuse. Lillian had overhead these nauseating details as a preteen girl. Her mother confessing them during Bible study class on a warm Wednesday evening in the middle of August while Lillian sat there mortified, perspiring in the humid air of the church basement, frowning at her mother's crocodile tears and trying to ignore the stares of self-righteous pity from friends and neighbors. Gertrude. The woman had been an incomplete human being. At least that was the most kind description. The unkind version painted Lillian's mother for what she had really been to the little frightened girl sitting beside her in that church basement, condemned to receive those sanctimonious stares for the rest of her life. A cold, demanding, hard-eyed woman who had taken out on that little girl who still believed in fairy tale happy endings all her own sins rather than face them honestly. A miserable creature who had compensated for her own failings and joylessness in life by sitting in church day and night to sanitize herself below those stained glass windows. As if she could somehow wash herself clean with holy water and her holier-than-thou intentions. And her daughter, too. As if her young daughter had anything to yet wash clean.

It wasn't long after Lillian had met Freddy.

Freddy Monroe Jackson.

Lillian and Freddy would ditch class and climb on the school roof and stare at the mountain and imagine what was beyond it and smoke cigarettes stolen from their mothers. Lillian could still remember the pleasant rush of nicotine streaming through her body. Like helium in a balloon, lifting her. She could still remember the way his long sandy bangs flopped over his eyes, yet were unable to hide their twinkle when he looked at her. He'd smelled of garbage. Of the dump. But that was okay. It was an earthy, textured smell. And he didn't talk much, but could say so much without hardly saying a word. Lillian had discovered a refuge in their shared silent conversations. Passing a cigarette back and forth.

It had been so intimate. Like kissing.

Gradually--

After the truth was finally revealed about what had really happened a decade ago in those dark woods beside that creek behind the rug mill, Lillian came to the difficult and courageous decision it would be unfair to allow Delbert to continue to suffer for her own failings and joylessness in life. For her own sins. For the past before he was born. Unfair for him not to know his father.

To not know Freddy.

It took a few weeks before Freddy healed well enough to be returned to prison where he would complete his convalescing in the medical ward on A Block. According to his letters to Delbert afterward, life was much easier on A Block. There were more windows and more sunlight. During the weeks before his transfer back to the prison on the mountain, Lillian had filled out the necessary forms and received visit approval for herself and her son.

Subsequently, she and Delbert took the slow-chugging county bus up the mountain to Gallows River State Prison high and deep in the Smoky Mountains. It was an exceptionally cold and clear day for the bus ride and when the thick pine trees briefly parted along that long, winding, climbing mountain road, even from behind the dingy bus window, it was like being on top of the world.

It took a half hour to be processed into the prison.

Inside those cold stone walls.

Lillian sat at a plastic blue table.

Freddy eventually appeared from behind a blue steel door and was processed into the visiting room. He was even thinner than before and looked tired. Still, he managed a smile as he sat down at the plastic blue table across from Lillian. There was an extra chair, but Delbert was absent. The boy stood behind an acrylic window in an anteroom behind another blue steel door. He waved at Freddy impatiently. Freddy sighed. Waved back. Studied Lillian.

"I'll let him come in after we've had a word," Lillian said eventually below bright fluorescent lights buzzing above them like luminescent beehives. "Been overdue maybe."

She sat back. Appraising him.

Plastic blue chair creaking.

"For the record," she said. "Just want you to know maybe you had an easier time of it here in that cell. Three squares. Roof over your head. Somebody looking out for you. Imagine me. Run out of town for what you done. Pregnant and barefoot, Freddy."

His head bowed.

"What?" she said, pushing forward, the plastic blue chair creaking louder. "You think I was supposed to stick around? Let that town take out on my son what was your cross to bear?"

His head remained bowed.

"That what you think, Freddy?"

She was arguing with herself.

She hated to argue with herself.

She could never win.

Freddy lifted his gaze.

Blinked in the bright fluorescents.

Eyes blue. Thoughtful.

"Just thinking you done good, Lily," he said. "That's all."

She gave him a questioning look. A cautious one.

"With that boy, I mean."

"You don't got to tell me that," she said.

"I want to."

"Not what I mean," Lillian said, sitting back again with a grunt, her thin pale arms folding across her narrow chest. "I mean you don't got to tell me somethin' I already know."

He shrugged. "Okay, then," he said.

Lillian sighed. Glanced about the room.

At the correction officers. The unarmed men patrolling the visiting room. The armed men with rifles and handguns in the tall towers outside. The inmates. Hard men with hard faces and mysterious tattoos sitting on more plastic blue chairs around more plastic blue tables with family and friends and counsel.

"I don't like bringing Delbert to a place like this," she said in a whisper. She pointed an unlit cigarette at him. It had been in her hand the entire time. Like a rabbit's foot. Lillian could already taste the rush of nicotine that would soon be streaming through her body just like when she and Freddy had sat on top of that schoolhouse staring at that mountain and wondering what lay beyond it. She guessed, perhaps, she now knew. "You need a good lawyer, Freddy," she considered eventually, frowning with contemplation. "And I, shit, well, I come into some money recently."

"I can't take your money, Lily," he said.

"Ain't my money," she sighed. "And that boy out there? He likes you and, truthfully, that boy don't like many people. But for some reason you hang the moon with him, okay?"

She managed a tired smile. A flicker.

Then stood. "I need some air."

Lillian motioned for Delbert to enter the visiting room. Delbert came eagerly. She passed her only son on the way out the door, ruffling his hair with her fingers to his consternation. His hair was a bit too long with sandy bangs that had to be routinely swept aside with an absent flick of the hand from his bright and intelligent blue eyes but for a stubborn cowlick which always seemed to stand at attention, floating above his head like a lazy cattail.

Lillian exited the anteroom for a designated patio area.

She lit her smoke. Watched from behind the acrylic glass.

Delbert sat across from his father at the visiting table. There was a brief awkward moment before Delbert pulled a small folded checkers board from his coat pocket along with a couple handfuls of well-worn black and red checker pieces.

"You play checkers, Freddy?" he said.

"Don't everybody?" Freddy said.

# 46.

**DELBERT WALKED HOME FROM SCHOOL** in no particular hurry. He was wearing his father's denim jacket beneath a gray winter sky, his backpack flung over a narrow shoulder. The denim jacket had been returned to him by the state police for his birthday, celebrated only the week before. He was now eleven years old. His ankle was fully healed and he hopped on it without thinking to avoid an icy puddle set deep against the sidewalk curb. Plump snowflakes fell with purpose from the gray winter sky and he stuck out his tongue to collect them. The snowflakes tasted wet and cold and substantial, promising an irreversible turn in the weather as Delbert approached the white clapboard house at the end of the dead end road. The boy stood before the small house, the snow swirling around him like fairies, muffling the sounds of the world, including the mill whistle and the rumbling of a train passing in the near distance. These were sounds he had begun to hear again in recent days. Sounds of this place welcoming him all over again. This town. He had fallen numb to its voice for a spell, but now he embraced it. Even as the falling snow promised to cover everything the eye could see in a fuzzy white blanket by morning as the small foothill town of Shady Creek hidden in the western foothills of North Carolina settled comfortably into its long winter nap. For this place was his home.

Delbert sighed and plodded slowly down the muddy driveway overgrown with all those wild things that would likely not survive the winter freeze. A familiar sports utility vehicle was parked in front of the white clapboard house still in need of fresh paint with a crooked porch still sliding off its crumbling foundation. The dentist sat inside the vehicle. Leaning on the horn. A double honk. He smiled at Delbert from a parka. Offered a creepy wink. Delbert climbed the uneven porch steps and entered the white clapboard house. The moving boxes were now gone. Unpacked. The cardboard boxes broken down and stored in the basement.

Delbert found his mother standing before the mirror at the bottom of the stairs. A pound of make-up. Hair teased and frozen in space with hairspray. A short summer dress which belied the late season. She stared at him in the cold flat glass. "Don't look at me like that," she muttered, sounding more self-conscious to him than usual. "You might need braces someday."

Another double honk from outside.

Muted in the falling snow.

"I'm coming," she said.

Her voice feathery.

A little out of breath.

She checked herself again in the mirror.

"Just give me a minute to collect my thoughts," she said.

She blinked at her shadowed reflection for a long beat before leaving her son standing alone in the foyer. She ducked inside the kitchen and pulled open the fridge, retrieving a vodka bottle from the ice box. She screwed off the lid with a well-practiced motion and took a long burning sip from the chilled bottle. Then another. Eyes watering as the hard liquor singed down her throat.

And noticed for the first time--

The yellowed, tattered photo on the fridge door.

Pinned beneath a magnet.

She wondered how long it had been there.

And how she had not noticed it before.

A magical window into the past.

The badly faded photograph revealed a much younger Freddy. A Freddy Lillian sometimes still dreamed about on sleepless nights. His strong, suntanned arm thrown casually over the shoulder of a pregnant, baby-faced Lillian. She had been on the precipice of a smile as the photograph had been taken as if the future held only magical possibilities, her sharp cheeks blushing like a little girl, her right hand caressing her large swollen belly like what was inside it contained all the treasure worth having in the entire world.

Her feathery breath caught in her throat.

She hesitated. Then slowly touched the photo.

The photo paper felt warm and crinkly.

Tears stood out in her eyes.

Slid down her cheeks.

A few moments later Lillian exited the house, shivering in a fake fur coat, shivering against the winter cold as much within as without, but leaving behind the vodka bottle in the kitchen sink. Upturned. Its contents gurgling down the hungry drain.

She stopped abruptly on the porch.

The screen door still slapping closed behind her.

The sports utility vehicle was backing out of the driveway without her, its engine whining a high-pitched scream, leaving behind a pair of curving muddy tracks in the snow before vanishing down the road, chugging with irritation as it passed a familiar unmarked black sedan parked idling beside a badly dented and paint-chipped old black mailbox at the edge of the property.

Captain Dwyer stood at the bottom of the porch. In the falling snow. Boots wet and muddy. Spinning snowflakes sticking to his state police coat and hat. "Told your boy I might make a habit of coming around," the captain said to Lillian. "If necessary."

He tipped his hat politely, then hiked back to the idling sedan, peeking up at the gray sky turning dark before ducking inside the car. He flashed his headlights at Lillian standing there on the porch as he pulled away, the sedan making a slow, deliberate U-turn, its tires crunching through the ice and the freezing mud in front of the big yellow dead end sign at the end of the street before heading off into the deepening shadows. The snow falling harder still.

The world suddenly caught in a shaken snow globe.

Lillian turned and discovered Delbert sitting on the porch swing. A satisfied witness. A large chunk of the porch swing's backboard was missing, a gaping hole blown to kingdom come by Harlan's searing shotgun blast. But the porch swing still hung there. Stubbornly, if slightly off-kilter compliments of that searing shotgun blast and the crooked porch roof. The porch swing swung backward and forward on its rusty chain, sliding back and forth over a large brown bloodstain that had settled in perpetuity into the dry rot of the rotten and buckled porch floorboards.

Lillian sighed.

Sat beside her son.

Sighed again.

Facing the oncoming winter.

Her face long and drawn.

Weathered.

"You think you're a man now?" she whispered, staring at all that falling snow. The snow had created a white curtain. That white curtain was obscuring everything, covering and softening the hard, sharp edges of the world. Wiping the world clean of them.

Erasing them from sight.

But she knew they were still there.

Just hidden.

"Is that it?" she said. "You think you can protect me?"

She almost sounded hopeful.

Her eyes almost pleading.

He nodded. Delbert. Her son.

Lillian smiled at the thought.

At the sincerity of it.

Its earnestness.

Her eyes closed and her arm gradually fell over the boy's thin shoulders, pulling him toward her bosom.

The porch swing moving beneath them.

# ABOUT THE AUTHOR

Russell Gilwee is a novelist and screenwriter. He lives in Northern California with his wife, Lauraleen, and their golden doodle, Sophie. He is busy at work on his second novel and several film projects, including the adaptation of Shady Creek into an independent motion picture.

Made in the USA
Columbia, SC
01 April 2019